WITHDRAWN

ALL
WE
BURIED

ALSO AVAILABLE BY ELENA TAYLOR

Eddie Shoes Mysteries (written as Elena Hartwell)

Three Strikes, You're Dead

Two Heads Are Deader Than One

One Dead, Two to Go

ALL WE BURIED

A Sheriff Bet Rivers Mystery

Elena Taylor

CROOKED
LANE

NEW YORK

This is a work of fiction. All of the names, characters, organizations, places and events portrayed in this novel are either products of the author's imagination or are used fictitiously. Any resemblance to real or actual events, locales, or persons, living or dead, is entirely coincidental.

Copyright © 2020 by Elena Hartwell

All rights reserved.

Published in the United States by Crooked Lane Books, an imprint of The Quick Brown Fox & Company LLC.

Crooked Lane Books and its logo are trademarks of The Quick Brown Fox & Company LLC.

Library of Congress Catalog-in-Publication data available upon request.

ISBN (hardcover): 978-1-64385-291-1
ISBN (ebook): 978-1-64385-312-3

Cover design by Nicole Lecht

Printed in the United States.

www.crookedlanebooks.com

Crooked Lane Books
34 West 27th St., 10th Floor
New York, NY 10001

First Edition: April 2020

10 9 8 7 6 5 4 3 2 1

For my darling hubby, JD Hammerly
R3

ONE

Sheriff Bet Rivers leaned back in her chair and gazed out the office window at the shifting light on Lake Collier. Bright sunlight cast up sparkling diamonds as a late-summer breeze chopped the surface—turquoise-blue and silver. The fragment of a song from her childhood teased her mind—*silver, blue, and gold.* She hummed the tune under her breath.

Red and yellow leaves turned the maple trees in the park across the street into Jackson Pollock paintings. Hard to believe Labor Day weekend ended tonight. Somehow summer had slipped by and fall had snuck up on her as she tended to her new position.

If she had still been in Los Angeles, she'd have been a detective by now. Instead, she was back in her tiny hometown with a job her father had tricked her into taking.

"I need you to cover for me while I get chemo," he said. "It's just for a few months. I'm going to be fine."

With the detective exam available only once every two years, it meant putting her career on hold. But her father had never asked her for anything; how could she say no?

He never said he would die, turning her "interim sheriff" position into something more permanent.

Her father always knew what cards to play. Competition. Family. Responsibility. Loyalty. Collier. A perfect straight. He'd used them all this time, as if he'd known it would be his last hand.

No easy way to extricate herself now, short of gnawing off her own foot.

The sound of instruments tuning up pulled her attention to a trio set up at a bench outside the market across the street. The raised sidewalk and false front of the old building made the perfect backdrop for their performance. Collier relied on tourism for much of its income, and the local musicians encouraged visitors to stay longer and spend more.

A beat of silence followed by a quick intake of breath, the unspoken communication of musicians well attuned to one another, and the trio launched into song.

Church of a different sort. Bet could hear her father's words. *I don't know if there's a God, Bet, but I do believe in bluegrass.*

The music produced a soundtrack to her grief. The banjo player favored the fingerpicking style of the great Earl Scruggs. Loss etched in the sound of three-part harmony, Earle Rivers's death still a wound that wouldn't close.

She recognized the fiddle player. She'd babysat him years ago. It made her feel old. Not yet thirty, she wasn't, but as the last generation of Lake Collier Riverses, the weight of history fell heavy on her shoulders. In a line of sheriffs stretching back to the town's founding, she was the bitter end.

Looking down at her desk, Bet eyed the new fly she'd tied. The small, barbless hook would work well for the catch-and-release fishing she did, and the bright yellow and green feathers pleased her. The only thing she'd missed while living in California. Surf fishing wasn't the same.

I should name it in your memory, Dad. The Earle fly. Her grandfather had named him after Scruggs, but her grandmother added the *e* because she liked how it looked.

Bet imagined her father's critical response to her work, the size of the hook too dainty for his memorial.

Bet "spoke" with her father more now, four months after his death, than she'd ever done when he lived. Another burden she carried. The conversations they'd never had. Things she should have asked but didn't.

She took a deep breath of the dry, pine scent that drifted in through the open windows, filling the room with a heady summer perfume. She should get up and walk around, let the community see she was on the job, but her body felt leaden. And it wasn't like anyone would notice. She could vanish for hours and it wouldn't matter to Collier; no one required her attention. Not like they had depended on her father. His death still hung over town like a malaise, her presence an insufficient cure no matter what Earle might have believed when he called her home.

Before her father's illness, she'd had a plan. First the police academy, then patrol officer, proving she could make it in Los Angeles as a cop. She'd envisioned at least twenty years in LA, moving up the ranks—something with Chief in the title—returning home with a long, impressive career before stepping into Earle's shoes.

Too late, she'd realized he wouldn't get better. He'd brought her home for good.

———

Stretching her arms above her head, she walked her fingers up the wall behind her, tapping to the beat of the music. Anything to shake off the drowsiness brought on by the hot, quiet day and long nights of uneasy sleep.

The coffee stand beckoned from across the street, but the sound of the front door opening and the low, throaty voice of the department's secretary, Alma, stopped her from voyaging out. A two-pack-a-day smoker for almost forty years, Alma sounded a lot like Lauren Bacall after a night of heavy drinking. She'd given up smoking more than twenty years ago, but even now, as she edged into her seventies, Alma's voice clung to the roughness like a dying man to a life preserver. Bet hoped the visitor only wanted information about the community and Alma could answer.

No such luck. The efficient clop of Alma's square-heeled shoes clumped down the scarred floors of the hallway, a counterpoint to another set of feet. Bet brought her hands down off the wall and automatically tucked a wayward curl of her auburn hair back up under her hat before Alma arrived, poking her birdlike head around the wooden frame of the door. Gray hair teased tall, as if that would give her five-foot frame a couple extra inches.

"Bet?" Alma always said her name as though it might not be Bet Rivers sitting behind the enormous sheriff's desk. Bet assumed Alma wished to find Earle Rivers there. She wondered how long that would last. If Bet threw the upcoming election and fled back to Southern California, leaving her deputy to pick up the reins, maybe everyone would be better off, no matter what her father wanted.

"Yes, Alma?"

"I think you'd better listen to what this young man has to say."

The "young man" in question could be anywhere under the age of sixty in Alma's book, and as he stood out of sight down the hallway, Bet had little to go on.

"Okay," Bet said.

"I think it's important." Alma waited for Bet to show appropriate attention.

"Okay."

"Seems he found a dead body floating in the lake."

TWO

Bet clunked her chair back down, her body no longer leaden. It wouldn't be the first death to occur in Lake Collier. Ominously dark due to depth, the waters were rarely calm, the rough water ill-suited for recreation. Lakers went other places for boating and swimming. Visitors found it difficult to access the shore. Daredevils had occasionally come to bad ends over the years, prompting the danger signs posted at the few public-access points.

But people still ignored the warnings and accidents happened. With four years of experience under her belt, Bet had performed death notifications before, the worst part of a law enforcement officer's job. A fatality in the lake would likely be a tourist, and the next of kin would have to be tracked down. Lakers knew to stay out of the water.

She swept the fly-making materials off the desktop and into the center drawer.

"Guess you'd better come in," Bet said to the shadow in the hall, wondering who would walk through her door.

As the "young man" came into the room, Bet guessed his age to be midforties. He was an awkward stick figure of a person; a few inches over six feet tall, but carrying all the bulk of a scarecrow missing his stuffing. An unruly mop of hair in a remarkable shade of orange rounded out his appearance. Wearing a neat, white, button-down shirt and tan cargo pants with one leg tucked into his sock, he looked a lot like Beaker from the Muppets, and

Bet had the fleeting thought he might open his mouth and nothing but "Beeep beep, mmeeeep meep" would come out.

"Peter Malone," he said in perfectly understandable English. He shook Bet's hand with a firmer grip than she'd expected from such a slender man. His handshake was warm and slightly damp. As if he'd just come out of the restroom after using one of the air dryers put in to save trees.

"*Doctor* Malone," Alma said, "is a college professor."

"I'm not a medical doctor, but I could play one on TV." Peter forced a laugh.

"How's that?" Bet asked.

"Just a little academic humor. PhD, not MD. I'm a scientist, really." Peter's voice trailed off. "I'm sorry, this is a bit outside my comfort zone." The professor shifted his bicycle helmet from one hand to the other.

Bet wondered if "this" was finding a dead body or reporting it.

Peter's eyes flicked up past Bet to the photo of her father in his sheriff's uniform, standing next to an American flag. The small metal plate at the bottom of the frame emblazoned with *SHERIFF RIVERS*.

"You're Sheriff Rivers?" His tone made it unclear if that was a statement or a question.

Before Bet could respond, her father's Anatolian shepherd, Schweitzer, squeezed his large body past the two standing in the doorway and stood between the strange man and Bet. The dog dropped to a sitting position, placing his sizable head level with the man's waist.

"I am." Bet watched Peter eye the big dog. She gave him points for not flinching when Schweitzer started to pant, showing teeth the size of a great white shark's not six inches from his belt buckle.

"Down," Bet said to the dog. He lay at Peter's feet with a low whine. "Good boy." She was pleased he responded so quickly to her command. After her father's death, Bet had become a dog owner overnight. She'd grown up around dogs, but Schweitzer was a one-person dog, and a working dog at that. The transition to Bet as his person hadn't been easy for either of them. She wasn't yet fluent in the language her father had developed with Schweitzer. As with many unfinished threads, he hadn't left behind an instruction manual.

She returned her attention to the man. "You found a body in the lake?"

"I did."

"Anyone you know?"

The question appeared to surprise him. "I don't think so."

"You aren't sure?"

"No."

"And that's because . . ."

Peter turned pale. "It's all so surreal. I found her . . . wrapped up in canvas."

Wrapped up in canvas. Something more than an accident, then. Unbidden, a recurring nightmare surfaced in Bet's mind. An object, the shape of a person, slipped through a hole chipped into the ice of the lake. Like a burial at sea, the shrouded figure vanishing into the water while Bet watched from the trees. Bet felt chills even in the heat of the room. She shook off the image. It didn't belong on the job.

"If it was wrapped up, what made you so sure of what was inside?"

Peter swallowed hard, an expression of anguish twisting his elongated features.

"I could see her hair."

Alma's hand flew up to cover her mouth and she shook her head, as if the action could change Peter's story. Peter swayed slightly, and Bet brought a chair over next to him. He thanked her and dropped into it, took a deep breath, and continued.

"I couldn't lift her in without tipping my canoe over, so I towed her back to my campsite. I beached my boat and hauled her up onto dry ground. I had to see if she . . . I had the thought it could be a hoax, you know, a dummy or something. I cut the fabric open. I think she's been dead a while, her face . . . No. I don't think I've ever seen her before."

Bet thought about the contamination of evidence but couldn't blame the man for his actions. She would have done the same thing. She didn't follow up on what the girl looked like. It would be better to see for herself. He explained there were no apparent injuries to her face or head and that he'd looked no further once he'd seen she was dead.

"Let's keep this quiet," Bet said to Alma on her way out the door with Peter. "I don't want people to get panicked or curious until I know what's what."

"Are you sure that's wise?" Alma asked quietly after Peter went out the door. "Maybe people need to be careful."

"It's not a shooting spree, Alma," Bet said. "We have no reason to think anyone else is in danger. We don't know yet how the woman died. It could have been an accident and someone tried to get rid of her body."

Disapproval showed on Alma's face. Bet resented that a secretary could make her question her own decisions, but Alma had decades of service in this office. She'd worked for Bet's grandfather first, then her father. She'd watched Bet grow up, so both of them were making the shift.

Sometimes Alma and Schweitzer looked at her with identical expressions. As if she were an imposter and they wanted Earle Rivers to come home and straighten things out.

"We have a town full of tourists," Bet reminded her. "The last thing we need is a story going viral about a body in the lake."

Alma pursed her lips. "As long as the upcoming election isn't why you don't want people to know."

Bet felt like she'd been slapped. She almost said the damn election was more important to Alma than it was to her, so of course it wasn't what she was thinking about. But that wasn't something she could admit out loud. She couldn't tell the community she'd been deceiving them for the last four months and all she wanted to do was fly south like the migrating birds.

"It's what Dad would do," Bet said, her voice hard as she started to leave.

Schweitzer stood at her side. His willingness to go with her made Bet happy, but she rubbed his ears and told him to stay at the station. It hurt to see the disappointment in his rich brown eyes, but with Peter's bike, there wouldn't be room for him in the SUV. Lately it felt like every time she turned around, she disappointed someone. She left without making further eye contact with Alma or the dog and found Peter at the bike rack. He'd unlocked his bike, and they loaded it into her vehicle.

"That must have been quite a shock for you," she said as he sat without speaking.

"It was . . . it is. It doesn't feel real. Even sitting here with you."

Bet knew firsthand how hard it could be to look at the face of a dead person. As a patrol officer in South Los Angeles, she'd attended numerous crime scenes. Even if she'd only done crowd control and taken witness statements, she'd observed the aftermath of vicious crimes, the images permanently carved into her memory.

Bet determined that Peter hadn't seen any people or vehicles near the lake since he arrived, then let him steer the conversation to get a better feel for the man. Malone explained he taught at the University of Washington, a top-ranked research institution out in Seattle.

"I'm a geomorphologist."

"*Geo*, earth. *Morph* . . . change?"

"Give the lady a gold star. I study the processes that change the earth's surface."

"What brings a geomorphologist to study Lake Collier?" She hoped he wouldn't call her the *lady* again.

"As you may know, this valley of yours was created by a glacier." Peter began to crack his knuckles, as if discussing his research made him nervous. "That makes the lake very interesting."

Bet skirted one edge of the lake while they talked, the roadbed chipped out of the adjacent hillside like the ridge of a scar. A narrow shoulder and a guardrail were all that protected drivers from an abrupt drop to the water below. On rare days the surface of Lake Collier remained calm, the water black. Now, rising chop and a cloud passing in front of the sun transformed it from this morning's turquoise to a forbidding, gunmetal gray.

Peter paused long enough for Bet to prompt an answer. "And you're here to study that?"

The professor looked around as if someone might be listening in on the conversation before leaning over to whisper, "Top secret stuff."

"I'm pretty good at keeping my mouth shut."

"I hope so. You never know who might be listening these days." The knuckle cracking increased in volume and tempo. "I'm kidding, of course. My research is unlikely to interest anyone outside of fellow scientists."

"I might surprise you. What's important about studying a glacial lake?"

"Ahh . . . but is it? There are rules to these things, you know. Is it a lake in a glacier or a glacial lake?"

"There's a difference?"

"To a scientist, yes." For the first time, Peter seemed to relax. Discussing his area of expertise must put him at ease, or at least put the dead girl out of his mind. If he'd lied about the situation, he'd be more likely to give something away if he was distracted.

"We have categories for everything," he said. "Glacial lakes can be formed a number of ways. Melting glaciers, blocked by ice, or dammed by a moraine—are you acquainted with that term?"

"Rock pushed up by a glacier."

"Close enough for our purposes. If a lake forms in a glacier not related to the glacier itself, it's a lake in a glacier."

"And you're here to, what, look for evidence of how ours formed?"

"Bingo."

It was a change of pace to have a scientist study the lake. Most people who arrived to "study" the area were either ghost hunters or looking for Sasquatch.

"And you're sure you never saw the dead woman before?"

Peter looked startled at her shift in the conversation, but he didn't change his story that Jane Doe was a complete stranger to him.

"Why does it matter?" Bet asked. "Whether it's a glacier in a lake or a glacial lake."

Comforted by his role as the expert, Peter continued. "We study glaciers for climate change research. I believe what you have here is a tarn."

"Tarn?"

"A tarn is a high mountain lake, but in glaciology, it's specifically a lake in a cirque."

"Got me on that one too."

Peter stretched back in his seat, his voice taking on a professorial air. Bet pictured him in front of a classroom. "Cirques have a very specific shape. Deep sides, kind of like an amphitheater. They usually form at the mouth of a valley, caused by a retreating glacier."

Lake Collier sat at the mouth of their hanging valley.

"Were you meeting anyone here? In Collier?"

Peter paused before he answered. "I don't know anyone in the area."

"That's not quite what I asked."

Peter turned in the seat to look directly at Bet, his next words clipped as if she'd struck a nerve. "No. I was not planning to meet anyone here in Collier."

Bet let the silence sit between them for a long moment. She pictured the shape of a tarn. Steep sided and bottomless. A long way down for something to fall.

"I assume you did your homework on the lake before you arrived," Bet said. "You must know our lake isn't considered safe for boating, swimming, or diving."

"I did." Peter sat back, looking out the window again, the questions back on solid ground. "But I'm well equipped. I always wear a life jacket and safety-cable myself to the canoe. I appreciate your concern for my welfare."

His precautions made sense, but if there were so many unex-plored lakes in the area, why choose one so dangerous?

"You're an adult; I can't stop you from putting yourself at risk. I just don't want to find your body floating in the lake too."

As she drove, Bet continued to watch Peter from the corner of her eye. It was true she couldn't stop the man from doing his research, but that didn't mean she would minimize the danger.

The lake stretched out in front of them now, the far end close to the bend in the road where it dropped out of their valley to the highway several miles below.

"Sorry I didn't come in to introduce myself before I went out on the water this morning. I was anxious to try out my equip-ment," Peter said. "I haven't even unhooked my truck from the trailer; that's why I biked in. But I did plan to come by and let you know I'm here."

He didn't need her permission. Maybe the scientist wasn't as confident now as he'd been before he left Seattle. Seeing firsthand how treacherous the lake was, perhaps he wanted someone in a position of authority to keep an eye on him. Not something Bet could do. Peter was on his own.

"It could be one of the deepest lakes in the region." Peter's voice rose in excitement. "Yet we know almost nothing about it. This area is so remote, what with only the single road coming in and heavy snowfall in the winter. No one has ever studied this marvel in our own backyard."

Outsider, Bet thought. *My backyard, not yours.* Tourists were appreciated. They supported the local economy, but Lakers resented visitors who spoke of the valley as "theirs." Bet pushed away the thought that she'd begun to think of herself as a Laker again.

"I guess I don't have to tell you how out of the way this area is," Peter said.

"I know something about it." Bet turned off Lake Collier Road and onto the private track at the east end of the lake. The main road continued out of the mountains to twist and turn its way down to Highway 97 and the larger towns east of the Cascades, Washington State's highest mountain range.

Bet stopped and put the SUV in park. Searching the ground, she found two sets of tire tracks in the dirt. One probably left from a large, heavy vehicle with a smaller set behind, which she guessed would match Peter's rig. She snapped a few quick pictures with the digital camera she kept in the SUV. Defense attorneys could confiscate cell phones, so Bet never used hers if there was a possibility a photo would be used in court. Lessons learned with the Los Angeles Police Department, second nature by now. After that, she drove around a section in case she wanted to come back and make casts.

Peter picked up the conversation where they'd left off. "Despite the posted warning signs, I was surprised to have the lake to myself." He paused a moment, fingers twitching. Bet wondered if he ever sat still. "I didn't see any boat ramps. Don't people swim or boat or fish out here in the summertime at all?"

"In addition to the constant chop, the water's always cold," Bet said. "Just over thirty degrees is a bit of a shock, even on a hot day. With nothing to catch, we Lakers tend to enjoy the beauty from a distance."

The relationship between the Lakers and the lake was an uneasy one and not something discussed with strangers.

"It's hard to believe there are no fish."

Bet wondered at his wistful tone. She chalked it up to something in his scientific soul. Or maybe he'd hoped to catch his own dinner while he was here.

"I can give you some suggestions for places out in the valley if you'd like to do some fishing."

Peter nodded, but didn't take her up on the offer. "It doesn't look like the buildings along the lake even take advantage of the waterfront," he said.

"The Lakeshore Tavern has a deck." She didn't explain it perched six feet above the dark water and didn't provide access to the lake. "There aren't any shallows. Most of the lake is like the deep end of a swimming pool. Step off the shore and you're already over your head."

Peter kept his eyes pinned on the water. "Don't you ever wonder what's down there?"

All the time.

He didn't seem to notice that Bet chose not to answer. The high peaks surrounding the lake and the dense patch of forest around the far side made the shore feel closed in and turned the road from bright day to false twilight. They crested the top of a small hill to one of the few places that provided a flat spot near the lake. A makeshift camp was situated off to their left. A mud-spattered blue Suburban with racks for a canoe on top and a trailer hitched behind sat half hidden under the trees.

"Do you have permission to be on this land?" Bet asked as she pulled the SUV in behind the Suburban.

"I do." Something flitted across Peter's delicate features. Bet thought for a moment it might have been fear. "I have permission from Robert Collier. In writing, if you want to see it."

"Collier says you can be here, that's between you and him." Bet pushed the shifter into park.

The original founders of the town—and the closest there was to aristocracy—the Colliers owned half the valley, including the long-defunct mine that had put the town on the map and the Train Yard, now leased to Jeb Pearson for the camp he ran for troubled teenage boys.

The Colliers hadn't been seen in town for years. Robert Collier the fourth had disappeared from town just after high school and his father had left not long after that, but they still profited from the land and buildings they owned. Their estate sat closed up a few miles away.

Lots of families disappearing around here.

She was the last of her line.

Peter hopped out of the SUV and stood quivering with energy as she stepped out. She began to understand why he was so thin. He reminded her of a hamster she'd owned as a child. The little orange puffball could spend hours running on his wheel. In the days after her mother's suicide, Bet's father had been concerned over how much time she spent sitting and watching a hamster.

"What's the attraction, Bet? He just goes around and around."

"That's what happy looks like."

She expected her father to leave the room, but he surprised her by pulling up a chair and sitting down. Their faces reflected back at them in the glass of the hamster cage.

Peter's voice pulled Bet back to the present. "Over there." He pointed. "By my canoe."

Her eyes followed his outstretched arm.

"Might be the only place to camp and launch a boat on the whole lake." Bet inspected the sandy stretch of beach.

"Lucky for me."

"I'm going to go confirm what you found. Why don't you wait here." Bet made it clear *no* wasn't an option, then moved forward alone, pulling on latex gloves. She could see the shape, wrapped in white canvas, lying on the sand. The section Peter cut open allowed sunlight to fall on the victim's expression, features frozen in a rictus of fear.

Bet had been back in Collier for six months. If natural causes, an accident, suicide, or an overdose hadn't killed Jane Doe, this could be her first homicide investigation as sheriff. How she handled the case could impact her reputation and ability to succeed back in LA. She wanted to get her life back on track, untangled from the complications her father had created when he died. This might be step one to resurrecting her plans.

Bet stopped short, adrenaline spiking at the sight of a body wrapped in canvas. "Her hair should be dark."

"Are you talking to me?" Peter called from his spot by the SUV.

Bet shook her head and managed to get the word "No" out, embarrassed to be caught speaking out loud. She wasn't going to admit to Peter she'd seen another woman, wrapped exactly like this, in a dream.

THREE

Bet had started riding along on patrol with her father after she turned sixteen. Even before that, he'd talked about the job, expecting it to be hers one day. He supported her decision to move to Los Angeles. It was smart, he said, to compete in the bigger pond. He hadn't expected her to replace him so soon, either.

Looking at Jane Doe now, Bet took a tactical pause. A trick her father taught her years ago. "Take a breath," her father would say when faced with something challenging. "Then divorce your thoughts from the personal and go through your checklist for the investigation. Do your job."

She shrugged off the similarity to her nightmare; coincidences happened. Déjà vu was an electrical malfunction of the brain. Something similar was impacting her here. This wasn't her dream coming true, just a tragic similarity to a childhood fear. *Focus on the victim.* She pushed off her anxiety. What mattered now was identifying this woman and determining how she'd died.

Homicides were rare in Collier. The few that occurred were usually clear-cut. Acts of domestic violence, drug deals gone bad in campgrounds, drunk driving. But she knew in her gut this would be something else. Instincts honed over four years on the streets and a lifetime of being Earle's child.

Bet took several photos of the dead girl and the area around her. Looking at the victim through the camera helped. She couldn't allow herself to be stopped by grief for a life cut short when faced with a job to do and an audience of one.

After she determined the campsite wasn't a crime scene, the body was real, and there was no immediate danger to the community, Bet called the coroner in Ellensburg. A veritable metropolis compared to Collier, E'burg boasted twenty thousand people and, more importantly, a morgue. But it was going to take at least an hour for the coroner to arrive in his van to take the body down to the medical examiner.

As Peter had reported he'd found the body floating in the lake, locating the crime scene might be impossible. Bet would have to search the entire lakeshore to try to find where someone had dumped the victim in. Further, there was no way to know at this point if she'd died at the lake or somewhere else entirely. Though why someone would bring her here, Bet couldn't guess.

After finishing her call with the coroner, she sat with Peter in the SUV. "Where on the lake were you when you found her?"

"So she's real?" he asked.

"Did you have any doubt?"

"I guess I still hoped it was some kind of hoax."

"But you touched her, right? You said you checked for a pulse?"

"She was so cold." Peter swallowed hard, his Adam's apple bobbing up and down in his skinny neck.

Jane Doe wasn't cold now. She'd warmed up in the sun.

"She's real." Bet thought about the difference between *dead* and *warm and dead*. Drowning victims in cold water sometimes survived if administered CPR before their body temperature returned to normal. Bet knew of drowning victims brought back after hours trapped in cold water. With body temperatures below eighty-six degrees, the human brain resisted hypoxia and survived with little oxygen. But Jane was no longer cold and temporarily dead. She was warm and permanently dead.

Bet hoped the woman couldn't have been revived if Peter had performed CPR after he brought her on shore.

"Where were you when you found her?" she asked again. The lake, with no easy access, posed challenges as a dump site. Could the body have been thrown in from the road? It would take a brazen individual to dispose of a body so publicly, no matter how late at night.

Bet felt a shudder at how the woman might have suffered if she went into the lake alive.

"There." Peter pointed to a spot where the shale from the mountainside poured down into the lake. There were several places made almost impassible on land because of the loose scree shed from the peaks.

Unlikely anyone had dumped the body from the point; far too difficult to get there. Most likely she drifted to the spot where Peter discovered her. Had the person who put her in the water expected her to sink?

Peter confirmed he had gone out on the lake at around nine that morning. He waited until the sun rose over the peaks and lit the waters. Starting close to camp, he experimented with his equipment. Using a submersible camera capable of going more than a thousand feet deep, he had a lot of lake to cover. He had been out on the water less than two hours when he noticed something on the surface a quarter mile away.

Curious about what might be adrift in the empty lake, he pulled the camera up and paddled over to find the body. She floated head down, almost completely submerged.

"At first, I wasn't sure what I was looking at," he said. "It wasn't until I saw her hair that I realized . . ."

"Then what?" Bet prompted when the scientist didn't pick up his train of thought.

"I debated about whether or not to leave her or bring her in," he said. "I wasn't sure if I should disturb anything." He stopped, as if he should say more but didn't know how. Bet inquired why he had decided to bring her to shore. "I thought there was a chance she was still alive, and I couldn't bear to leave her alone in that water."

"Because it's cold?" she asked.

"Because it's dead."

He laughed self-consciously and shook his head. "I may be a scientist, and I may be thrilled at what I can learn about this lake, but now that I'm here, now that I have been out on this water . . . between you and me? Something about it gives me the shivers. And not only *after* I found the girl."

Bet didn't respond, though between the blackness of the water and the lack of life, she could have told Peter most everyone in town felt that way.

The coroner arrived in his van, declared the woman dead, and loaded her up for the long drive down the mountain. Bet signed all the forms and watched as the van disappeared with the mystery corpse.

Protocol dictated that the coroner and medical examiner do their jobs first, but she felt apprehensive letting her only tangible evidence drive away. She knew the steps to take for an investigation, but that didn't mean she'd get it all right.

This was her opportunity to have something to show for her time in Collier. Help her pick back up where she'd left off when the chance arose. Otherwise, her hiatus would just put her behind in her quest to make a name for herself separate from her father's. She would have nothing but a leave of absence for personal hardship on her record, a cause for pity, not promotion. Sheriff of a town of less than a thousand wasn't going to impress anyone. But if she solved a murder, that would look good to command.

Jane Doe had also left behind someone who cared for her. No matter what had caused her death, her life mattered. Bet wanted to give her friends and loved ones answers, even if that wouldn't take the grief away. She understood the pain of unanswered questions.

"Are those the clothes you wore when you pulled her out of the lake?" Bet pointed at a shirt and a pair of pants spread out over a low bush to dry in the sun.

"They are," Peter said. "I got wet hauling her onto shore and changed before I biked to your station."

"I need to take them with me."

"Will I get them back?" he asked, with a step toward his clothes.

"I'll take care of that." Bet pulled an evidence bag out of the crime scene kit she kept on hand. Bet would leave the clothes with the crime lab after she went to the morgue. Peter watched as she put the clothing into the bag, sealed it with evidence tape, and labeled it with a Sharpie.

"You can't think I had anything to do with this," he said.

"Standard procedure; nothing to worry about. We have to be able to identify anything that transferred from you or your clothes onto her. I'll need your fingerprints for the same reason."

Dr. Malone acquiesced, and Bet quickly processed a full set of fingerprints.

"I'll have some follow-up questions for you." She moved toward the driver's side door of her SUV. "How long do you anticipate being around?"

"School starts the third Monday of this month. I plan to get home a day or two before."

"Not a lot of prep work before classes start?"

"I'm ready to go." Malone dropped his eyes away.

Bet opened her door.

"Do you . . . that is to say—" Peter stopped, searching for the right words.

"Are you wondering if you're in any danger?"

"That wasn't what I was going to ask, but now that you mention it."

Bet considered the best information to tell the man. "I'll know more once they get the body unwrapped and see what happened to her. But I think it's unlikely this is the act of someone who would be a danger to you."

Peter looked unconvinced, so Bet continued.

"Statistically this was either domestic or a drug deal gone bad. It's possible she died accidentally or by suicide and someone disposed of her. I doubt she's local unless she moved here very recently, or I would have recognized her." Bet had been gone long enough that she wouldn't necessarily recognize everyone who lived in the valley, but she didn't want to admit that to Peter. "If her death was a deliberate act, whoever disposed of her body is probably long gone. But if you feel unsafe, you could consider staying in town."

Peter shifted his weight back and forth, as though movement could help him form words.

"So this doesn't have to be a murder, then? Someone just ditched her like this because they didn't want to explain how she died?"

"Anything is possible. Currently it's just a suspicious death."

He struggled with whatever it was he wanted to say. "I've . . . I've never found . . ." He tipped his head forward as if in prayer. "I've never seen anyone dead before. Not like this." He looked at Bet again. "She's so young."

Bet put her hand on his arm where it rested on her window-sill. There wasn't anything she could say to that. He needed reas-surance, but her responsibility was for Jane Doe, which meant heading to the morgue. "I need to get going."

"You'll be back?" he asked, hand on the doorframe, eyes never leaving the lake. Bet could see tiny bronze hairs on the knuckles of Peter's hands.

An intimate detail.

What he really wanted to know was how long he'd be alone. "I'll be back."

Peter nodded, never taking his eyes from the water. "I'll be here." He stepped away from the SUV.

"You aren't going to be calling a bunch of people to tell them what you found, are you?" Bet asked, starting her engine up.

"No. This isn't what I want people to remember about my research."

Bet hoped that was true and pulled out onto the dirt road to start her trek out of the mountains. Just before she rounded the curve that would block his campsite from view, she looked in her rearview mirror. He hadn't moved at all.

The images from Bet's recurring nightmare returned as she drove. The silhouette of the man who carried the body came into focus. He wore a beard and moved with a halting step.

Was her imagination filling in the blanks? Or were these parts of the dream she'd never remembered before?

"It doesn't matter," she said out loud. A habit she'd picked up since moving back to Collier and driving in a patrol car alone. "It's just a dream. All that matters now is what I can prove in the real world."

FOUR

Fifty minutes later, Bet arrived in Ellensburg. On the way, she called Alma on her cell phone and reassured her she didn't recognize the victim.

"That's a relief." Bet waited in silence, knowing Alma had something else to say. "Still someone's daughter, though, isn't she?"

"We'll figure out who she is. I promise."

Alma hung up without another word, though Bet could guess what troubled her: Bet in charge of the investigation. If Jane Doe had died by another's hand, this would be Bet's first homicide investigation as sheriff. While it was possible the woman had died from natural causes, an accident, or suicide, someone had disposed of her body, and that was still a crime.

If this was a homicide, with no obvious crime scene, no identification for the victim, and a watery dump site, the investigation wouldn't be easy. Bet didn't want her first homicide to remain unsolved. She'd taken on the election in her father's place when her dad was in no condition to run. Collier was her responsibility now.

Before his death, her father had voiced legitimate concerns about Deputy Dale Kovač.

"Dale isn't sheriff material," he'd said as part of his plea for her return to Collier. "He doesn't have your experience. Or your instincts."

It was true. Both had been through training academies, but Bet had four years on the streets of Los Angeles and a lifetime of her father's wisdom. Dale had a year in Spokane and a few years working for her father in Collier. He hadn't been in the trenches like she had.

But she'd never solved a homicide by herself, either. What if her father's belief in her was misplaced?

Bet sat at one of the few lights on Ellensburg's main drag, thinking about how he'd convinced her to come home.

You knew exactly what would happen if I came back here, didn't you, Dad? she said. *You knew I'd feel compelled to see this through.*

Admit it, she could hear him say. *You want to solve this case and prove you can follow in my footsteps.* Bet turned up the radio to drown out the conversation taking place in her head.

A few minutes later, the hospital appeared. It was a modern building of gray concrete that stood out from the ubiquitous brick buildings and false-front architecture of downtown Ellensburg. Incorporated in 1883, the town showed its western history, though not to the extent Collier did. Founded on trapping, mining, and trading with the local tribes, Ellensburg only hinted at its past; it didn't dwell in it. Hayfields and cattle still took up much of the valley, but the lines of wind turbines that marched down the surrounding hills gave testament to technological advancement and the ever-present wind.

Pulling into the hospital lot, Bet drove around back and parked. She called the medical examiner and waited for her to come up to the loading dock to escort Bet to the morgue. Carolyn Pak appeared, a colorful tie-dyed shirt under her white lab coat, black hair—peppered with gray—pulled into a tight ponytail.

"Hey, Red." She gave her usual greeting and reached out for a handshake. "Nice to see you."

Bet had been coming to the morgue since she was a child, first during the summertime when her father didn't want to leave her at home alone. Once just after she'd moved back to Collier and a person died from natural causes unattended by a physician. But the last time she'd walked these halls was when her father died. She hadn't watched the autopsy, but she stood vigil in the hallway.

"How's the new job treating you?" Carolyn's eyes were kind.

"I'll let you know after the election."

"You know if I could vote in your area, you'd have mine."

As part of unincorporated Kittitas County, Collier had its own sheriff, voted in by town residents.

"I appreciate that."

No one visiting a sick loved one wanted to see sheet-covered bodies on their way to autopsy, so the morgue sat in the basement, outside the areas of public view. Carolyn walked down various hallways to an elevator most people didn't know existed, Bet jogged to keep up with her fast stride.

Arriving in the morgue, Bet saw that Carolyn had already removed all the ropes keeping Jane Doe trapped in her shroud. Peter had cut through only one to reveal the woman's face.

"Those are interesting," Carolyn said, pointing to the knots laid out on another table.

"Someone knows more than a basic half hitch." Bet inspected them. "Do you know what kind of knots these are?"

"Nope. Knots are not my specialty. Maybe one of your deputies was a Boy Scout."

"Clayton, maybe," Bet said. "I can't see Dale being quite that regimented."

Carolyn removed the canvas, and Bet had her first full look at Jane Doe. She swallowed hard, relieved the body showed little trauma. The first time Bet attended an autopsy, she'd thrown up in a trash can—a detail she didn't share with her dad. By now she knew what to expect, and the clinical nature of the process made it easier to stomach than a crime scene, though she never would get used to the smell.

Someone had stripped Jane Doe naked before wrapping her up and abandoning her in the lake. Carolyn clucked sympathetically over the youth of the dead woman.

"I'm guessing somewhere between eighteen and twenty-five," Carolyn said. "But you know that's just speculation on my part. She could be a few years on either side of that."

"I know, nothing is verified until you've done the autopsy. We'll move forward with the assumption she could be a minor."

After Carolyn turned Jane over, they could see a hole in the woman's back.

"Looks like a gunshot wound," the medical examiner said.

So this was going to be a homicide. Now Bet had to discover who had committed the crime and whether or not it was intentional. She might have missed the detective exam in LA, but there were no homicide detectives in Collier to swoop in and take over the case. Finding the perpetrator was up to her.

"Was her death instant?"

"I'll find out if there's any water in her lungs. Despite her hair having spilled out here at the top, she was sealed up pretty tight. It's possible water couldn't reach her even if she was still breathing when she went into the lake. Look at this, though." Carolyn gestured toward the fabric. "There's almost no blood inside. You said she was floating? There must have been pockets of air caught by the canvas to keep her from sinking. If she was still bleeding, we'd see it here."

"Could it have seeped out?"

"Maybe, but we're talking about a lot of blood, and there're no bloodstains on the body." Her fingers rubbed the material as if she would learn something tactually. "This canvas is waxed to be waterproof, which is also a little strange."

"Strange how?"

"If you want waterproof fabric, the synthetics are a lot better, lighter weight, more efficient. Waxed canvas went out of favor decades ago. I'll send a sample over to the lab and see if they can trace any information about where it might have come from or what it was used for."

Bet felt relief that the girl had been dead long before Peter Malone found her. If she'd died solely from drowning, Bet would have been haunted by the thought she could have been revived.

Standing five feet four inches tall and weighing one hundred five pounds, the young woman had not been a large person in life. Reduced to a corpse and lying on the cold, metal table in the morgue, she appeared even smaller. Her features, what Bet could see of them despite the rigor mortis pushing her face into that awful grimace, were dainty. A slight, upturned nose, a spray of freckles scattered across her cheekbones, and wide-set eyes combined to create a pixielike girl.

"How long do you think she's been dead?"

"Cold slows the rigor," Carolyn said, referencing the stiffened muscles of a corpse. "Hours, sometimes even days." She shrugged.

How long had Jane Doe floated out there? It was possible someone else had seen her on the lake, not realizing she was anything other than trash.

Carolyn made a noise under her breath as she looked down at the wound to the left of Jane Doe's spine. "There's no exit wound, but something's odd about this track. I think the killer dug the bullet out of Jane here before getting rid of the body."

"Smart killer," Bet said.

"Certainly a careful one. Probably small caliber, not to go through her, though she could have been shot with something larger from a distance. If the bullet is gone, you know I can't guess the type of weapon or compare ballistics even if you do find the weapon your shooter used."

"But you're sure it was a bullet that made that hole."

"Safe bet, Bet," she said, smiling at the comment she always made to assure Bet of one of her findings. Carolyn had enough experience for Bet to trust her judgment. "I'll know more once I cut her open. But I've seen a lot of gunshot wounds in my day," she said. "It looks like the bullet came in at an angle and embedded itself in her vertebrae. Interesting, but probably not useful."

"What's wrong with her fingers?" Bet asked, looking down at the girl's hands.

Carolyn picked up the girl's right hand, looked closely, then swore under her breath. She reached over and picked up her left hand, inspected it, and swore again. Carolyn raced over to a cabinet and pulled out the materials needed to take fingerprints from a corpse: black powder like that used at crime scenes, tape to lift them, and cards to mount them on.

"What is it?"

"I'm going to guess some kind of acid. Possibly poured on to destroy her fingerprints."

"Postmortem?"

"I'll have to do more tests. First I'm going to get whatever is left of her fingerprints and scrape under her nails. Of course, the acid will impact that evidence as well."

Bet watched Carolyn work on Jane Doe's hands. After attempting to recover fingerprints, she scraped under Jane Doe's fingernails, placing the residue in evidence bags. Bet hoped Jane scratched her attacker, leaving DNA under her nails.

Carolyn finished and shook her head at Bet's unasked question. "I'll let you know what I find, when I find it. There's always a possibility the killer left latent prints on the body. I'll look for those before I do the autopsy."

Next, Carolyn inspected the young woman's head, looking for other signs of trauma. "Definitely strange. Look at this."

"What?"

The medical examiner pointed to a section of Jane's hair. The woman's long tresses hung matted in sections, still wet from the lake. Carolyn carefully pulled apart some of the tendrils. "Unless there's some new hairstyle I don't know about, someone cut off a hunk of this girl's hair."

Bet and Carolyn exchanged a glance. Everyone in law enforcement knew signatures were the sign of a serial killer. Hair and fingers were common body parts for a serial killer to keep as trophies. With Washington State being one of the top five producers of serial killers, it was the kind of crime Bet had to consider.

"Could that have been through rough handling? Gotten caught on something in the water? Or during transport?" Bet asked.

"Could be. The hair was clearly cut with scissors or a knife. See how sharp the line is? Not torn. But it could have snagged on something and someone cut it to get her untangled."

"Let's hope so," Bet said under her breath. She craved more action than Collier provided, but that didn't mean she wanted people to die so she had something to do.

Bet left the morgue knowing Carolyn would do everything she could to identify Jane. The girl had been young, pretty, and—other than the bullet wound—apparently in good health. Someone would be looking for her.

Whoever had killed Jane hadn't panicked. The killer had probably removed Jane's clothing either because it gave an indication of how to identify her, such as an affiliation or a location, or to minimize the chance of any transfer from their body to hers. Carolyn would check for signs of sexual assault, but Bet's intuition said this wasn't a crime of passion or rape turned murder. It felt more like an execution. Psychopaths were out there who killed for fun, but it happened a lot less than the crime shows on television would have people believe. Jane Doe might just have been in the wrong place at the wrong time.

Bet hopped back into her SUV and headed up Highway 97 toward Blewett Pass and the two-lane turnoff to Collier. She'd already asked Dale to block off the two roads on either side of the lake. Alma had given Dale the rundown on what happened that morning, so Bet didn't have to explain the situation. Bet had also made sure Alma described Peter to Dale. Peter could come and go on his bicycle. She had already compared the tread on Peter's Suburban and trailer, and they matched the tracks she found on the eastern road. Dale could block it off completely, as no one needed to travel on it; it ended not far from Peter's camp and no one else lived in the area.

Bet had requested that Dale look for tire tracks on the road at the west end of the lake. There wasn't much traffic on that road either, as it led to the empty Collier house and the home of the caretaker, George Stand. If anyone in the community asked about the blockades, Dale would report a mountain lion had been sighted and they were taking precautions.

The valley was filled with wildlife wandering around, and with tourists still in for the end of Labor Day weekend, Lakers would understand Bet's concerns. If the rumor took hold, it would keep people out of the woods.

Before Bet left the hospital, Jane Doe's features relaxed, providing Bet the opportunity for a better photo to use for an ID. She planned to print out copies from the computer at the station to show around town. People died in the backcountry every year from falls, exposure, hypothermia. Bet would let people believe Jane Doe's death had been an accident while they worked to identify her.

No use asking around about the sound of gunfire without a time of death. Gunshots weren't unusual. A firing range sat in the valley outside town, and the loud, popping sounds echoed because of all the granite peaks, making it hard to guess the point of origin. Even if anyone heard the report of a distant shot, most people would assume it came from the range. If someone had thought there was anything suspicious, they would have called it in already.

"One step at a time," she said as she drove up into the mountains. "You're the sheriff. You can handle it." Her mind went over everything she'd learned as she prepared for the detective's exam. If this investigation went well, it would help her career, even if she was currently stuck in Collier.

Bet arrived to find Dale, solid as an International Harvester, in place at the west end of the lake. Her deputy stood an inch shorter than Bet but was twice her width, all muscle. The dark hair of his Croatian heritage dropped over his forehead and stood up in the back in a hairstyle Bet thought they called a "duck butt" back in the fifties; however, she never said that out loud. Dale had a sense of humor, but not about his hair.

Dale put in his bid for sheriff when Bet's father grew ill. That action prompted Earle's call to Bet. Arriving just in time to submit her application to run in her father's place, she found Dale stoic about her slipping into the role of sheriff. He'd been her father's deputy, and now he was hers. But she sensed him biding his time, resentment quietly building up.

After six months of working with him, however, Bet agreed with her father's assessment. Dale wasn't ready for the responsibility that came with the job.

A few tire tracks lined the western road where it turned onto the dirt-and-gravel parking lot next to the lake.

"Holiday weekend; probably people using the picnic area," Dale said, passing his cell phone over for Bet to scroll through the images of tire tracks. "Eating hot dogs, no doubt." Dale shook his head. "Do you know how many chemicals are in those things?"

Bet thought about the hot dogs she'd eaten for dinner last night.

"At least we can compare these tracks to a vehicle if we ever come up with one." She handed the cell phone back, wondering why he didn't use the camera in his vehicle. He knew his phone could be subpoenaed just as well as she did.

"Clayton is on his way in." Bet referenced the part-time deputy she regularly called in from the nearby town of Cle Elum when she needed an extra pair of hands. "Did you explain the ROAD CLOSED sign to George?"

"Yeah. Found him in town before I headed over here. He was on Django, so he doesn't need to drive a car on the road."

Django was George's big red quarter horse. Caretaker for the Collier estate and handyman and manager for all the buildings the Colliers owned, George often traveled on horseback. He could cross the valley easily on a horse, rather than the long way around that the road required.

"Tell him the story about a mountain lion sighting?" Bet asked.

"Yep."

At least Dale agreed with her use of the story to keep people out of the woods.

"Route calls back to your cell?" he asked.

"Please."

Routine calls went to Alma's desk and emergency calls routed to Bet's phone, or Dale's if she was off duty or out of the area. Dale turned his attention to his phone and made the switch.

"Hey, before you go, I have a question for you."

Dale looked at her, his expression neutral.

"I'm wondering why you used your cell phone for photos instead of the digital camera."

He waited a beat too long to answer. It wasn't a challenge, exactly, but it was close.

"Judgment call. I don't think any of the photos I took here are going to be part of a court case."

She understood his reasoning, so she let it go. But for her, he'd gone with convenience over what would be better in the long run. It was the kind of detail her father would have used to assess Dale's fitness for the top job—cutting corners on the easy stuff. More proof Bet shouldn't leave Collier in Dale's hands.

Dale hopped into his patrol vehicle, parked to the left of the *ROAD CLOSED* sign, and started it up. The biodiesel he always bought made his SUV smell like french fries, and Bet felt her stomach rumble with hunger. She swung back into her SUV, and they headed into town.

Along the way she passed a *DALE KOVAČ FOR SHERIFF* sign. She hated the politics and the situation, but she didn't see an easy way out. In addition to her belief that Dale wasn't up to the job, if she went back to Los Angeles now, she might not have the opportunity to step into the job later as she'd always planned. She would be the woman who abandoned Collier after her father died, which might not be forgiven. If Dale took the job, it could be for life.

Arriving at the station, Clayton's battered silver Isuzu Trooper pulled into the lot behind them. The big man unfolded himself from behind the wheel.

"Hey, Sheriff," Clayton greeted her. She'd given up trying to get him to call her Bet months ago.

Easygoing, broad shouldered, and blond, Clayton looked like an all-American farm boy. But the guileless innocence in his smile masked a man who could kill with one finger. With a black belt in tae kwon do and a few other martial arts Bet had never heard of, Clayton could drop a drunk-and-disorderly to the ground with the simple twist of a wrist.

The three of them headed into the station, where Alma pulled out the extra chairs and they circled up around her desk, the best place for all of them to meet as Alma took notes on her computer. Once everyone settled, Bet went over the events of the day. She passed around the photo of Jane Doe, unsurprised that no one recognized her.

"The first thing we need to do is identify our victim. Without a crime scene, determining her identity takes priority."

"Don't you want to look for the crime scene too?" Dale asked. "Check out the lake?"

"We'll do that first thing tomorrow morning," she said to him. "You and I will do a circuit of the lake once it's light. We're unlikely to have success in the dark, and I want to talk to people in town first."

Dale usually worked Friday, Saturday, and Sunday nights, and Monday and Tuesday during the day, along with all holidays and special events. Because he'd had to work Thursday night this past week, he should have tomorrow off.

"We're going to have a lot of overtime on this," Bet said. "You're free to work extra hours, right?"

Dale nodded, pulling out his cell phone and sending a text. "Yep." He put the phone back in his pocket. Bet thought he might have a new girlfriend but had yet to meet the woman.

Bet was in the office Wednesday through Sunday during the day and on call every night. Today both Dale and Bet worked, but a loud-music complaint had taken Dale out to a campground several miles away when Peter arrived at the station. Bet felt relief she'd been the one at the station to take the case.

Investigations in Collier mostly constituted finding a lost hiker in the woods, not violent crimes. Bet called backup if she needed it, such as to break up a domestic disturbance. A lot of people in the area exercised their Second Amendment rights and Bet didn't walk casually into anyone's house, even if she'd known them her entire life.

Between the two of them, Bet and Dale covered over five hundred square miles of isolated communities, campgrounds, roads, and trails. Though they had help from the National Forest Service and the other sheriff substations in the area, they relied primarily on each other and Clayton.

Turning back to Clayton, she said, "Depending on what we find, I may need you to work extra hours as well."

"I'll negotiate with Cle Elum." Clayton worked part-time for her and part-time for the sheriff in the small town thirty minutes south of Collier. "I could use the extra hours."

"Still trying to recover from last year's fires?" Alma asked. Clayton and his wife Kathy owned an organic farm that she managed. A severe fire season last year had impacted their yield, the smoke so thick it blocked sunlight and limited crop production. The health hazards of the air had kept farmworkers from picking ripe crops on time.

"A little." Clayton shook his head. "But that's not the real problem. We hope Kathy can work less. We weren't going to say anything yet, but . . . Kathy's pregnant again. Her doctor wants her to take it easy."

They all knew how much Clayton wanted children. Over the last few years, Kathy had suffered multiple miscarriages, and the subject remained a painful one.

Everyone congratulated Clayton, but Bet could see the news wasn't entirely positive.

"Everything is okay, though?" she asked, after Alma finished telling Clayton she'd get busy knitting booties. It crossed her mind Kathy might want Clayton to leave law enforcement and help her on the farm.

"So far, so good," Clayton said. "We just don't want to get too excited until she gets past her first trimester."

Bet could tell he didn't want to talk about it further, so she turned the conversation back to the investigation. "We should start showing the photo around town. We also need to search for abandoned vehicles. Jane Doe might have driven up here alone and left her car somewhere."

On the drive home from Ellensburg, Bet had considered various lines of investigation. Now she laid out her plan.

"Let's do a grid search for abandoned cars downtown. Clayton, you start there. Also flag anyone with outstanding warrants for violent crimes or drugs. While you're at it, take a copy of the photo into the open businesses and see if anyone remembers seeing her. If she made a credit card purchase somewhere, we can get her name. State her death is accidental for the time being. Ask that people not talk about her, as we haven't identified next of kin."

Clayton asked how long she wanted him to search.

"Search until nine. It's going to be slow running plates and talking to store personnel. Most places are closed by nine, so you can pick back up in the morning.

"Dale. I want you to search the campgrounds. Check for any vehicle or campsite that appears abandoned. I'll contact the ranger station, but we both know they're even more understaffed than we are."

Alma piped up from behind her computer screen, "What should I be doing?"

"Print off copies of Jane Doe's photo for us to take with us. The photos are already uploaded onto our server. Then head home. We'll all reconvene in the morning, and you can run a background check on Peter Malone." She turned to her deputies while Alma worked on the prints. "But call me immediately if anything suspicious turns up."

She kept her eyes pinned on Dale until he acknowledged her request with a nod. The thought that he might use the investigation in some way to get ahead in the polls troubled her. She might have mixed feelings about the position, but the town deserved her full attention.

"What are your plans?" Dale asked as he prepared to leave.

"I'm going to have another chat with the good professor and check in with George and the Collier estate."

This time she could bring Schweitzer. Her heart lifted at his excitement to go with her instead of staying behind under Alma's desk.

"Good boy, Schweitz," she said as he danced at her feet. His happiness felt like progress.

———————

As she paralleled the lake on her way to his campsite, Bet spotted Peter paddling to shore. The tall peaks cast shadows across the water. She guessed the fading light had ended his workday, too.

Not to mention that the physical challenge of navigating the canoe and equipment around the rough lake all afternoon, on top of the stress of his morning find, had likely worn him out.

She reached his trailer as Peter dragged the canoe onto dry land. The bottom scraped loudly against the ground, the layer of sand thin over the granite. Bet let Schweitzer out of the SUV, and he bounded down to the edge of the water in delight, wading out on legs so long his belly stayed dry.

Peter scratched Schweitzer under the chin before he leaned over to lift his equipment out of the boat.

"I meant to ask you what kind of dog that is," Peter said.

"Anatolian shepherd."

"Good-looking dog."

"He knows it." Schweitzer stood out in the lake, halfheartedly lapping up some of the cold water. "Want a hand with that?" Bet gestured toward the equipment still in the boat.

"Sure. Take this." Peter handed her a monitor while he carried the camera. Schweitzer followed them to Peter's trailer.

"What's it look like down there?" Bet hoped to be invited inside so she could have a look around without a warrant.

"You can see for yourself in a moment," Peter said as they reached the door.

While Bet was in E'burg, Peter had disconnected the Suburban and leveled the trailer with jacks. Bet could see propane tanks on the tongue of the hitch and a generator nearby, ready to provide power.

Peter unlocked the door and secured it open with a hook on the side of the trailer.

Stepping inside, he held open the screen door to usher her in, exactly as she'd hoped. Bet gave Schweitzer the hand signal to sit/stay, and he stretched out in the shade of a small pine tree to wait.

Bet stooped automatically to get through the doorway. Once they were inside, however, even Peter stood upright easily. Bet planted her back to the door and surveyed Peter's tiny kingdom. She didn't expect to find obvious signs of a struggle or blood spatter on the walls to prove Jane Doe had died here, but she'd love for something useful to come to light. Peter didn't appear nervous to invite her inside, but he could still have something to hide.

To her right was a table with bench seats. Directly across from her, a child-sized stove, sink, and refrigerator took up the middle section. To her left, the section where ATVs and motorcycles usually parked had been converted to a mobile science lab. A big monitor to edit digital video sat alongside extra storage shelves. All manner of equipment Bet couldn't guess at was secured for safe transport. As she looked around, Peter took the camera out of its waterproof housing and hooked it up to the computer. It would be tough to shoot someone or wrap up a body in such a tight space.

"I have a couple marine batteries to power all this," he said with a wave of his hand. "And that generator outside to recharge the batteries."

"Very efficient." Bet wondered what benefactor footed the cost for his research. She didn't think college professors paid for their own research projects, and even one as simple as this carried a price tag.

"This is a great travel trailer," she said to explain her snooping around. "I've always wanted one of these myself." She peered under the table as if marveling at the clever design. "This folds out into a bed?"

"It does." Peter didn't look up from his equipment. "It might be more comfortable than my bed at home."

Bet could see dust on the floor. While it wasn't proof Peter hadn't just cleaned up a crime scene, it did make it unlikely, especially combined with his nonchalance about letting her inside.

Finished hooking up cables, Peter turned on the computer. Bet saw a warped image of the scientist fill the screen. The camera caught a shot of his face as he lowered it into the lake. Through the film of water, the camera pushed his features out of proportion, face rippling and changing. Peter's eyes scrunched together, teeth gritted in concentration. His mouth and jaw stretched out until they filled the screen.

Dr. Jekyll and Mr. Hyde, two personalities in one body. A tingle of apprehension shot down her spine. She turned abruptly to look at the scientist but saw only his open, friendly face intent on the work in front of him.

Once it began to descend, the camera slipped past the choppy surface and into the crystal-clear water below. While light spilled through from above, the only objects the lens could find were occasional specks.

"What are those?" Bet stood behind Peter and pointed to the tiny spots on the screen.

"Fine grains of rock."

The two continued watching as the camera dropped one hundred, two hundred, three hundred feet. No fish or plant life save an occasional leaf sinking slowly into the depths. A flash of something white made Bet gasp, only to have the camera focus in and reveal a plastic grocery bag making its way to the bottom.

"How deep did you end up?" she asked, after a few minutes revealed nothing different.

"Three hundred and twenty feet or so. And I was nowhere near the middle of the lake." His voice held awe, and Bet felt the stirrings of his excitement.

"How deep do you think it goes?" Bet's mind turned to all the objects rumored to have disappeared under the water.

Peter shrugged. "It could certainly go much deeper than I went today." Clearly the professor hoped it would.

"Does it look like a cirque?"

Peter laughed. "That's not how this works. I have to map the entire bottom, do a number of calculations, analyze the composition of the rock. I won't be announcing my findings anytime soon."

"Is it surprising no scientist has ever come out here before?"

"Not really," Peter said. "There are a lot of lakes in these high altitudes and not enough of us to study all of them. Even an easily accessible body of water like Lake Chelan, which is considered the twenty-fifth-deepest lake in the world, by the way, still hasn't been fully researched."

On the monitor, the equipment found the bottom. As the camera moved slowly across the plateau, Bet could see the pristine condition of the stone. No algae, no plant life at all, just patches of sediment that looked like the same sand as on the shore. The light on the housing illuminated only a few feet, so despite the clarity of the water, visibility remained minimal in the dark.

"Did it all look like this?"

"Yep. I covered this area of the lake bottom, and it all looks the same. It does slope off toward the middle of the lake, but that's all I know. Nothing to see but rock, sand, and water."

"What were you hoping to find today?" Bet anticipated something about glaciated surfaces. Peter looked at her with a grin on his Muppet face.

"Might be fun to find the train."

FIVE

Bet said yes to Peter's offer of coffee, her curiosity piqued by his interest in the train and her continued sense he was hiding something. He secured the camera equipment while she sat at the tiny table at the front of the trailer to stay out of his way. From her perch, she could look out the window and see Schweitzer under his tree. He rolled over on his back, scratching his shoulders against the sandy soil with all four feet in the air. Behind him, the waters of the dark lake lapped the shore near the beached canoe.

Peter stooped over the burners on the trailer's miniature stove as the flame glowed propane-blue under the kettle. Rather than a coffeepot, Peter pulled out a reusable mesh coffee filter, which sat atop the cup in a plastic housing, brewing one cup at a time.

"How do you know about our train?" Bet asked as Peter puttered with cream and sugar, though she waved him off putting any into hers.

"A colleague told me about it, a friend in the history department. He heard I was coming here for research and wanted to make sure I knew about your colorful past."

"How much did he tell you?" Bet was curious if her own understanding of the town's history matched some professor's from Seattle.

"I know the first Robert Collier homesteaded this area in 1870," Peter said. "Three hundred twenty acres, I believe."

"One hundred and sixty originally; he added another hundred and sixty when he married," Bet corrected.

"Interesting, interesting," Peter said. "Let's sit outside to drink these. It's hot in here."

Bet stepped out ahead of the scientist and walked to one of the two camp chairs he'd set up under the trees. Bet looked out over the lake and thought about the question of the train, which might or might not be rusting in the inky depths.

"I guess Collier recognized mining would pay out a lot more than farming this area ever would," Peter said.

"True." Bet saw Schweitzer look over at her as if weighing the value of walking the ten feet from his spot on the ground to her side. A nap won out over the potential for dog biscuits, and he lay his head back down and closed his eyes. She trusted his instincts: nothing suspicious about Peter's body language.

"A lot of people here in Collier must have worked in the mine."

"What did your friend the history professor tell you?"

"I know a lot of people died when the mine collapsed. Early 1900s, right?"

"Nineteen ten. Same year as Halley's comet."

"No one ever tried to reopen it?"

The Colliers could have, but the mine no longer held much attraction to them.

"The owner died not long after the collapse and his son took over, but I guess the mine wasn't valuable enough to dig through all that." Bet gestured at the enormous slide of rock and shale that covered the lower half of the mountain across the lake in front of them. "Most of the coal had already been removed, and the accident made the mine unsafe."

"They're still in there, then? All the miners who died?"

"Still there."

"That's quite a legacy," Peter said.

"Anything goes missing around town, we blame it on the miners' ghosts," Bet said. "Not that I've ever seen one." Bet knocked her knuckles against the chair's armrest. It wasn't wood, but the motion should suffice for luck. The closest Bet came to communing with the dead was the never-ending conversation with her father's voice in her head.

"A lot of people worked in the mine." Bet returned to the conversation. "Or supported it in some way. We had over two thousand residents at the turn of the last century. People traveled long distances to work here."

A lot of towns with names like Black Diamond, Ruby City, and Newcastle had sprouted across the Pacific Northwest, littering the foothills and mountains as men drove holes into the ground and hauled black gold out of the earth. Some of the towns had survived the mining years, others becoming nothing more than ghost towns along roads no longer traveled.

"That explains how you are so ethnically diverse."

"You've been out to our cemetery, have you?"

"Not yet. But I've read about it. Is it really twenty-five different graveyards all pushed together?"

"It is. Once prospectors found coal here, workers came from all over Europe. Each group has their own graveyard. Italian, Croatian, Slovakian. During a wage dispute in the late 1800s, Collier brought African American miners in as strikebreakers. The territorial governor finally stepped in and the strike ended, but a lot of the black miners stayed and raised families here."

Bet watched a car across the lake on its way out of town. Trees hid Peter's campsite, but from her spot she had a good view of the road. If Peter had killed Jane Doe somewhere else, he could have slipped her into the water from here. But why the ruse? Why pretend to find her? If he'd killed her elsewhere, why bring her out to Collier? Or if he did, why not bury her in the woods? The lake made a poor dump site, unless she was supposed to sink. Maybe Peter had dumped her at night, expected her to sink, and then when she didn't he covered his mistake by "finding" her instead of trying to hide her in broad daylight.

Peter broke into Bet's thoughts. "But then all the miners waged another strike against Collier. Apparently under the prophetic streak of the wandering comet."

"Yep," Bet said. "They wanted better treatment and better pay, and they held Robert Collier's locomotive captive. Collier threatened to bring in miners from Appalachia as strikebreakers this time around, so the miners holed up inside the mine to keep anyone from coming in and taking over their jobs like before."

"And then it all went boom," Peter said, referring to the explosion that shut the mine down forever.

"What do you think set it off?" Bet asked, curious about a scientific opinion.

"A methane leak makes the most sense," Peter said. "Though I've also heard the theory the miners accidentally set it off themselves. What do you think?"

"I think the cause doesn't matter. Whatever it was, every miner in those tunnels died, buried under tons of rock. One hundred and twelve men and boys."

"Except one."

"You know about Seeley?"

"That I do. Lucky number one hundred and thirteen. The only one to live."

Bet wondered what it would have been like for fifteen-year-old Seeley Lander, who escaped the mine collapse because he'd been outside. While on duty guarding the hijacked locomotive, idling outside the mine entrance, Seeley, against orders, had left the locomotive unattended and climbed halfway up the mountain for a peek at the comet lighting up the night sky.

"So you're interested in history too," Bet said. "Not just tarns in cirques?"

"Interested in a good mystery," Peter said. "Either someone made off down this mountain with that train after setting off the explosives that buried all those men, just as Seeley Lander said, or there's a locomotive at the bottom of your lake. You can't tell me you've never wondered if Robert Collier had all those men killed."

"That was a long time ago. I deal more with the here and now." Bet didn't have to hear her father's voice to know that was a lie. Bet was mired in the past.

Peter took a sip of coffee, his eyes drifting toward his canoe, where Jane Doe's body had lain just that morning. "I've heard there's plenty of ghost sightings around town. Spirits of the dead miners trying to find their way home. You said yourself, Lakers blame the ghosts when things go missing."

"I didn't think an educated man like you would put much stock in ghost stories."

"What do you believe?"

Bet wasn't sure if he was referring to the train or to the ghosts. "My money says the train is in the lake."

The lake has always held our secrets.

"Speaking of the lake." Bet pulled out Jane Doe's photo and handed it to Peter. "See if you recognize her now that her face isn't contorted from rigor." His reaction interested her as much as getting an ID for the girl. She watched his face carefully as he took in the image. No recognition dawned in his eyes, nor did he register any signs of guilt.

He handed the photo back to her. "Sorry. I don't. But she looks like half the students I've had over the years." He rubbed his face in his hands as if to shake off the image of the dead girl. "She's just a kid."

"She is," Bet agreed, though any violent death bothered her. "She was." The two fell silent again, a brief pause to acknowledge the tragedy. "I should get back to work." Bet tucked the camera into her pocket and stood up with her cup in hand. "Thanks for the coffee."

"I'll take that for you." He held his hand out for her mug. "Aren't you going to search the lakeshore?"

"I can't talk about an ongoing investigation."

"Understood. Not a lot of daylight here in your part of the world, is there?" Peter referenced the late sunrise and early sunset created by the ring of peaks.

"We Lakers have a saying—there are only two kinds of Collier days: short and shorter." Bet offered a smile, then turned to her dog. "Come on, Schweitzer." He rose, tail wagging. He gave a quick bark and spun in a circle, happy to be headed back to the SUV. He was always up for a new adventure.

"Long day for you," Peter said.

"Comes with the territory."

As darkness settled into the valley, Bet drove away from Peter's camp and on to the next step in her investigation.

"Let's see what we can learn from George," she said to Schweitzer, his expression bright in the rearview mirror. The dog let out a quick yip as if to say he had her back.

For the first time since leaving LA, Bet didn't feel alone.

SIX

From Lake Collier Road, Bet turned into the picnic area parking lot, where the white-and-orange temporary barricade Dale had set up stood in place. She passed the *END COUNTY MAIN-TAINED ROAD* sign not long after and traveled the Colliers' private drive while the trees closed in around her.

As she pulled up in front of George's house, a motion detector light popped on, and she waited. If George was home, he would come out on the front porch.

In the glow cast by the outdoor light, Bet could see the nose of George's old Willys pickup truck sticking out from behind the cabin. Bought new by George's grandfather, it now had more rust than green paint, but George kept the drivetrain in perfect running order.

After a few moments went by and no one stirred, Bet stepped out of her vehicle. The air turned cold now that the sun had set. She let Schweitzer out of the back and asked him to heel. He fell in, the reassuring weight of his shoulder against her leg.

"Hullo!" The stillness of the forest swallowed her voice. Not even moonlight could reach the cabin, backed up against one of the granite peaks and surrounded by stately old-growth Doug firs. A gray layer of lichen covered the trees, and the forest felt hushed in anticipation. The logs of the house were almost black and moss and ferns grew from the cedar-shingled roof, as if the forest claimed the building as its own.

"George?" She could smell wood smoke and meat. George kept a herd of goats, and Bet wondered if she'd find one of them hanging alongside deer or rabbit or whatever else George might have killed. Schweitzer wagged his tail and gave out a whine Bet guessed to be from the thought of a snack, not imminent danger. He looked up at her and his tongue rolled out of his mouth.

"No meat for you." She dug into her pocket and came up with a biscuit. "This will have to do."

Polishing off the treat in one big crunch, Schweitzer faced front again. Bet walked along the side of the house, the big dog matching her step for step. As they rounded the rough-hewn wall, another motion detector light popped on and Bet could see the old smokehouse. A gray cloud puffed from the exhaust pipe on the sharply pointed roof. Roughly the size of a tall phone booth, the front door closed with a simple latch. Django stood in a nearby corral. He whinnied softly and trotted over to see who'd come calling.

Bet crossed to the smokehouse. A horror-movie fantasy of finding a body hanging on a meat hook, turning into a slab of bacon, shimmered in her mind. She swung the door open to find strips of meat in neat rows.

"No way that's anything but goat or rabbit," Bet said to Schweitzer, who licked his chops in agreement.

After closing the door, Bet crossed over to stroke Django's neck, the big animal leaning against her outstretched hand.

"George's out somewhere tonight without you, is that it?" Django's eyes slid to half-mast as Bet scratched the crest at the base of his mane. George owned another horse, an older mare named Constant. Though the elderly horse was mostly a companion for Django, George still rode Constant on occasion. She anticipated he'd be home soon now that night had fallen.

Bet pulled out her flashlight and lit up the pathway leading from George Stand's house to the Collier residence and decided to walk on the trail. The road would be closed at the Colliers' locked gate, so she couldn't drive there anyway. With a final scratch for Django, she started off through the trees, relieved that the community caretaking exception to the Fourth Amendment allowed officers to access private property without a warrant, locked gate or no locked gate.

The driveway curved around the small manmade lake the Colliers had dug out a century ago and stocked with fish, whereas the path led directly between the two homes. In the past, the pond had been open to the local community. Bet remembered fishing there with the Chandler brothers, her closest childhood friends. Dylan, the same age as her, and his older brother Eric, the boy she had idolized as a child. The brothers both moved away after they had turned eighteen. Their father Michael had left years ago and their mother Tracy died last year. The people who'd felt most like family were gone.

Bet reached out to put her hand on Schweitzer's head as he strode along next to her. "It's just you and me, buddy."

Access to the Collier property ended when Robert Collier Senior moved and closed up the house, though Bet knew local teenagers still snuck in sometimes. The rumor of huge trout in the forbidden pond lured them in.

The Doug firs that kept George's house in darkness thinned into the open glen where the Collier mansion stood. The light of the moon glinted silver on the trees but did little to light her way. The path came out on the east side of the house, which loomed over her in the dark. As she expected, no lights were on in the building. The Colliers had built the structure in the late 1800s from local timber and granite. It resembled a hunting lodge more than a house, with a grand entrance of stone steps and huge, solid double doors fronting the three stories. Bet wondered what it would be like to keep such a big house clean.

As they moved around to the front, Schweitzer's ears perked up and he looked in the direction of the garage, originally designed to hold horses and buggies and later retrofitted to house five cars. Bet stopped for a moment to listen.

Someone moved in the garage.

Bet put her hand on her service weapon. Had someone broken into the place? This could be her crime scene, complete with killer.

The large rolling doors on the front of the garage were closed, but a side door stood propped open, light spilling out onto the ground. She made her way over to get a better look. A figure bent over the engine compartment of a black Ford Bronco. Light shone from under the hood, but Bet couldn't get a clear view.

"Hello in there," she said in her no-nonsense sheriff voice. "Sheriff Rivers here. I need to ask you a few questions. Can you come out here, please?" Schweitzer crouched, waiting, the hand on her gun signaling him to high alert.

The figure backed away from the Bronco and turned toward Bet. She felt a ripple of unease at the looming shadows the action created. With no light shining on his face, Bet couldn't see his features, but she could tell by body weight and height it wasn't George Stand, the only person who had any right to be inside the building.

With his head turned sideways, she could see the outline of his beard, neatly trimmed. She reeled back as images from the nightmare flooded her mind. It was the same silhouette as in her dream, just before the shrouded body slid through the hole in the lake.

Her heart beat fast and heavy against her chest. The vision felt real, as if it wasn't a dream but a memory.

"What's wrong?" she could hear her father's voice ask her on that long-ago night when she got home from the lake. "You're trembling. What happened?" That wasn't a usual part of the dream. That fragment of dialogue was something new.

The shadowy figure started to reach behind him.

Schweitzer growled.

"Please keep your hands where I can see them." Bet unsnapped her holster. Her hand shook from adrenaline and fear.

"Well, now," the voice drawled. "I was just going to wipe off the oil." He held his hands up. "See?"

He stepped out into the glow of her flashlight. "Name's Robert Collier. My family owns this property. Want to explain what *you're* doing here?"

SEVEN

"How about you show me some identification." Bet dropped her hand off her weapon. Schweitzer sat down next to her, tense, but off the high alert her previous actions had prompted.

"Sure thing," the man said. "But I do need to wipe the oil off my hands."

Brown doe eyes crinkled in amusement as he kept his hands in front of him, just above waist level. He turned slowly around so Bet could see a red automotive rag in the back pocket of his jeans.

"Mind if I take that out?" he asked.

"Go ahead." If Bet remembered correctly, Robert Collier would be in his thirties. He stood a few inches over six feet, a barrel-chested man with a reddish-brown moustache, neatly clipped like his darker beard. The hair on his face accented the strong line of his jaw rather than hiding it, as it might on a lesser man. The hair on his head was dark and shot through with strands of silver.

He turned back around and appraised her while he rubbed the oil off his hands. "Elizabeth Rivers," he said. "Followed in your father's footsteps, did you?"

She ignored the question. "You have that ID on your person?"

He pulled his wallet out of his pocket, then slid the driver's license out and handed it over to Bet. Bet did believe he was Robert Collier; she remembered him. He'd cut a commanding figure even then, but curiosity about what the ID would tell her kept her quiet. Robert John Collier was thirty-six years old, six feet four inches tall, and two hundred thirty-five pounds. The ID showed an address in Arlington, Virginia.

While Bet studied the card, Robert studied the dog. He extended a hand, which Schweitzer sniffed, then ignored.

"Want to tell me why you're sneaking up on me in my own garage?" he asked as Bet handed back the ID. His voice carried amusement, the emotion mirrored in his eyes.

"Haven't had any of you Colliers around in a lot of years," Bet said. "Valuable property you have here. I wouldn't want anyone breaking in."

"I 'preciate your concern for my family's welfare."

"What brings you back here?"

"I don't know that's any of your business."

"I meant no offense, sir," Bet said. "Just making polite conversation."

"None taken."

"When did you arrive, Mr. Collier?"

"Please, call me Rob. All my friends do."

"You drove all the way from Virginia? That's a long drive."

"My horse doesn't fit in a plane." Rob pointed to a horse trailer parked behind the garage that Bet could just make out in the dark. "Besides, it's a beautiful country we have. Not every day a man gets the chance to cross it. I made a lot of stops before I arrived here."

"And that was . . . ?"

"About two hours ago."

"You drove across the country, arrived two hours ago, and decided you just had to change your oil."

Rob looked at Bet, his eyes sparkling. He didn't appear bothered by her presence or her questions, but in Bet's experience, wealthy men rarely thought they could get into trouble for anything. He could be a stone-cold killer with no fear of getting caught.

"The engine had cooled."

"You come all that way alone?"

"Well, there's the horse."

"That wasn't quite what I meant."

"I'm a single man, Sheriff. If I get lonely, I can find company here in town."

Bet pulled the photo of Jane Doe from her pocket and handed it to him. "Have you seen this woman?" She was curious how he would react to the photo of a dead woman.

Rob scrutinized the photo. "Nope. I haven't seen anyone since I arrived."

"Notice anything disturbed in your house or this garage?"

"Not a thing." Rob held the photo out to her. "What happened to her?" Bet didn't take the picture from Rob's outstretched hand.

"Accident." Why did he barely react to the photo of a dead woman? Most people were either repulsed or fascinated.

He kneeled down then, face level with Schweitzer.

"Good-looking dog," he said. "Don't see a lot of Anatolian shepherds."

"This is Schweitzer." People rarely recognized Schweitzer's breed, and Collier's comment took her by surprise.

"The man or the mountain?"

"You know Idaho, Mr. Collier." Everyone assumed her father had named the dog after Albert, but Bet and her dad loved to ski Schweitzer Mountain.

"I've been a lot of places, Elizabeth."

"Plan on staying here long?" Bet was determined to take back control of the conversation, even if only in her own mind. Rob Collier's quick response to her dog and his name threw her off. She took the photo he offered again as he stood back up.

"Don't know my plans yet." Rob turned to go back into the garage. "Come on by anytime, though, Elizabeth," he continued. "Nice to know the law is looking out for me and mine." She heard him chuckle to himself.

"Let me know if you notice anything disturbed." She held out one of her business cards.

"You'll be the first person I call." Rob closed the door behind him.

It irked her that he'd managed the last word, but before she could figure out a context to reopen the conversation, the sound of a horse whinny echoed through the woods from the direction of George Stand's house. He must be home with Constant.

Bet turned her back on the Collier estate and jogged down the road to George's place, curious if Rob had put the locked chain back on the gate. Schweitzer ran at her side, clearly hoping for a race.

Arriving at the gate, Bet found the chain cut and the gate left open.

Why would a man need to break into his own house?

Bet picked up speed. Maybe George had seen something in the woods more helpful than ghosts.

EIGHT

Bet stopped before she reached the cabin and called out George's name. George's tendency to go around armed meant Bet didn't want to startle the man, especially showing up after dark.

"Round back," he called out in reply. She and Schweitzer came around the side of the house to find a coyote slung over Constant's back. The dead animal stared vacantly in soundless appeal from eyes that reminded her unsettlingly of Rob Collier's, though they contained none of the sparkle. Tearing her eyes away, she turned her attention to George.

George moved with the speed of a man half his age. His face broke into a friendly smile that almost reached his eyes. Smooth skin belied his years. He looked barely out of his forties, though the hair visible under the brim of his hat showed more gray than black.

"Evenin', Sheriff Rivers the Younger. You're out late."

George had called Bet *the Younger* for as long as she could remember. As a child she'd been *Rivers the Younger*, then when she returned to town, *Deputy Rivers the Younger*, and finally, on the day of her father's funeral, George had given his condolences and called her *Sheriff Rivers the Younger*. Bet could think of no clearer way to be passed the torch. If she never had children, she'd stay the Younger until the day she died.

Like Rob Collier, George pulled a handkerchief from his back pocket. His hands were smudged with blood, however, not Quaker State.

"That's a big animal, George." Bet estimated the coyote weighed close to fifty pounds. George himself didn't weigh much over one hundred forty-five, a small, compact man with the barreled legs of a bronc rider.

George wiped his hands methodically before he spoke again. "Don't need a permit in this state when a coyote"—he pronounced the word with only two syllables the way most Lakers did—"threatens livestock on private land. You know my hunting license is up-to-date."

"Going after your goats?"

"That's right, and they make Django nervous. That's why I was out on Constant here; nothing bothers her."

Bet considered asking why he went out into the woods to find the animal if it had targeted goats behind his house, but she wasn't here about George's hunting practices, and if they went down that road she'd get little help from the man. Then she took a closer look at the knots George was untying.

"What kind of knots are those, George?" Her heart beat faster at the similarity to the ones on Jane Doe.

He looked up at her with an odd expression on his face. "Slipped constrictor knots. Why? You need to tie something up?"

"Where did you learn how to tie those?"

George laughed. "Don't know, Rivers. I've known how to do them so long . . ." His voice drifted off. "You know, I think Mr. Collier might have taught me those when I was a boy. The father of the Elder that is, three generations back."

"Are they common?"

"Don't think so. Military folks would know how. Truckers and riggers." George thought another moment. "And me."

Not to mention the rest of the Colliers. Bet debated about asking for more information but wasn't sure how it would help.

"How long have you known Robert Collier planned to visit?" she asked instead.

"Mr. Collier the Elder?" Bet read George's surprise.

Bet clarified that she meant his son.

"The Younger?" This seemed to surprise George even more. "Well, I'll be. Didn't think he'd ever set foot on the old place again."

"Why's that?" Bet's antennae quivered with the thought that the past feud might get explained.

"The Younger and the Elder didn't get along so well. I think everyone knows that." George wiped the sweat off the back of his neck and face with his red bandana, leaving a smear of blood, darker than his own skin. "I'd best get over there." He finished untying the coyote and lifted it to the ground. "I didn't know anything about the Younger coming to stay."

Bet started to ask for more information, but he cut her off. "I really need to get over there, Sheriff. I've kept the place up fine, but it's not ready for someone to live in. I should get it aired out, furniture uncovered. Lots to do. Wonder how long he's staying."

"Just a few questions first. I promise I'll be quick." Bet pulled the photo of Jane Doe out of her pocket. "I need to show you a photo of someone from the morgue. All right?" George dipped his head, which she took for a yes. "Do you recognize this woman?"

George took a long, hard look before he handed the photo back. "Never seen her before. Poor girl. What happened to her?"

"Accident. I need to find out her identity."

"Sorry, Sheriff. Can't help you."

Bet decided she wasn't going to learn anything useful with him so antsy to get over to the big house.

"I'll see you soon, George," she said. Schweitzer walked over to the coyote and sniffed at the corpse, a low whine rumbling in his chest.

George ruffled the big dog's ears. "Don't you worry, Schweitzer. You're safe from me."

Bet gave Schweitzer the hand signal to come, and the dog fell in next to her.

"Unless you go after my goats, that is," he said under his breath as they turned to go. She stopped and looked back at the tightly drawn man.

"You see anything in the woods recently that didn't belong there?" Bet asked.

"Just the ghosts. They're back again."

"I'm looking into your sightings." Bet picked up her pace to get around the side of the house. She loaded the dog into the SUV and began the drive to town.

Schweitzer sat up in the back, eyes pinned to George's house, as if his thoughts remained on the coyote.

"I didn't like seeing him that way either, Schweitz," Bet told her dog. Schweitzer whined again, and he didn't stop looking until the house disappeared from view and only the plume of smoke hung in the trees behind them.

NINE

Bet's stomach grumbled as she reached the edge of town. She headed over to the Lakeshore Tavern for dinner before going home. She parked the SUV in the side lot and opened the back for Schweitzer to hop out.

They walked into the neighborhood bar, where the rough pine walls and solid beams that supported the pressed-tin ceiling made up one of Bet's favorite safe havens. Autographed photos of bluegrass musicians who'd stopped by to play over the years hung on the walls.

The heels of her hiking boots thunked on the planks of the hardwood floors as she crossed the main room. The locals called out their greetings and she waved at the bartender, who hailed her with a hearty "Bet!"

"New tattoo, Rope?" Bet asked the bartender as she crossed over to say hello. Between his strange name and his penchant for body art, Rope managed to stand out in a town of unusual characters. The beefy man peeled the white gauze down off a patch on a forearm reminiscent of Popeye's and held it out for inspection.

"What do you think?" He admired his latest acquisition. His shaved head glimmered with a sheen of sweat in the warm room, and Bet could see the rows of rings, barbells, and other bits and pieces of iron sticking out of his face and ears in direct contrast to the vintage western clothes he wore when he worked behind the bar. He looked like a futuristic cowboy.

Tomás arrived with a fresh bowl of water for Schweitzer. She showed him Jane Doe's photograph, but he also shook his head.

"Sorry, Bet. Do you want a minute with the menu?"

She said yes, and Tomás left her with a promise to return soon.

Bet decided on her order and leaned back to listen to the buzz coming from inside the lively restaurant. She took a deep breath to release the stress of the day. Her mind went to Rob Collier's appearance. What was the likelihood he'd randomly reappeared in town at the same time a woman showed up dead in the lake that abutted his property? He could be lying about when he arrived, having rolled into town last night in time to drop Jane Doe in the lake before Peter found her this morning. He would know how to tie those odd knots.

It wasn't long before she started to imagine her father's voice. Conversations from the past. Tips for her future in law enforcement. She never knew what gem would surface at any given time.

"Don't get me wrong, Bet. The first shot in a gunfight is important," she remembered him saying not long before he died. "But never underestimate longevity in battle."

Bet let her father's voice continue. Since his death, she'd replayed old conversations, looking for clues into how he thought. Had he really fallen from a trail he knew like the back of his hand? Or had the cancer fight been one battle he couldn't face? Had he really intended for Bet to fill in for a short time, or had he lured her back to stay?

"Never run out of ammunition. An empty gun is just a chunk of metal getting heavy in your hand." The combat veteran her father had been never fully returned to civilian life.

Sometimes she added questions she wished she'd asked but never had the courage to bring up while he was still alive.

Wasn't easy for Mom, was it, Dad?

Bet's perspective on her parents' relationship had changed over the years, she realized, looking at it now with adult eyes. Her mother Fiona had been more outgoing than her father, though neither was particularly gregarious. Fiona had enjoyed small groups

"That's the best-looking bat tattoo I've ever seen. It balaɪ really well with the Celtic design here." Bet pointed to the tatɪ above it, hoping she'd said the right thing. His broad grin sweɪ across his face and his eyes lit up.

"Thanks, Bet. I knew I could count on you to appreciate it. You going to sit in here and listen to music? Folks are going to pick tonight," he said, referencing the live bluegrass jam sessions that took place regularly.

Bet loved to hang out when the local musicians played around the hearth, the fireplace empty in the summer heat, but she shook her head. "I'm heading out to my table, but I'd like to show you something first. We had a young woman die in an accident nearby, and I need to make an identification."

Rope's expression turned serious as he took the photo from Bet's hand. He looked closely, but shook his head. "Sorry, Bet. I don't remember seeing her."

"Okay. Thanks. I'll check with Tomás when I see him."

Rope handed the photo back to her. "Do you know what you want?"

"I need a minute."

"Burger patty for Schweitzer?"

"Yep." Bet patted the dog on the head. "You know how he likes it."

"Rare and now," they said together.

"I'll send Tomás out." Rope caught his partner's attention and signaled him to follow Bet outside when he finished up with his current customers, communicating wordlessly as only lovers and coworkers could do.

Bet went out onto the porch, trailed by the sound of instruments tuning up and the scent of burgers on the grill. Schweitzer squeezed his body under Bet's favorite table at the far end of the deck, high above the water of the lake. She was glad she'd pulled her coat out of the SUV, knowing the temperature would continue to drop. High elevations after dark were often colder than the flatlands.

of people. Three or four musicians would come over to play and sing, out in the backyard in the summertime or squeezed into the living room in the dead of winter. Bet remembered sitting at the top of the stairs, tucked around the corner out of sight, listening long past her bedtime. Between songs, their voices would rise and fall with music all their own, amusement at jokes Bet didn't understand, shushes when anyone laughed too loud, reminders that a child slept upstairs.

One night she crawled farther out above the stairs than usual, a particular song catching her ear, and without realizing it she crept into her mother's line of sight. Glancing up, either because of motion in the corner of her eye or from a mother's intuition, Fiona locked eyes with her five-year-old. Bet froze, certain that punishment hung over her head for climbing out of bed so late, but her mother winked and returned to the song.

At the time Bet had felt solely relief, but now, years later, she realized it had been a pact made between mother and daughter to keep a secret from the man who made the rules. Bet wondered what other secrets Fiona kept. Like why suicide seemed the best option.

When Bet was ten, her mother had hung herself from a beam in the garage. An act that brought Bet's father home early from his latest deployment and ended his military career, returning him to civilian law enforcement—deputy to his father first, then sheriff after him, as all the Rivers men had done. Keeping the links in the chain unbroken since the time Collier was nothing more than a few prospectors from the railroad looking for coal.

Bet had started to relive her father tearing down the garage when a voice broke into her memories.

Peter had walked out onto the deck, Tomás trailing close behind. "Hello, Sheriff. Mind if I join you?"

"Following me, Professor?"

Peter laughed. "Not a lot of choices in town."

"Pull up a chair." At least it would quiet her father's voice.

———

Bet wanted to learn more about Peter, so she encouraged him to talk about his work. It was clear he loved what he did, though he remained vague about the project that had brought him to Collier. She asked questions about his students, how many he had each year, graduate or undergraduate.

"Do you find more women going into the hard sciences?" she asked, curious about his contact with young women.

"I do, yes," he said.

Jane Doe was college age, the University of Washington in Seattle by far the largest university in the state. Ellensburg was closer but less than half the size.

"Do you advise many female students?"

Peter looked uncomfortable. "Why do you ask that?"

"Curiosity. I know what it's like to pursue a career in a male-dominated field. I'm wondering what it's like for women at U-Dub."

"We have a number of women on the faculty as well."

"They're more popular with the students coming in?"

Peter laughed, though it had a bitter tinge. "Are you asking if I'm considered a dinosaur?"

"I looked to the experienced women on the police force for guidance. I thought your female students might too."

Peter nodded, an expression that might be sorrow on his face. "I can understand that. To answer your question, yes. Female students tend to gravitate to female professors as advisers."

"That bothers you?"

"It does. I'm there to teach every student, regardless of gender. I like to think I have something to offer everyone."

Bet thought he might be telling the truth, at least as he saw it.

"What piqued your interest in our lake specifically?"

"There's a lot going for it. It's remote, but still accessible by road." His eyes searched for something to focus on besides her face.

Which also made it a good place to dispose of a body. But she still couldn't see a reason for dumping the body in the lake. Jane Doe would have been less likely to be found out in the woods.

Maybe someone wanted her found.

"There are plenty of remote lakes in our area," she said. "There must be more to it than easy road access and a rumor about a train."

Peter changed the subject. "I've talked enough about me. Tell me something about you. What do you do besides fight crime and keep the streets safe for the citizens? Hobbies? You must have hobbies."

The thought of surfing the net looking for photos of missing girls who matched Jane Doe rose in her mind's eye. She pictured her father with stacks of Polaroid photos from a crime scene. Pouring over them late at night when he couldn't sleep, positioned like tarot cards on his desk. Bet would sit quietly next to him as he rearranged the photos over and over, ruminating on clues hidden in the images.

Bet decided to let the conversation move away from Peter for a while. She'd circle back around later. "Fly-fishing, I guess. Though I'm not sure if that's a hobby or a religion."

"Fly-fishing. That's great," Peter said. "Let me guess, you have an older brother."

Bet pictured Dylan and Eric Chandler, her surrogate brothers. She'd learned to fly-fish with her father, Dylan and Eric, and their dad, Michael, before the scandal sent Michael out of town. The five of them would string out along a river, waiting for the fish to rise. Bet's father and Michael Chandler had both survived their deployments, first in Kosovo, later in Afghanistan.

Still beats fishing in the Nerodimka, the two men would say when the fish weren't biting.

"I was my father's only child," Bet said. She wondered if Jane Doe had siblings. How many people waited for her to come home?

"What do you fish for? Cutthroat trout? Rainbow? Small-mouth bass?"

"Are you an avid fisherman yourself?" Bet remembered his wistfulness at the fact that no fish lived in their lake.

"I'm not, but tell me what you love about it."

Bet laughed; usually it was only other anglers interested in her fishing. She launched into a description of the perfect cast. The ten and two o'clock wave of the arm, line, and fly. She described a few of her favorite fishing spots, though her mind kept returning to the lake.

The lake that shushed softly beneath them, the water reflecting light back through the cracks in the floorboards of the deck. The strings of white Christmas lights tacked to the wall threw a warm glow onto the aged wood of the porch and lined the obsidian-black water below.

During a pause in the conversation, music flooded through the open back door, the Appalachian hills of her mother's homeland made present through song.

In Scarlet town where I was born, there was a fair maid dwelling . . .

"Are you singing?" Peter asked.

"Just a little." Bet picked up her glass to cover her self-consciousness. She hadn't meant to sing out loud.

"You've a real pretty voice," Peter said. "Those all local musicians in there?"

Bet said they probably were, and the two sat quiet to listen.

"They sound good, too," Peter said.

The air, tinged now with a chill blown up from the surface of the lake, made them shrug on the jackets they'd brought with them—Peter's a rugged, heavy cotton, the type worn by men who labored with heavy machinery, baggy on his lanky form; Bet's a supple leather. Mist rose from the lake and spread across the surface, turning the black to gray.

Bet brought the conversation back to his arrival at the lake. "You've never been here before? To the lake?"

"Nope, nope, this is my first trip here to your lovely hamlet."

"Why now?" she asked. "Something must have prompted your research project."

"It's been on my mind to do for a long time, and I need to . . . well, let's just say I hope to find something worth publishing. Tenure beckons."

Bet had started to ask another question when Peter swallowed the last of his beer. "I'd better find the men's room." He cut off her words and picked up Bet's empty glass as well. "Need anything, Sheriff?"

"I'm fine."

Bet watched him go through the door into the main room. Though he didn't strike her as a psychopath who'd killed a girl then "found" her as a way to insert himself into the investigation, he kept secrets. She made a mental note to run the license plate on his trailer. If it didn't belong to the professor or the university, maybe she could find out who funded his study.

———

They parted ways in the parking lot. Malone pedaled off to his campsite after a firm handshake and a caution from Bet about biking the narrow road at night. She and Schweitzer climbed back into her SUV.

Arriving home, she paused for a moment outside, looking over her house. Earle never rebuilt the garage after his wife's death. Bright moonlight cast the two-story craftsman into shades of electric blue. The house sat under tall evergreens, which covered the roof with needles.

Her father would tell her to get out the ladder and clean the gutters before the fall rains came.

The house could also use a fresh coat of paint, at least on the front, faded from sunlight, but the window boxes overflowed with multicolored pansies, while the cheerful faces of white and yellow daisies lined the walkway. Bet didn't have a green thumb, but she'd managed to keep them alive through the summer.

"I should plant something other than a few flowers, Dad," she'd said to him not long before he died.

"Gardening was your mother's job."

Bet remembered fresh vegetables when she was a child, though she'd been too young to appreciate them. Working with her mother out in the backyard, Bet had liked to dig into the cool earth and find earthworms, which she held, wriggling in her hands, fascinated by creatures who could survive underground.

Bet walked across the creaky front porch. A white patch glowed in the dim light. Someone had left her a note.

She unfolded it, shining light from her cell phone on the paper.

Outsider.

Just a single word typed on the page.

She let herself in through the front door, unlocked as always, and made her way through the house without turning any lights on, the note in her hand. The house hadn't changed since Bet was a child. Up she went, knowing where every piece of furniture sat, hulking in the dark hoping to bite a shin; the exact spot where the carpet runner needed to be retacked on the stair, requiring that she step to the side to keep from tripping; the number of steps it took to reach the bathroom in the master bedroom.

Bet hadn't fully shifted into her father's space. First she'd moved her toiletries into the master bathroom. Next she'd emptied her father's closet, taking everything to the Goodwill in E'burg and bringing her own clothes in. She had yet to finish that chore, so both closets were half empty. Just like her job—half in as sheriff, half out. There was so much to do here in Collier. Sell the house? Keep the house? Win the election and stay for four years, then go back to Los Angeles? Hope Dale could grow into the job and take her place? Or lose the election and leave now? Let down her father and the entire town?

Apparently at least one person hoped for the latter. But why leave a note on her door? What did they hope to accomplish? She bristled at the implication that she no longer belonged, then wondered why it mattered now.

The antique standing mirror of her mother's reflected the light Bet turned on in the bathroom. As a child, Bet had believed her mother regretted her decision to take her own life and tried to communicate with her daughter through the glass. If ever an object was haunted, it was the tall mirror, hand carved in Appalachia by

Bet's great-great grandfather. The frame was scrolled with fanciful creatures and strange faces. But all Bet caught tonight was her own image in the warped glass.

She brushed her teeth and washed her face, then went down the hall to her old room. She tucked her Glock 21 under one side of the bed and encouraged Schweitzer to climb up on his.

Earle never slept with his dogs. "Dogs belong on the floor," he always said. It still felt like defiance when she brought Schweitzer up at night, but she loved the sense of security he brought.

It was crazy she was sleeping in her childhood bed with a dog his size. She should splurge on a king-size bed and move into the master. Maybe she'd do it when Schweitzer finally felt comfortable enough to spend the full night with her. He still hopped down partway through the night. Sometimes she felt guilty, using him to comfort her. If she returned to Los Angeles, what kind of life would Schweitzer have? He'd be better off staying with Alma. But now that he'd started accepting her, she wasn't sure she could give him up.

As she pushed thoughts of her future aside, her mind cycled back to Jane Doe. She'd known it would happen sooner or later, her first homicide case. If she solved it—when she solved it— maybe she'd finally live up to the expectations of a dead man.

TEN

The icy air burned her lungs as Bet stood panting under the trees. Snow covered the ground between her and the frozen lake. She clutched something in her mittened hand, a bone-white coffee cup. Why was she carrying that? A noise broke through the winter hush, someone trudging through the snow. She tucked behind a tree. No one should be out this late. The boogeymen of childhood stories ricocheted through her imagination. The silhouette of a man appeared, a dark outline against the white snow that glittered in the light of the moon.

He lurched to a spot on the ice, unsteady with the weight of his burden. It had the shape of a person and was wrapped in white cloth. He dropped it on the ice. Black hair spilled out against the ground.

Bet woke from her nightmare again and again throughout the night, so many details she'd never remembered before sharp now in her mind. She told herself it was the similarity to Jane Doe. She fought against letting it take on significance, no matter what tricks her mind played on her. Schweitzer whined, eyeing her from his place on the floor. She patted the bed and he hopped up, leaning his bulk against her.

"Earle never needed reassurance, did he, buddy?" she asked the dog as she put her arm around him. But she wasn't her father. Her father had hoped she'd be sheriff, but he never said she had to become him to do the job. She put that on herself.

"You're in charge," he'd said, once she'd taken over and asked him for input on a decision. "It's up to you."

After a few minutes with the dog, she slid out of bed. Daylight coming through the windows finally let her give up on sleep.

She and Schweitzer got ready for the day, a quick shower for Bet, breakfast for both, Schweitzer's nails clicking as he tap-danced on the linoleum of the kitchen floor while she set down his bowl. His tail beat out happiness. "Must be nice for life to be so simple," she said as Schweitzer licked the bowl clean.

Driving to the station, Bet replayed the scenes from the dream. Usually she dreamt it only once a night, not on a never-ending loop. Could this be signaling something new? Or was it just a manifestation of stress over her future and solving the mystery of Jane Doe?

Unrefreshed from her restless sleep, Bet walked through the front door to find Alma watching her closely. "Rough night?" the woman asked.

Bet considered telling Alma about her nightmare. Alma knew everything that happened around town. Had someone disappeared who wasn't reported? Could Bet be remembering something her father had talked about years ago? Or would Alma think she was crazy and wish that much harder for Earle's resurrection? If Bet was going to commit to this job, she didn't want Alma to have any reservations.

"I worked late," she said instead, and started to go into her office to wait for Clayton and Dale to arrive.

"I owe you an apology," Alma said, stopping Bet in her tracks. "For yesterday."

Bet couldn't keep the surprise from her voice. "For what?"

Alma laughed. "Your father would have asked that too. We both know what I'm talking about, but you want me to say it out loud."

Why would Alma have needed to apologize to Earle?

"I was out of line asking if the election impacted your decisions. I know you're better than that."

Dale came through the door with Clayton behind him, both ready to get started on their day. It broke the moment with Alma, who started pulling out chairs.

The group went over last night's events. Neither Clayton nor Dale discovered anything useful in his search.

Bet took a breath and put her thoughts in order. "What do we know about Robert Collier?"

"Robert Collier?" Dale repeated. "The rich guy?"

"Senior or junior?" Alma asked.

"Both." Bet described her interactions with Rob Collier and George Stand. "It doesn't seem like anyone knew Rob Collier was coming to town."

"You think Rob had something to do with killing Jane Doe?" Alma said. "That doesn't fit with my memories of him."

"What do you remember?" Bet asked.

"He was a very polite boy." *Polite* was one of Alma's highest compliments for people under the age of eighteen. "He'd carry your groceries to the car, stop to help if you had a flat tire, that kind of thing."

"What about the dynamic with his father? George hinted things weren't great."

"When he was young, he and his father were real close. I remember that. We all know what happened to his mother."

"I don't," Clayton said.

"Really?" Alma said.

"He didn't grow up here, Alma," Bet reminded her. "That was old gossip by the time Clayton started working for us."

Alma looked at Bet with raised eyebrows. Bet indicated for her to go ahead and tell the story.

"When Rob was about ten, his mother left town, except rumor has it she left because of an affair." Alma paused dramatically, a consummate storyteller raising the tension. "With Michael Chandler."

"Who is Michael Chandler?" Clayton asked.

Alma laughed. "Oh, boy. You really are out of the loop, aren't you? Michael Chandler was married to Tracy Chandler. He's Eric and Dylan's father. Did you know any of them?"

Clayton shook his head. "The names don't ring a bell."

"Tracy never filed for divorce," Bet said. "That I do know."

"After Rob's mother Lillian left, no woman ever took her place in the Collier household, though plenty were interested. Robert Senior's sitting on a fortune and he was a handsome man, but he never dated anyone here, so it was just him and Rob, thicker than thieves. And then they weren't anymore. Some kind of rift. Right before Rob graduated from high school."

"You don't know what the fight was about?" Bet asked.

Alma shook her head. "Rob packed up and left town the day after his high school graduation, and we never saw him again."

"How is this ancient history going to help us figure out who killed Jane Doe?" Clayton asked.

"Interesting timing. Dead girl. Him in town," Dale offered.

"And he's been gone a long time. Who knows what he's like now," Bet said.

"It doesn't make sense, though," Clayton said. "If Mr. Collier killed her, why would he stick around? He could have left and no one would ever know he was here."

"Arrogance?" Bet said. "Maybe he thinks he's untouchable. If he's back here at the family estate, his father didn't disown him. Though he did have to cut the chain to get in the gate, so maybe his dad doesn't know he's here." She went on to explain about the knots George used on the coyote and where he'd learned to tie them. "Rob would likely know those knots too," she said.

"You wanted me to do background on Peter Malone," Alma said. "What's more important, info on Peter or Rob?"

"Start with Peter, but put Rob on the list," Bet said. "Both of them arrived in town at the same time the woman was shot, so they're both persons of interest to me. Our most important task is an ID for Jane Doe."

Bet turned to the plan for the day. She told them she hoped the killer didn't know they'd found the body yet, giving him or her a false sense of security.

"Dale, I'd like you to start out on the west end of the lake. We need to do a complete circuit on the chance we can find evidence of a crime scene, or at least where Jane Doe went into the water."

Clayton would work his way through town again, then start to visit houses out in the valley. He skipped a number of businesses that had been closed last night, plus different people worked during the day that he wanted to show Jane Doe's photograph to.

Bet planned to walk the east end of the lake and handle the regular business of the office should anything come up. Alma would start with a search on the internet for missing women matching Jane Doe's description. Missing-children sites and *be on the lookout* notices—BOLOs—could all include pictures of Jane, especially if she was under the age of eighteen. Carolyn had estimated eighteen to twenty-five, but as that wasn't confirmed, they had to assume Jane Doe could be a minor.

Alma would also send copies of the photo to other law enforcement agencies in Washington State and follow up with the ranger station about abandoned cars in campgrounds outside of town. Once she finished with that, she'd start in on the background for Peter Malone and Rob Collier. The group would reconvene at noon.

Bet and Schweitzer walked outside with her deputies. She paused a moment to look around town, quiet now that the holiday weekend was over.

The red-brick sheriff's station sat near the intersection of Lake Collier Road and Bullitt Lane, the dead center of the commercial district. Bet loved all two streets of it. Standing in front of the station, she could see most of the stores. The tiny Ace Hardware, the used-book store, Backcountry Climbers where you could buy an ice ax, a high-tech tent, and an espresso—places she saw every day. She knew the owners and the employees and most of the patrons. It was nothing like her job in Los Angeles, where people were always strangers.

The buildings were a mix of wood and brick. False fronts from the late 1800s stood above raised sidewalks, some the original wood planks, the rest replaced with concrete. Scuff marks along the curb showed where tourists had misjudged the height of the sidewalk and scraped their front ends parking too close.

A wooded hillside rose behind town and the cemetery kept watch over the living. Each section was surrounded by iron fencing, marking the territory of the ethnic groups. The factions lay side by side, not unlike how they'd lived, diverse but not harmonious.

The Collier Market now served the best coffee in town, thanks to Sandy Stuart and her coffee cart, parked just inside the front entrance. Even before Bet came through the front door, Schweitzer close behind, Sandy had already started making Bet's latte.

"Mornin'," Bet said, taking her hat off as she crossed the threshold.

"Mornin', Sheriff." Sandy tossed a dog biscuit to Schweitzer. "Come to talk strategy?"

As soon as Bet announced her bid for sheriff in the upcoming election, Sandy had offered to help with the campaign. "Women have to stick together," she said when Bet asked her why. "I know what it's like to be underestimated."

Sandy stood five feet tall and five feet wide. She had the unaffected smile of a child and the brain of a rocket scientist. People underestimated Sandy because of her size. People underestimated Sandy because she worked standing at an espresso machine. But they never underestimated her twice.

After growing up in Collier, a descendant of one of the African American miners brought in as a strikebreaker, Sandy had gone off to law school in Seattle. She'd worked as a high-powered attorney until a heart attack almost killed her at age forty-five. The health scare brought her back to Collier to regroup.

Now she worked the coffee stand six mornings a week. She'd told Bet the morning shift gave her reason to get out of bed in the morning. She rode her bike in from her house seven miles away. Back in town for a year, she'd lost fifty pounds. She said she never missed the courtroom. Bet almost believed her, though her exuberance about helping with the campaign made her wonder if Sandy was getting bored. Maybe she wanted to practice law again.

"I want to show you a photo," Bet said, picking a fresh-baked muffin out of the basket on the counter. She could feel its warmth through the cellophane wrapping.

"Something tells me it isn't a picture of hot, naked men."

Setting the muffin down on the counter, Bet put the photo of Jane Doe next to it. "It's from the morgue, okay?" Sandy nodded. She'd seen plenty of crime scene photos from her time in the courtroom. "Have you seen this woman?"

Sandy picked up the photo, her fingers rubbing the edge of the glossy photo paper. Her face showed no reaction. "How'd she get dead?"

"Single gunshot wound to the back."

Sandy winced. She took the photo over to the window to shed a little more light on it, then handed it back to Bet.

"Where'd you find her?"

"Floating in the lake."

"She came in Friday morning for coffee."

Bet hadn't expected to hit pay dirt so soon. "You get a name? Credit card receipt?"

Sandy shook her head. "Sorry, she didn't talk much. And paid in cash. She came in early, just after I opened. Bought two drinks and a blueberry muffin."

"Two?"

"But I didn't see who she was with."

Bet contemplated that information for a moment. "Did you see what she was driving?"

Sandy shook her head again.

"Anything stand out about her?"

"She asked what time you would get in."

Bet rocked back on her heels. "She asked about me specifically? Or she just asked about the sheriff's office?"

"She asked, 'What time does Sheriff Rivers get in?'" Sandy finished making Bet's latte. She turned back to the counter and set the drink down, her brow furrowed and her mouth puckered.

"I've seen that look before," Bet said, before taking a sip. "Something else?"

"I didn't think much of it at the time, but something struck me just now."

Bet waited while Sandy put her thoughts together. Sandy never said anything she wasn't sure about.

"I said," Sandy continued, "'Usually around eight,' and the woman said, 'I guess I'll have to wait to see him.'"

"Did you correct her?"

"No. I just assumed she read E. Rivers somewhere and guessed you were a man. People were always doing that with me. S. Stuart, criminal defense attorney; must be a guy, right? I knew she'd figure it out when she saw you."

"But now you don't think it was just a wrong guess on her part?"

"Maybe it was something else."

"Like what?" Bet asked, curious what Sandy had in mind.

"I wonder if she was specifically looking for your dad, not as sheriff, but because of something about him."

It wouldn't be the first time someone had come looking for Sheriff Rivers and thought they would get Earle, not Elizabeth. When Bet took over for her father, she hadn't changed anything in the printed or online material. Her father had been E. Rivers, Sheriff, and now so was she. It was one of the many things Sandy wanted her to change for the election that Bet hadn't had time to deal with and wasn't sure she wanted to.

"Huh," Bet said.

"Yeah. Huh."

Bet took a sip of coffee. If Jane Doe expected Earle, maybe she'd been in Collier before.

"Have you been out to Pearson's?" Sandy asked.

"Not yet. It didn't feel like a link. Pearson's is solely for boys."

Sandy shook her head in mock despair, "Bet, Bet, Bet. Don't you know where there are boys, you'll find girls not far behind?"

Bet gave herself a smack on the head. "Duh," she said.

Sandy chuckled and leaned over the counter to pat Bet on the shoulder. "You would have thought of it eventually."

"Thanks. By the way, I know I don't have to ask you to keep this quiet. The gunshot isn't public information, or that we found her in the lake." Luckily for Bet, when outsiders died from falls or accidents, the locals mostly ignored it. As long as they didn't know it was from a gunshot wound, her death wouldn't pique their interest.

Sandy crossed her heart. "I know nothing."

Just before Bet reached the door, Sandy called out, "Next time, bring photos of hot, naked men."

"I'll see what I can do."

Sandy was right. Clayton would have taken a photo out to Jeb Pearson eventually, but Sandy's quick connection to his organization made Bet feel foolish. She should have made visiting him a priority.

As she left the market, Bet's mind turned to her father again, as it usually did when she questioned her abilities. The medical examiner ruled her father's manner of death after the fatal fall in the backcountry accidental, but Bet didn't quite believe it. Her father didn't make those kinds of mistakes. And why had he taken a walk in the woods that day, yet left Schweitzer behind?

She'd poured over the autopsy reports, but just because she couldn't fault Carolyn's findings didn't mean Carolyn's assessment was right. Her father's cancer had been worse than he admitted to Bet. Maybe he'd decided to treat his illness his own way in his own time.

After he lured Bet home.

Her father had always stepped up if she asked for help. Could she really turn her back on him now that he was dead?

Bet crossed the street and went back into the station. She set the lemon poppy-seed muffin down on Alma's desk as a peace offering. "Thank you."

Alma smiled. "Don't feel bad. I second-guessed your father sometimes too."

Bet felt as if she'd passed a test. "I have a question for you." She thought about her conversation with Sandy. "Did anyone come in looking for me on Friday?"

Alma grabbed her notebook where she marked down events of the day. She paged backward to Friday. "George Stand came in wanting you to know the ghosts were back in the woods again."

"What did you tell him?"

"Told him you had a meeting scheduled with the Paranormal Society in E'burg at the end of the month and for him to check back then."

Bet chuckled. Definitely not the kind of issue she'd dealt with down in California. "What about someone you never met before?"

Bet sipped her latte and broke off a piece of the muffin. Alma swatted at Bet with her bony claw of a hand. "Get your own muffin."

"I'm only eating the stump," Bet teased her. Alma had a thing about muffin stumps. She always complained it wasted good dough.

"No one came in looking for you, but we did get a phone call at nine forty-one AM. Female. Didn't identify herself; asked was Sheriff Rivers in."

Bet remembered she'd driven down to Cle Elum for a quick meeting that morning.

"By any chance, do you remember if she asked for Earle?"

Alma shook her head. "Just Sheriff Rivers. Why?"

"Maybe nothing, just something that caller might have said to Sandy, if it's the same girl. Did you say *she* or *her* about me?"

Alma thought for a moment. "No, I just said, 'The sheriff isn't in.'"

"Okay. Did the woman ever call again?"

Alma shook her head, mouth full of muffin.

"You recorded the number from the call though, right?"

"Yep."

"Find out who that phone is registered to."

"Will do."

"I'm going to head over to Pearson's. Please contact Clayton and let him know he doesn't need to drive out there." Bet signaled for Schweitzer to come along, and the two started to leave.

"Here," Alma said, holding out the muffin stump. "Got to keep your strength up."

———

It didn't take long before the last building in town slipped behind her and the openness of the Train Yard spread out all the way to the base of Iron Horse Mountain. She thought about the glacier that formed their valley. U-shaped, the basin was flat bottomed and steep sided. Ponderosa pines, with their distinctive red bark hatch-marked with black crevices, rose in giant stands above the valley floor.

The forest ringed the Train Yard, an area clear-cut years ago to build the town and make way for the roundhouse. The open valley hosted livestock—horses and cattle—along with a roving elk herd, protected by law from hunters unless they strayed too far off the valley floor.

Bet felt something in her chest release at the beauty of her community. An ability to breathe she'd never felt driving around Los Angeles.

Neatly painted white fence marked the beginning of Pearson's Ranch. Jeb firmly believed Mark Twain had it right and painting fence could turn the roughest Tom Sawyer into a fine, upstanding citizen.

Sometimes he was right.

Turning onto the drive in front of the main building of the complex, Bet could see Jeb putting up storm windows on the boys' cabins, battening down the facility for winter. During the winter months he rented some of the cabins out to snowmobilers, cross-country skiers, and snowshoers, but he closed the bulk of the buildings for the season. The round building in front of her had once sat at the end of the Colliers' private railway line. The giant turntable it housed spun the locomotives around to head back down the mountain. Pieces of track still glinted in places across the meadow, peeking through tall grass, but most of it had been pulled up and used in other locations around the state.

Jeb's dog, a huge, slow-moving Newfoundland named Grizzly, uncurled himself from his spot by the door and wandered over to join Jeb in greeting Bet. Even from her seat in the SUV, Bet could reach out and pet the bear-sized dog. Though Schweitzer stood an inch taller at the shoulder, the Newfie had a good fifty pounds on him. His hair was more black than the brown of his namesake, but Bet thought the name was perfect.

Standing at the side of her SUV, Jeb scratched Schweitzer, who had stretched his neck out over the back of the rear seat to get some attention. After greeting the dogs, Bet and Jeb turned to each other.

"Howdy, Bet," Jeb said. Now well into his fifties, the only evidence he wore from his years of hard drinking were scattered red trails of broken capillaries across his craggy face, his wiry body taut from manual labor and clean living. "Everything okay?"

"I'm trying to identify someone. I need to show you a photo from the morgue." She handed him a copy of the photo.

Jeb looked at it carefully before he shook his head. "Not sure. It's hard to tell with her like this."

If the young woman had known Earle Rivers, she might have a connection to a boy who ended up at Pearson's. Earle had volunteered during the summer teaching fly-fishing to the boys Jeb rehabilitated, and sometimes to the family or friends who came to visit. Bet had taken on her father's role here this summer too. If Jane Doe met Earle that way, it would have been at least a year ago, maybe longer.

"She might have visited someone here. It could have even been a few years ago, so try to picture her younger."

Jeb looked at the photo again. "Pretty little thing, isn't she?"

"She was," Bet said.

"What happened to her?"

"Accident." Law enforcement officers didn't have to tell the truth about an ongoing investigation.

Jeb looked down at the image again. "I don't know, Rivers. It's possible I've seen her before. I meet a lot of kids out here."

"Hang on to that, would you? It might spark a memory. Call me if you think of anything."

Jeb nodded. Bet headed back to the lake. She needed to start walking around it, taking the route opposite the one Dale was examining. Perhaps the lakeshore held evidence of a crime scene.

―――――――

A few hours later, Bet stumbled across the loose rubble covering the area where the mine mouth had once opened above the lake. Standing a hundred feet above the water, she could see Peter out on his little boat at the far end. Today the lake surface was quiet, and where she stood the air was still. The white-and-silver granite stone of the mountainside glowed visible at the edge until it plunged into the water and the darkness created by depth swallowed it whole; a great, white whale into the sea.

Neither Bet nor Schweitzer found evidence of a crime scene on this side of the lake. Schweitzer scanned the lakeshore with his nose while she searched with her eyes. Jane Doe could have traversed the rocky shore of the lake with a companion-turned-killer. Bet hoped to find where the victim bled out. She knew the stats: more than half of female homicide victims were killed by men they knew, intimate partners or family members. Jane could have gone hiking and tried to break up with someone, triggering anger that turned violent.

After completing her section of the lake, Bet traveled higher up the hillside to get a larger view. As she let her eyes scan away from her, the flash of something metallic caught her attention. Carefully picking her way over, she found a section of train track poking out of the rock. Bet picked up a few loose pieces of stone, her fingers brushing the metal, hot from the sun. She tossed the rocks in the direction of the lake. Schweitzer traced their arcs, as if he might need to recover them later. He looked up at her.

"Good boy."

He tilted his head, assessing her comment. She crouched down next to him, taking his face in her hands. "We're going to be all right, you and I."

The dog touched his nose against her cheek. She felt him give her a tentative lick before he sat back. His face said he expected a scolding.

She reached out and scratched his chest. "Earle wasn't much for physical affection, was he?"

The dog grumbled in his chest as if agreeing with her comment, though it might just have been appreciation for the attention.

"I'm not my father, Schweitz. You can give me kisses anytime."

Bet stood back up and balanced on the old track. From where she stood, she could look back and forth at where the train had run over a hundred years ago. The hillside showed a slight flattening the length of the landslide, where the train had stopped to be loaded at the mine. Somewhere below her, all the miners lay buried.

In the distance, Dale worked his way around the other end of the lake. He hadn't found any evidence of a crime scene either. When they spoke on the phone, he reported that even the picnic areas showed no footprints near the water's edge. Several people had used the scattered picnic tables, there were footprints in the parking lot, and flattened spots still showed under the trees, but he found no blood pool on the ground and no obvious tracks led to the lake.

Bet's phone rang, breaking the silence.

"Carolyn, what have you found for me?"

"Hey, Red. Here's what I know so far. It was a bullet hole. The bullet was removed, probably with pliers, most likely needle-nose from the thin gouges left behind. No sexual assault. No water in her lungs."

"Anything else?"

"I found fibers in the wound, leading me to believe she was dressed when she was shot. I sent them over to the lab, but I wouldn't hold out hope it will tell us anything more than whether she wore cotton or a poly blend."

"Were you able to save any fingerprints?"

"The chemical poured on her fingers was lye. It's highly caustic and destroyed the ridges of her fingerprints. I also didn't find anything under her fingernails. She may not have scratched at her killer, or if she did, the lye dissolved any tissue left behind."

Bet asked about latent fingerprints on Jane Doe, but Carolyn reported she had found none.

"I'm still working on TOD," Carolyn said, referencing time of death. "I'll call you back when I know more or get blood and tox reports back from the lab."

"Okay," Bet said as they ended the call. "Thanks for the update."

Bet considered other options for identifying Jane Doe. DNA was rarely useful for victim identification without something to compare it to. DNA tests could take months, and the likelihood that Jane Doe was in a criminal database was negligible. Fingerprints might have identified the woman if she had been entered in a database, such as for a job in education or health care. Now their best chance of identifying Jane Doe would be through a missing persons report or a plea to the public with her description. If their attempts to find her identification failed locally, Bet would move to a wider audience, which would also expose her investigation, making it available to public scrutiny.

Looking across the lake at the road, Bet couldn't believe someone cautious enough to remove all of Jane Doe's easily identifiable characteristics would risk dumping a body from there. Despite the small population of Collier, the likelihood that someone would drive along at the exact moment the perpetrator was pushing a body into the water would be too great, especially during a holiday weekend. The shoulder along the stretch of road by the lake was narrow; parking a vehicle would stand out to anyone passing by.

The voice of Earle Rivers came through loud and clear. *If the only options you have don't make sense, there must be another option.*

"What other option would that be, Dad?" Bet asked out loud, as no one else was within earshot. Schweitzer looked at her as if expecting a command.

If the body didn't get dumped in the lake, maybe it came in some other way.

"How could a body get into a lake except by being dumped?"

Out on the water, Peter Malone caught Bet's attention again. "Guess if I want to know something about a lake, I should ask an expert."

Bet thought her father would approve and turned to make her way back across the loose rocks to talk once more with Professor Malone.

ELEVEN

On the way back down the hillside, Bet's phone rang again, an unfamiliar number on the screen.

"Sheriff Rivers?" a woman's voice asked.

"Yes. Who is this?"

"This is Jamie Garcia. I'm a reporter for the *Seattle Times*. I understand you're investigating a homicide in Collier."

The woman's comment stopped Bet in her tracks. Schweitzer gave a low growl as if reading her distress.

Bet made a rookie mistake. "Where did you hear that?" She knew the woman's answer before she gave it.

"I'm not at liberty to reveal my sources."

Of course she wasn't. Bet paused, uncertain how to respond. She'd never had to deal with the press as a patrol officer, and nothing newsworthy had happened in Collier during the last six months except her own father's death, which hadn't made the news in Seattle.

How had this?

"How about you tell me what you know, and I can confirm or deny."

She hoped to discover that the woman knew nothing and was just fishing for information. The long pause made Bet think this might be true.

"I understand you have a Jane Doe who died under mysterious circumstances. That you're new to your position, and at this point don't have any leads. Is all that accurate?"

It was, but Bet certainly didn't want that to be the entirety of the reporter's story.

Now it was Bet's turn to pause. She didn't want the media to take control of the situation. What could she offer the woman in exchange for time?

"Tell you what," Bet said. "I'm getting ready to step into a meeting. Let me call you back in, say, an hour? We can talk more then."

"The story is going to come out with or without your help, so I look forward to hearing from you."

Bet took a few deep breaths after ending the call before she continued to her vehicle. She wanted to research the reporter and find out who she was dealing with. She might need to ask the press for help in identifying Jane Doe, but not until she was ready. Currently, Jane Doe's killer might not know her body had been found. Bet wasn't ready to give up that advantage. Maybe she could get the reporter to hold off in exchange for an exclusive story.

With Schweitzer loaded up, Bet realized it was ten minutes to noon. Peter Malone and researching the reporter would have to wait. She drove over to the station to check in. Clayton towered over Alma where they stood together on the front steps, waiting for the rest to gather. Even with Alma on the top step and Clayton on the bottom, she barely reached his shoulder, but the old woman had a spine of steel and showed no sign of slowing down.

"I might have something, Sheriff," Clayton said, as Bet walked up.

"Let's talk inside." The three went in and sat down around Alma's desk.

"I ran the few license plates in town I didn't see last night," Clayton said, after getting settled on the wooden office chair, which creaked under his weight. "None came back owned by someone who could be our Jane Doe, and I managed to track down all the owners. But I found another car near the Ruby Creek Campground. It was parked off the road with a bent rim, so it wasn't drivable. I called in to the DMV for a name and phone number. It's registered to a man in Tacoma named Tim Reed. I called and reached his wife."

"What did the wife have to say?" Alma sat poised next to Clayton, fingers on her keyboard, taking notes. Alma kept a log of everything each one of them did for the investigation, printing out her notes and keeping them in a binder to track their progress. Bet could look back over the material anytime she needed to assess what had been done.

"She said her husband came up here this weekend with his daughter, Trisha, as a quick vacation before school started up for her again."

"She said *his* daughter," Bet said, "not *theirs*?"

"I caught that too," Clayton said. "It's her stepdaughter. Trisha is nineteen years old and a student at Tacoma Community College."

"Did you get a description?"

"Her hair is long and blond and she has blue eyes just like our Jane Doe. The stepmother reported they aren't due back to Tacoma until this evening, so she wasn't worried about them. But she couldn't reach her husband on his cell phone."

Cell phones regularly went out of range, so that wasn't unusual. Still, they had to track the two down.

"Here's the interesting part, though. The stepmother said the trip was in part because Tim and Trisha weren't getting along very well. Her father wanted her to consider moving back home for the school year. She didn't spell it out, but it sounded like they might be struggling financially and the girl might have a drug or alcohol problem on top of that."

Bet was always amazed at what people would say to authorities over the phone.

"I also had the sense the stepmother didn't really want Trisha to move home."

Domestic trouble. She wondered what the relationship was like between Trisha and her father. Could there have been an accident?

"We need to find out if Tim Reed owned a gun." Washington State didn't require gun owners to register firearms, so there wasn't an easy way to check. "Alma, find out if he has a hunting license or a Concealed Pistol License. That will give us a place to start."

Alma started clicking on the computer keys.

"The wife gave you his cell number?" Bet asked Clayton.

"She did. I'm going to call and make sure his daughter is still with him. I didn't want to bring it up with the stepmother that we have a young, blond Jane Doe in the morgue with no evidence at all that it's Trisha."

Dale came through the door, balancing four cups and a muffin on a to-go tray.

Alma had him trained too. Dale put the coffees down on Alma's desk and reshaped his pompadour, ruffled by the wind.

"You look fine, pretty boy," Alma said, picking up her muffin.

Dale, stone-faced, removed a black plastic comb from his back pocket and began to run it slowly through his slicked-back hair, eyes locked on Alma. Alma stared him down but couldn't make him blink. She threw up her hands with a laugh. "You win."

Dale's poker face broke into a grin. Despite the difference in their ages, he and Alma had always shared an easy relationship.

"Good work, Clayton." Bet took a sip of her latte. "Keep me posted." It was a long shot that the man had killed his daughter and dumped her in the lake, but if there had been an accident, he could have panicked.

"Do you really think a man could accidentally kill his daughter, then get rid of her that way?" Clayton asked.

Bet's mind rebelled at the thought of a man disposing of his daughter in such a strange and callous fashion, but she knew not to discount what people would do when faced with tragedy.

"We don't know they were out here alone. Someone else could be involved. For all we know, Tim Reed is in trouble too."

Clayton nodded, his face grim. Bet imagined impending fatherhood would impact his reaction to investigations moving forward. She still feared Kathy might want Clayton closer to home. She didn't want to lose him to the farm.

"Did you ask the stepmother to email you a photo of Trisha?" Bet asked.

"I wasn't sure if I should."

"Alma can call her back." Bet looked at Alma, who nodded, her eyes not leaving her computer. "What about leaving a note on the car?"

"That I did. I left my card with a note to call the station, as we were concerned about the well-being of the driver. I noted that we would be following up with the registered owner. Hopefully he'll call us."

Clayton went on to explain that he'd shown the photo of Jane Doe around, but no one admitted recognizing her. He'd visited all the open businesses in town. "I thought I'd continue to work my way outward from town. If she was in the market getting coffee Friday morning, someone might have seen her."

"Good, do that after we break." Bet thought about how the girl's "accidental" death would be talked about among the locals. "Did you ask people to respect the privacy of the girl's family and request that they not talk about her publicly?" If an article came out online from Jamie Garcia, she might have a bigger problem.

"I did," Clayton said. "I reminded them we wanted to identify her so we could let the family know."

"Clayton knows the drill." Dale's tone was harsher than the situation warranted.

After an uncomfortable pause, Bet responded. "We all do," she said. "But this isn't the type of thing we usually deal with. It doesn't hurt to check in with each other as we go."

"Okay," Alma said, ignoring the dynamic in the room. "I have a Tim Reed with a Tacoma address and a deer and elk license along with a small-game license. He probably owns at least a rifle or a shotgun. No CPL."

It didn't prove anything, but it pointed toward Reed as a gun owner. He could still own a handgun, even though he didn't have a Concealed Pistol License.

"Alma," Bet said. "When you call the stepmother back to get a photo of Trisha Reed, ask about firearms in the home. She may not tell us the truth, but it can't hurt to try. If she's forthright, it will give us a better sense of what we're dealing with. Find out if he planned to meet anyone here."

Clayton waited to make sure Bet had finished talking before he picked up where he left off. "I'm also going to look for other abandoned vehicles farther out."

The downtown area was small, but homes were scattered throughout the valley. A network of forest service roads also extended throughout the area, and private roads, often little more than dirt tracks, disappeared into the forest, providing numerous locations to leave a vehicle. People sometimes camped on private land. There were plenty of places Jane Doe might have left a car.

Bet thanked him and turned to Dale, keeping her voice neutral as she asked for his report. She wondered if she needed to have a talk with him about keeping the peace between them through the election. Friendly competition was one thing, but he couldn't let it impact their working relationship. The edge in his tone supported her father's speculation about his unreadiness to lead.

Dale reported nothing suspicious in the section of the lake area he'd searched.

Bet turned to Alma. "And no luck with the missing persons sites or other agencies?" She knew that if Alma had found an ID for Jane Doe, she wouldn't have waited to tell them.

"No, but I do know who owns the phone that called in here last Friday." Alma handed Bet a piece of paper with a name and a phone number. It was definitely not a name Bet expected. Alma cackled at Bet's reaction. "Thought that might get your attention."

Dale cracked his neck and rolled his shoulders, his chest pulled tight against his work shirt. "Going to let us in on it?"

"Seeley Lander," Alma said.

"Wait, isn't that the kid from the mine?" Clayton asked.

"Are you sure this is right?" Bet asked.

"I asked them to spell it for me three times. I couldn't believe it either. At first I thought it belonged to a man long dead, but then I started thinking about family names. So I did some looking on the intranet."

"Internet," the other three said automatically.

"Intra, inter, whatever." Alma pulled another sheet of paper out. "According to what I found, our Seeley Lander moved to another little mining town called Jaxon just forty-five miles away, where he found Jesus and started his own church." Alma paused in her recitation to look around. "I've only ever driven through Jaxon; not much there."

"They have a big car show every year," Clayton said.

"How come I don't know about that?" Alma said. "I could take the 'Cuda."

"So he moved to Jaxon." Bet kept her on track.

"Right." Alma refocused on her notes. "He had a son named Boston, who had a son named Winston, who had a son named—"

"Seeley," Bet finished for her.

"Voilà." Alma set her notes back down. "This Seeley is a student at the University of Washington."

"Good work, Alma. Did you try calling that number?"

"Figured I'd leave that to you, Sheriff."

Bet wondered if her use of the title was a rebuke for Dale, a reminder of who was in charge.

At least for now.

Bet pulled her personal cell phone out of her pocket. She didn't want the sheriff's office phone number showing up on Seeley's caller ID.

The phone rang four times before it went to voice mail. Bet pushed the button for speakerphone so everyone could hear. To Bet's ear the voice on the message sounded like a man in his early twenties.

"Hey, you've reached Seeley. Can't answer the phone right now. Leave a message. I'll get back to you when I can. Adventure called. It might be a few days."

Bet hung up without leaving a message.

"Alma, see what you can discover about this Seeley Lander. Residence, police record, vehicle registration, whatever you can find. His parents might still live in Jaxon or the Wenatchee area. I don't want to leave a voice mail until I know more about him."

"Think he killed that girl?" Alma asked.

"Most women are killed by people they know. If he was with her but didn't kill her, he might be dead or injured himself."

"Interesting a strange woman called from his phone looking for you on Friday, and Monday a professor from the same university finds a Jane Doe in the lake," Alma said.

"I'm way ahead of you, Alma," Bet said. "See if you can find me a picture of him through the—"

Alma stopped Bet's request by handing her a printout. "I found this on the U-Dub website. Young Seeley Lander apparently won some kind of science award as a freshman."

The photo looked like it had come from a high school yearbook. It showed a serious young man. Thin, Caucasian, with dark hair that looked naturally disheveled rather than expensive-salon-disheveled. A pink butterfly of acne spread across his cheeks and the bridge of his nose. Alma handed Clayton and Dale copies as well.

"Anything else?" Alma asked.

"What about social media?" Clayton asked.

"Good idea," Bet said. "Alma, see if he has any accounts."

"I'll start with Facebook." Alma clicked a few keys. "Here we go. He shows nine hundred and sixty-eight friends." She turned the screen around to face the group.

"Can you access them?" Bet asked.

"I can. Want me to get started with this?"

Bet thought about the priorities. "First, a photo of Trisha. Second, the information on Malone and Rob Collier. Then start on Facebook and any other social media accounts he has."

"Isn't it more important to ID the woman Sandy saw Friday morning?" Dale asked. "Seems like social media is the better lead."

"We don't know how much Jane Doe uses social media. Trying to find her that way could send Alma down a rabbit hole.

Alma can get a photo of Trisha with one phone call to her step-mother so we can take her off the list. For all we know, Seeley Lander came up with Trisha and her father, so Trisha could still be Jane Doe. Plus, if we find Seeley, he may know Jane's identity. If Malone or Collier are involved in some way, that's an important avenue of investigation too."

Alma looked back and forth between Dale and Bet with an expression Bet couldn't read. Was she weighing who would make the better sheriff or just hoping everyone kept getting along?

"I'm on it." Alma turned her computer screen back around on her desk. "I'll call on the photo for Trisha first thing."

"Dale?" Bet asked.

"One more section of the lake to walk."

"I've got some work to do at my desk," Bet said. "Then I'm going to pay another visit to Dr. Malone."

On the computer, Bet did a search on Jamie Garcia. She found the woman had a degree in digital journalism from Central Washington University, the same school Bet had graduated from. Jamie had worked on the school newspaper and graduated in June. Bet couldn't find any bylines for her in any papers in Washington, and certainly not the *Seattle Times*.

Apparently Jamie Garcia was looking for a break and someone with information about Jane Doe thought Bet's case was it.

"She's just trying to make a name for herself," Bet said to Schweitzer, who had followed her into the office and now lay on the dog bed she purchased after her father died. Bet understood the challenge of starting a career, but that didn't mean she wanted the woman to interfere with her case.

Bet pulled out her cell, and Jamie Garcia picked up.

"Hello, Sheriff."

Bet laid out her plea to Jamie about holding off until she followed up on a few more leads to identify Jane Doe. "The family hasn't been notified," she said, hoping to play on the woman's sense of decency. "If I can't make an ID, I'll need the media's help. You'll be the first person I call."

"One week," Jamie said. "And an exclusive interview with you. I know you'll run a photo on all the media outlets if you want the public's help to make an identification, so that's not an exclusive for me. But you can give me more insights for a bigger article. Like why you held back on making her death public sooner."

It wasn't exactly a threat. But it felt close.

Bet agreed to the time frame, hoping to have an identification and a suspect before the week was up.

They ended the call with Bet feeling even more pressure to move the investigation along.

"The last thing I need is some wannabe journalist putting random information out on the internet."

If only she knew who'd provided Jamie Garcia with the heads-up about Jane Doe in the first place. She and her deputies had spoken to a lot of people when they showed Jane Doe's photo around town, so it could have come from anyone. Except why did Jamie believe Jane Doe's death was under suspicious circumstances rather than an accident?

Pushing thoughts of a failed investigation made public aside, Bet headed out to have another chat with Professor Malone.

Sitting in the driver's seat, Bet noticed something tucked under her windshield wiper. Looking around as she stepped back out of the SUV, she didn't see anyone on the street nearby.

The white slip of paper looked identical to the note left on her door.

Go back to LA, it read. Nothing more.

But Bet's imagination filled in the missing words in the sentence. *Or else.*

TWELVE

Bet stuffed the note into her glove box, determined not to let it rattle her, and drove out to the lake. She arrived just in time to help Peter pull his boat out of the water.

"I think you saw me coming and decided to wait for me," she teased him as she walked down to the shoreline.

"I'm not a man to ever turn down assistance, Sheriff, no I am not," Peter said.

They carried his equipment to the trailer while Schweitzer curled up under his new favorite tree. His tongue hung out, sides heaving, as he panted in the late-afternoon heat that had yet to dissipate even though the sun had disappeared behind the peaks. After Peter unlocked the door, Bet followed him inside, the screen door closing behind her with a bang.

Bet observed the professor in silence while he hooked the equipment up to the computer in the trailer.

Peter hadn't slept well. Dark circles appeared under his eyes. Bet wondered if the bed wasn't as comfortable as he'd claimed or if something else prevented a restful night. Maybe he had nightmares too.

"A question for you, Professor," Bet said.

"Let's go outside. Hotter than Hades in here. Least there's a breeze off the lake." Peter opened the windows of the little trailer to let it air out. "Beer?" he asked, pulling open the door to his tiny fridge.

"Still on duty."

"Suit yourself." Peter pulled out a Mac and Jack's African Amber and tossed the cap into a garbage bag hanging on the inside of the door. Bet ducked her head through the doorway and followed him out. Schweitzer beat his tail against the hard earth, but he didn't get up from his spot under the tree.

"You've the right idea, don't you, champ?" Peter stopped to scratch the dog behind the ears, and Schweitzer made approving noises deep in his chest. He rolled over and gave Peter access to his tummy for a rub.

"Make a friend for life with that action." Bet observed the man with her dog.

"I've always liked dogs."

The professor rose slightly in her estimation.

Peter gave Schweitzer one last pat and walked over to one of the chairs under the trees. Bet sat down in the other.

"Expecting company?" Bet asked. Peter looked perplexed. "You had two chairs set out before I arrived the first time," she pointed out, "Someone else going to join you?"

"I'm an optimist."

The two sat for a moment in the silence and enjoyed the view of the lake. Small waves lapped the shore. How many secrets hid under the water?

Shaking herself from her reverie, Bet pulled the photo of Seeley Lander out of her pocket and handed it over to Peter. "Ever seen this man?"

Peter looked it over, but no recognition showed in his face. He gave it back with a shrug. "I don't think so. Is he involved in the girl's death?"

"Remind me what time you arrived at the lake on Saturday?"

"Sunday," Peter corrected her.

"Right, Sunday. What time did you arrive on Sunday?"

"Were you seeing if I would change my story?"

"Why would I do that?"

Peter narrowed his eyes and took a sip from his beer. "Am I a suspect?"

"I'm just asking questions. You might have seen something you don't know is important."

"I must have arrived around nine thirty at night," he said. "I didn't look at the time, but I left Seattle just after seven, and it's about a two-hour drive."

"Why leave so late at night?"

"I had things I needed to do before I left."

"No stops along the way?"

"Gas in North Bend." He named a town on the west side of Snoqualmie Summit, the pass where Interstate 90 crossed the Cascade Mountain Range. "Would you like to see my gas receipt?"

"Sure."

Peter hesitated. "I have to keep all my receipts because of the project funding."

"I don't need to take it with me."

Peter stood and went into the trailer. He came back out with a manila envelope. He pulled out a stack of receipts and shuffled through them. He slipped one out from near the top of the stack and handed it over to Bet. She looked at it and verified that the time stamp read 7:48 PM with Sunday's date. She pulled out her camera and snapped a quick picture of it.

"I have to keep records too," Bet said, handing it back to him. He tucked it into the envelope with the rest of them.

"Does this mean you know when that girl died?"

"Just covering my bases."

Peter nodded and set the envelope on the ground, as if it might bite him.

"A project like this must be expensive," Bet said.

"Not compared to most. It's local, and it's just me, right? It gets a lot more expensive when an entire team of scientists travels to a remote location."

"Does the trailer belong to you?"

"No. I borrowed it from a colleague in my department."

Bet waited to see if he would add more.

"His name is Ed Winter. Do you want to contact him?"

"I'll let you know. Why did you choose this project?"

"I don't need to go far to find amazing things. Think about what's right here, all around us. Did you know this mountain range is part of the Pacific Ring of Fire? Connecting us to Japan?"

"I do," Bet said. "You can't live near a fourteen-thousand-foot active volcano and not have some interest in them."

"Mount Rainier is rather impressive, isn't she?"

"I appreciate the power of the rock I live on. But we were talking about why you chose this lake."

Peter paused a moment, considering Bet's question. "As I've said to you before, I've always been interested in our local geographic composition. This lake is just one more example of what makes the area so special."

"Did you go into town on Sunday?" Bet asked.

"Nope. First time I went into town was when I went to see you."

"Which Collier did you make arrangements with?"

Annoyance flickered across his face, and Peter didn't answer right away. "What does that have to do with anything?"

"Curiosity. I wondered if you being here has anything to do with Robert Collier showing up."

"What?" Peter's voice held a note of something more than surprise.

"You didn't know he was coming for a visit?"

"I didn't think his health allowed him to travel." His reference to health indicated that he'd negotiated with the elder Collier.

"Junior, not Senior."

Peter digested this information. "I don't know anything about that."

"Did you happen to notice a big black Ford Bronco around here anytime since you arrived?"

"Should I be looking for one?"

"I'll take that as a no."

"I told you I hadn't seen anyone or any vehicles out this way."

"I believe you."

"Then why are you asking me all these questions?"

"Can objects find a way into a lake without being dumped?"

"Sure. Float in on a river or stream."

"And if there isn't a river or stream?"

"Could be an underground spring or river or some other fissure under the lake surface. You don't think the body was dumped?"

"You found her; you tell me."

"It never crossed my mind she hadn't gone in at the surface."

Peter didn't pause before he said that, a strong indicator he told the truth.

Upon seeing Bet stand, Schweitzer heaved himself to his feet. "Thank you for your time, Professor."

"Women I've had dinner with can call me Peter."

"I'll keep that in mind."

Bet and her dog walked over to the SUV, and Schweitzer waited patiently for Bet to open the back for him. She did, and he leapt into his spot.

"Sure you don't want to stay and have a beer?" Peter asked from his chair under the trees.

"No rest for the wicked," Bet said, getting into the driver's seat. She started the engine, ignoring the little voice in her head that said it would be more fun to stay and have a beer with Peter Malone.

Bet drove to George's house and then the Collier estate to see if either recognized Seeley Lander, but both houses sat still and dark. Bet and Dale met up at the station to check in with Alma and Clayton. Clayton had reached Trisha's father, who agreed to come by the station. Clayton struck out finding any other abandoned vehicles or anyone recognizing Seeley Lander, including Jeb Pearson.

No missing persons report matching Jane Doe's description had been filed anywhere in the state during the last month. Bet could have Alma turn her attention out of state, but if Jane Doe hadn't been gone long, it was possible no one had reported her missing yet. At least her photo had been circulated with other law enforcement agencies now, so an ID could be made if a report did come in. Unfortunately, these things took time.

Bet asked Dale if he'd found anything useful around the lake.

"Granite," Dale said. "Granite, trees, and cold, dark water."

Alma had discovered Seeley Lander owned a 1997 red Ford Ranger Extended Cab, for which she put out a BOLO to state law enforcement agencies. The truck registration listed an address in Seattle.

"I hope you stated there is no probable cause for arrest," Bet said. "Just for identification."

"Are you checking to see if I know how to do my job too?" Bet heard annoyance in Alma's voice.

"That is my responsibility."

"Yes, Sheriff. I included no PC for arrest. ID only." This time Alma used Bet's title as a rebuke to her.

"Good. Thank you."

Alma continued, her feathers ruffled. "I called the apartment building and spoke to the manager. He said a couple of young men lived in that apartment last school year, but only one name was on the lease, not Seeley's. They've all moved out and no forwarding for Seeley. I'm trying to track down his roommates. I did find a W. Lander in Jaxon; I'm guessing they are related. I called, but it went to voice mail. I left a message asking that they call the station. I hope that's okay."

"That's fine, Alma," Bet said. "Thank you. Keep trying their number. What did you tell them in the message?" Bet refused to let the woman's annoyance bother her.

"That we were trying to track down a Seeley Lander, who might have witnessed a traffic accident. I said we'd caught his license plate on a traffic cam."

Bet chuckled; there were no traffic cams in Collier. "Perfect."

"Hopefully he'll show up safe and sound at some McDonald's somewhere," Alma said.

"Not too safe if he's eating at McDonald's," Dale said.

"Health nut," Alma grumbled under her breath. "A Big Mac now and then never hurt anyone."

Dale leaned over and kissed Alma on the cheek.

"Shoo, you," Alma said gruffly, fighting a grin. Their close relationship sent a spark of envy through Bet. Bet had known Alma her entire life but didn't have that sense of closeness. Sometimes Bet felt like she didn't know how to be easy with anyone.

"What have you learned about Peter Malone and Rob Collier?"

"Well now," Alma said, "that's been rather interesting." She went on to explain that the good professor apparently had a gambling problem, with two mortgages on his house and maxed-out credit cards.

"He spends a lot of time at the casinos. I'm thinking blackjack or poker," Alma said thoughtfully. "A thinking man's game."

"Smart people don't gamble," Dale said.

Alma grumbled at Dale. "A little gambling never hurt anyone. You just have to know when to stop."

"Good info, Alma," Bet said, before she could start extolling the virtues of nickel slots. "What about Rob Collier?"

"That man has me stumped. I found very little through my usual channels. I have to get back to you on that one."

"So you started in on the Facebook pictures, then?" Bet asked, hearing the sharpness in her tone as the words came out. She guessed Alma had moved on to social media so fast because Dale wanted her to and it would keep her neutral during the fight for the sheriff's seat. Alma had done the basics on Rob Collier and would no doubt return to investigating him once she got through Seeley's Facebook account.

"Nothing so far that matches Jane Doe." The look in Alma's eyes told Bet she'd heard the sharpness too.

Bet softened her tone. "How many more photos do you have to look at?"

"About a hundred. I also kept a running list of names with no identifiable profile photo and a private setting. I'll have to track them down individually to find out what they look like or if they're missing. I'll keep at it."

"Thank you, Alma." She looked at Dale. "I agree with you, following up on social media is important too."

Bet looked over her own notes before giving her report. It also bought her a little time while she debated whether or not to bring up Jamie Garcia. She decided to let the issue with the reporter go for the time being. She liked to think she had it handled and the sheriff's station wasn't a democracy.

"I spoke with the medical examiner today," she said instead. "There were no fingerprints to run through IAFIS, and with no crime scene, we don't have a lot of clues for what happened. We'll have to work from the other direction, figure out who she was and who might have killed her."

"Unless it's random," Alma said.

"Right," Bet said. "There is that."

"What if it's not *who* but *where*?" Dale said.

"What does that mean?" Alma asked.

"If the girl was shot because of where she was instead of who she was, then we should be looking at what's going on at the lake," Dale said.

"You mean Peter Malone? We're already looking at him," Alma said.

"Wait a minute. What if it's not the lake." Bet followed Dale's train of thought.

"But that's where the body was found," Alma said.

"Right. Found. But not where she was killed. More importantly, why put her in the lake at all?"

"Now you've really lost me," Alma said.

"Where's that topographical map of our area?" Bet asked Alma.

"Over there." Alma pointed to a tall cardboard tube in the corner behind her desk.

"Help me with this, would you?" Bet asked as she pulled out the expansive map. The four of them spread it out over Alma's desk, each holding a corner to keep it from rolling up again.

"There're probably other ways to access the Collier property. Service road, fire road, something." Bet's eyes searched the map. "Here." She pointed to a thin white line on the map. "That might be another way onto the far north corner of the Colliers' property."

"How does that help us?" Alma asked.

"We think Jane Doe bought coffee for two from Sandy on Friday and asked about me, or at least Sheriff Rivers. A few hours later, an unknown woman called from Seeley Lander's telephone, also looking for me. It would make sense it was the same woman. Three days later Jane Doe ends up dead in the lake. Seeley Lander and Jane Doe could have been here together, as we think she used his cell phone. But if they were here in town Friday morning, why not just walk into the station? Why call?"

"They went somewhere else," Dale said.

"Right. They went somewhere else, but the girl ended up in the lake. So where did they go that they didn't just drive the fifteen minutes back to town?"

"Other side of the mountain." Dale pointed to the spot Bet had found on the map.

"To get to this area," Bet said, "you'd have to go back down Highway 97 and out to Ingalls Creek Road."

"But why would anyone want to get onto the Colliers' land? There's nothing out there but more woods," Clayton said. "What's over there you can't get over here?"

"I asked Peter Malone how an object could get into a lake without being dumped from the surface. He mentioned an underground spring or river."

"You think there's an underground river into our lake?" Alma asked.

"I do," Bet said. "And I think it starts in the old mine."

"But the entrance to the mine is covered with a ton of rock," Clayton said.

Bet pointed to the thin track on the aerial map. "But what if there's another way in?"

THIRTEEN

They'd finished going over the map when the door opened and a tall, dark-haired man came in. He introduced himself as Tim Reed and said Clayton had requested he come in before he left town.

"Is everything all right?" he asked, eyeing the four of them gathered in the front office.

Bet thanked him for coming and introduced herself as the sheriff. "We understand you're here with your daughter?"

"I am," he said, a line of sweat appearing on his brow.

"We'd like to speak with you both."

"She's back at the campground."

"You aren't headed home tonight?"

Tim shifted his weight. "I think you'd better tell me what this is about."

"We found your car abandoned off the road," Bet said. "We're just confirming you're all right and plan to get it fixed."

Tim looked relieved. "I'm having a new rim delivered from Cle Elum tomorrow. I didn't have a spare, and it's too bent to put a new tire on."

"How did the accident happen?"

"No one else was involved."

Bet didn't like Mr. Reed's cagey answers. She caught a glimpse of Dale's expression. She could tell he didn't think much of them either. She knew he judged her for how she interviewed the man, just as she judged his work.

"That's not what I asked you."

"A deer came out of the trees. I swerved and hit the rock instead."

Deer were common in the area. He could be telling the truth.

"How did you get here from the campground?"

"A friend drove me over here. He's waiting outside."

"Why don't I drive you back to your campground so I can see for myself your daughter's all right?"

Bet could tell Tim Reed didn't think much of that idea.

"I have a better thought." Tim Reed pulled his cell phone out and pushed a few buttons. A moment later, Bet could hear a young woman's voice. Tim held out his phone and spoke to the screen, explaining the purpose for the video call. He held the phone up for Bet to see.

Bet leaned over to see a young woman with tousled blond hair.

"What's up?" the woman asked, her eyes unfocused. Bet recalled their speculation that the girl might have a drug or alcohol problem. If she'd crashed the car under the influence, it would explain Mr. Reed's nervousness. She appeared to be inside a tent, asleep early.

"Trisha. Tell this nice police officer you're all right," Tim said.

"I'm fine."

"Were you in the accident, Trisha?" Bet asked. "That left the car disabled?"

"No. I was here at the campground."

Bet asked her to hold her driver's license up to the camera so she could check her ID, then thanked her and hung up the phone.

"It was your daughter driving that car, wasn't it?" Bet said, holding on to Mr. Reed's phone. It was possible he'd admit it if it was true, but there was nothing Bet could do if he didn't.

"We'll have the car fixed in the morning and get out of your hair," he said, not meeting Bet's eyes.

Bet handed him the phone. "You have a safe trip home."

At least they knew Trisha Reed wasn't Jane Doe.

Bet sent Dale and Clayton home for the night, and Alma trundled off a few minutes later. Now she sat in the silence of her office and thought back over the case. The dark wainscoting and wooden accents of the room always made it feel like a warm, dark cave. The furniture—a heavy desk, the chairs, the wooden file cabinet and glass-fronted gun locker—was all vintage to the town's founding, just like the building that housed the station.

What do you know? Bet heard her father ask. *Always go back to what you know.*

I know Trisha isn't our Jane Doe. Bet looked at the photo of Earle Rivers on the wall. *I don't know who Jane Doe is, but she might be a friend of Seeley Lander, a student at the University of Washington. But even if Jane Doe is a student there too, that's alongside forty thousand other students. Worse than a needle in a haystack.*

Sandy speculated that the girl might have been looking for Bet's father. That implied she had prior knowledge of Earle Rivers. For Jane Doe to know Earle Rivers, she could have met him at any time in the past. Bet contemplated cases involving a young woman or teenage girl from out of town, but soon stopped herself.

She could have been a witness or a friend of a friend of a victim. Bet continued to talk to her father in her head while looking at his picture on the wall. *There's no way to know why she looked for you or if she even met you before.*

Bet cycled through the unsolved cases still open in her office. Bet's father hadn't believed cold cases died, so he always kept the files accessible. There were only two that involved homicides. One occurred a few years ago—a strangled hitchhiker found dumped near the junction of Lake Collier Road and Highway 97. The hitchhiker had been left in a ditch and was found by a passing motorist who stopped after seeing the flash of color from the victim's red jacket. Thirty-three years old, the hitchhiker had suffered from psychological problems and walked away from her family in Portland, Oregon, showing up near Collier three months later.

The other cold case had even less in common with current events, dating back to Earle's early days in law enforcement, not long after he'd come home from Afghanistan for good. The body of a middle-aged man was found in the woods at the far end of the Train Yard. He was never identified. The body was also too badly decomposed to confirm cause of death. Earle always believed the case his own personal failure.

I should have been able to find out who he was, Bet could hear her father say. Though he rarely spoke of it, Bet would occasionally find him going through the old file. Bet could picture the first time she found him doing it. She'd gone to his den, where he kept an office. Current crime scene photos were spread out on his desk, the old file open on his lap. Asleep in his chair, he woke with a start when Bet appeared in the doorway. Her father never slept deep.

"What are you looking at, Dad?"

"The one that got away, Bet."

He handed the file over to her.

"Why is it your fault? No one could figure out who he was."

Bet's father took the file back from her and closed it, placing it in the bottom drawer of his desk. He slowly restacked the photos of the current crime and placed them in their file before answering.

"Someone has to be responsible. If you're serious about pursuing law enforcement, you'll have a case like this of your own one day. Then you'll understand."

Had she already stumbled over hers? Her first six months on the job?

Rob Collier's reappearance in town at the same time Jane Doe floated in the lake felt like too big a coincidence. What did it mean that Alma couldn't find him through her regular channels?

Bet logged on to the internet and did a basic search, finding almost nothing about the man. A few old posts about football games at Alabama. No social media. No job listings. He didn't appear on LinkedIn.

At least she didn't find any arrest records.

Why wouldn't he have a presence on the internet? she asked her father's portrait. Not that Earle would have been much help; he'd had little use for social media himself, with no online footprint except the website for the station.

Maybe Rob protected his online identity because of his family wealth.

Bet sighed and turned away from her father's portrait. Leaning back against the wall in her chair, Bet closed her eyes and let herself relax, blanking her mind. The image surfaced of the body dumped in the lake, and she let herself go. She could feel the cold and hear the heavy breathing of the man as he struggled under the weight. Long dark hair spilled from the top of the bundle. Why did her dream feel so real? It never had before. Maybe it was the similarity to Jane Doe that caused her mind to add details. Or maybe something else was going on.

Bet woke up her computer and looked up a phone number. She expected to get voice mail, so the voice on the other end surprised her.

"Professor James?" she asked.

"Yes. Who is this, please?"

Bet explained who she was, hoping he remembered her.

"*Sheriff* Rivers," he said. "So you did go into law enforcement. Good for you. What can I do for you? Looking for insights into the criminal mind?"

"No. I'm wondering about repressed memories someone recovers later in therapy. I've heard about that working, but I can't remember talking about it in any of my classes."

"That's because most of it is a lot of bunk. A fad for the nineties, false memories put in place by a lot of well-meaning therapists who made things worse for their patients."

Bet wondered why she felt disappointed. She'd called because she wanted reassurance that her dream was nothing but a nightmare, her imagination filling in details because of Jane Doe. So why wouldn't it make her happy that repressed memories couldn't be true?

"So there's no way someone could forget a traumatic event," she said, more to herself than to the professor.

"I didn't say that."

Bet felt something in the pit of her stomach. A sense of dread. She held her breath.

"Repressed memories are bunk when a therapist uses psychotherapy to guide a patient to remember something. That process can actually insert information into a patient's mind and make them think they are remembering something they experienced. But people can suppress traumatic events."

"How is it different?"

"What matters most is external evidence of the event. For example, if the individual uncovers a diary from someone else outlining the event or something tangible that provides information external to the individual. Photographs. News reports. If that happens, it could mean the person experienced a condition called a dissociative or a psychogenic fugue."

Bet's fear rose. Dissociative? That sounded ominous.

"What is that?"

The professor went on to explain that a traumatic event could trigger reversible amnesia. "An individual can forget memories, an event, even aspects of their own personality."

"How long would the state last?"

"The length of time the person is in the fugue? Or how long the person forgets the experience that caused the initial trauma?"

"Both."

"The fugue could last less than a single day or a month or even years. People in that situation often stay on the move. There are case histories of people who traveled for years before returning to their 'original' personality. The DSM-5 calls that 'a state of bewildered wandering.' I always found that rather poetic."

Bet remembered the DSM-5 was the American Psychiatric Association's listing of mental disorders. She didn't know if the description was poetic or not, but she definitely didn't like the sound of it. "And how long do they forget the trauma that caused it?"

"That varies. Oftentimes the sufferer dreams about the event or experiences flashbacks that they attribute to imagination. Then, if something specific triggers the original memory, it can come back in larger chunks. Do you have someone who committed a crime describing these kinds of symptoms and using them as an excuse? Is there any way to find confirmation outside their 'memories'?"

"Not a criminal. But maybe someone who witnessed a crime as a child. Would that be traumatic enough?"

"Possibly, depending on the crime. A young child's mind can be incredibly good at protecting itself. If it came on top of another personal trauma, that could certainly do it."

Like her mother's body hanging in the garage. The creak of the rope as she swayed when Bet opened the door. The chair knocked over on the ground beneath her feet.

"What should the person recovering her memories do?"

"Her?" The professor's tone changed to one of compassion. Bet said nothing.

"I would still recommend they speak to someone," her professor said. "But the therapist can't focus on the memories themselves; it's too likely to create false ones. The therapist should focus on current events impacting the individual's state of mind. I'd be happy to provide a referral. Does this person live in the area?"

"Close enough," Bet said. She took down the names. "One last question."

Professor James waited while Bet tried to figure out how to ask something she wasn't sure she wanted an answer for. "Would this kind of situation indicate the individual was unstable?"

"You report this individual didn't suffer the event herself, correct?"

Bet made a noise of assent.

"If this was an isolated incident, the individual could live a perfectly normal life. It doesn't indicate other psychological issues, if that's what you're wondering about. Has this individual suffered blackouts or lost time?"

Bet said no.

"Then I wouldn't worry unduly about this person's mental status."

When Bet didn't respond right away, he continued, "For example, if this person were, say, in law enforcement, it wouldn't prevent her from doing her job."

Bet heard the careful way he worded the sentence. He had always been an intuitive man. And one who kept confidences.

"Thank you, Professor. I'll be in touch if I need anything else."

"Anytime."

She hung up. Despite his confidence that it didn't indicate other problems, she felt apprehensive. Could she be remembering a real event? If she was, did it relate to what happened to Jane Doe all these years later? And did it mean she wasn't as qualified to be sheriff as her father had thought?

Bet's mother had died seventeen years ago. So the blocked or forgotten trauma most likely happened immediately after that. If another body had been found seventeen years ago, wrapped in canvas, Alma would have remembered. And a woman's disappearance that had been investigated but not solved would be in the cold-case files.

She tried to remember the first time she'd had the dream. Bet and her father were adjusting to a lot. He'd been deployed much of Bet's early years, making him a virtual stranger. Bet spent a lot of time with her best friend, Dylan Chandler. They were inseparable. His father Michael had already left town, his visits coming further and further apart, so Dylan knew what it was like to have an absent parent. It was winter, just after Christmas. School started again, so maybe the second or third week in January.

Back then, school was a single building from kindergarten to ninth grade. Starting in tenth grade, kids were bused down to the bigger high school outside Cle Elum.

"That was the last year I saw much of Eric Chandler," Bet said out loud. She and Dylan had looked up to Eric, and he'd spent time with them back then, but once Eric went off to high school, their little group began to disintegrate. When Dylan and Bet followed him later, Eric didn't want to be shackled to his little brother and the too tall, gawky girl Bet had become. Dylan focused on football and baseball and whatever else kind of ball and left Bet to her own devices. Eric graduated, and with Dylan and his motorcycle, even their time on the school bus ended. Bet shied away from the later memories of Eric, when they reconnected at Central Washington University and Bet fell head over heels in love with her childhood friend.

"The Colliers," Bet said out loud to dispel memories of Eric Chandler. "The Colliers were still around when that dream started, and now Junior is back in town."

Bet thought about people vanishing from Collier. Michael Chandler's last visit would have been around then, too. Bet had never thought about the timing of him finally fading away. Did it have anything to do with Earle coming back to Collier full-time?

She ran her fingers over the list of names the professor had provided. Even if he was right and she should talk to a professional, it would have to wait. Between her investigation and the election, she couldn't drive out to E'burg to lie on some shrink's couch. Maybe if she solved the case, the memories would integrate on their own.

She shuddered at the thought of what else she might remember. Had she recognized the man who carried the body and slid it into the lake? Was it someone she knew? Was that part of the initial trauma?

Maybe she should go back to Los Angeles and let sleeping dogs lie. Maybe she shouldn't work out her personal issues as sheriff. Maybe Dale was the better choice.

She opened the top drawer of her desk to stick the list of therapists in her center drawer on top of the fly she'd abandoned after Peter Malone came through the door.

The fly was gone.

She felt a creeping sensation up her spine. Digging around, she thought perhaps she'd pushed the fly, and the materials she'd used to make it, farther back in the drawer.

Nothing.

Why would someone come in and take such an innocuous item out of her desk? She searched through her other drawers and checked through the papers on her desk. Nothing else was disturbed.

She thought about the people with access to her office. She had to admit, it could be anyone. Alma didn't lock the door if she left at lunch or to run an errand, and Bet never locked her office door. They had a gun safe for firearms and the cells were behind a locked door, but the offices could be easily accessed.

Like the notes on her door and windshield, it wasn't a threat. Just something to make her feel uncomfortable, watched. Slightly unsafe. Was that the intent? To keep her on edge?

If so, it was working.

But it also made her want to dig in her heels.

"Nothing I can do about it now, except start to lock my office door. Let's go, Schweitz," she said to her dog, who rose from the floor, excited at the thought of dinner. "That's right, buddy. One of your favorite times of the day."

Stepping out of the building with Schweitzer at her side, Bet could see the last streaks of light behind the peaks to the west. Troubled by her new demons, she didn't want to go home, so she walked to the tavern instead.

Schweitzer knew right away where Bet headed, and his excitement at the thought of a burger patty made just the way he liked it was palpable. As she approached the building, she saw a number of vehicles out front, including Robert Collier's Bronco.

"Maybe I'll learn a little more about the prodigal son, Mr. 'My-friends-call-me-Rob' Collier."

FOURTEEN

Bet spotted Rob the moment she walked into the tavern. Even with his back to the door, he stood out in the crowd. Though built like a barrel, he wasn't a fat man. Instead, he wore his bulk like a Brahman bull, someone you wouldn't want to mess with. Although he was dressed like the other men in the room—blue jeans, cowboy boots, denim shirts—the quality of his clothes separated him from the others. His cowboy boots, worn at the heel, were custom-made, no doubt from the skin of some exotic animal.

Bet remembered one of her professors at the university talking about social class. "Old-money people don't care how others see them. And more importantly, they play by their own rules."

Rob Collier was old money.

He stood in profile as she walked into the bar, and she shivered at the resemblance to the figure coming clearer from her dream—or a memory, depending on what tricks her mind was playing. She hoped Professor James was right and she wasn't compromised psychologically. She'd passed the psychological testing required for the Los Angeles Police Department, so at least she knew she had the appropriate traits to fulfill her duties.

But it didn't mean she wasn't crazy.

She paused at the door, debating whether to take the empty seat next to him or sit by herself at her favorite table out on the back porch. The crowded bar might not be the best place to have a chat with the man.

As if sensing her eyes on him, Rob turned and met Bet's gaze. The amusement she'd seen on his face when they first met returned, and he stood to push out the barstool next to his with exaggerated gallantry.

Bet didn't have to see herself in a mirror to know what she looked like as she walked over to sit down. She wore the tan-and-brown uniform of her station, her bulky duty belt weighed down with the hardware of her profession. Her hair had escaped long ago from the bands and pins she used to keep it tucked up while she worked, and the natural curls sprang out from under her hat in runaway ringlets. Rob looked calm, cool, and collected—refined and confident in a way only the rich seemed to pull off in hot weather. Bet ignored the voice inside her head telling her to straighten her uniform and do something about her hair. She sauntered over, determined not to feel inferior just because of a social status that shouldn't matter, yet somehow did.

"Evenin', Sheriff," Rob said, as Bet unhooked her fanny pack. Plunking it down on the bar next to the beaver fur hat Rob had neatly balanced on its crown, Bet realized her only accessory looked a little worse for wear. Never mind that Rob's hat probably cost more than Bet earned in a month, the sweat stains on the inside of her fanny pack made her feel not just cheap but tacky.

Bet deftly slid the fanny pack off the bar and hung it over the back of her barstool. She stepped on her insecurities and sat down. Schweitzer squeezed in under her feet and scrunched himself into a remarkably small ball. Rob waited until she'd situated herself before he sat down again. Bet wondered if that was a display of chivalry or the opportunity to stand over her for a moment, asserting physical dominance. Bet had learned long ago that a lot of men were intimidated by her height, even more than they were by the fact that she carried a gun.

"Out for a night on the town?" Bet asked, as Rob held up his hand to get Rope's attention.

"Not much to eat at the old homestead," Rob said as Rope hustled over and greeted Bet.

"How's the new tat healing?" Bet asked the bartender.

"Stopped feeling like a herd of bees used my arm for target practice," Rope said with a grin.

Bet put in her order, including Schweitzer's patty, and Rope glided off to the kitchen, calling over his shoulder to Tomás about an order up at the window. He raised his voice over the din of conversation, but Bet thought Tomás would have heard him even if he'd whispered. Bet felt herself relax in the familiar atmosphere, despite her unexpected dinner companion.

"George would have gotten the larder stocked if you told him you were coming."

"I can carry my own groceries," Rob said. "I'm not accustomed to hired help."

"What? No staff of domestics at your place in Arlington? You shop and change your own oil. Do you cook and clean, too?"

Rob snorted in amusement and took a sip from the tumbler sitting in front of him. The amber liquid glowed in the warm, low light of the bar. Bet guessed expensive, single-malt Scotch.

"Have I ruffled your feathers in some way, Elizabeth?" Rob asked, after he savored his drink and put the glass back down.

Rope reappeared with a glass of water. He knew she never drank alcohol in uniform. It gave Bet a moment to reflect. No sense riling Collier up. She'd never learn anything that way.

"Have you decided how long you're going to stay in town?" Bet asked.

"Nope."

Must be nice to come and go as you please.

She wasn't sure why Rob brought this prickly side out of her. His wealth, the stress of Jane Doe's murder, or the fact that he looked like the memory surfacing in her mind—none of these explained her strong reaction to the man.

"You've been gone a long time." Bet made her tone as neutral as possible.

"Yep."

"Did you move straight to Arlington when you left here?"

Instead of answering, Rob sang a few lines from Lynyrd Sky-nyrd's southern anthem "Sweet Home Alabama" in a low, clear tenor, well suited to the song.

"I didn't know you had such a fine voice, Mr. Collier."

"If I remember right, you do too. Your mother and you used to do duets right here in this bar."

Bet felt herself blushing at the compliment. *Rob Collier remembers me from when I was a child?* She'd never thought of herself as memorable.

"University of Alabama?" Bet asked.

"Full ride."

Bet didn't tell Rob she already knew this information.

"A few years in Tuscaloosa were enough, though. Arlington is more my style."

"Not that you needed a scholarship. Your father could have paid for any school you wanted."

"Not everything is about money."

"Football?" Bet asked.

Rob nodded. Even Bet knew the reputation of the Crimson Tide.

"Were you any good?"

Rob laughed. "You are blunt, aren't you, Elizabeth?"

"Either you were or you weren't. Regardless, it was a long time ago. Something tells me you aren't stuck in the past of your glory years."

"Yeah. I was good. Just not good enough."

"You wanted to play pro?"

"At the time."

Bet thought about all the reasons a person wouldn't show up much online and the various covert institutions and companies headquartered in that area.

"How did you end up in Arlington?"

A silence stretched out between the two of them that made Bet wonder if he'd heard the question. It seemed innocuous enough, but maybe there was more to Rob than a sizable inheritance.

"Had to go someplace." The two fell silent as Rope came around the front of the bar. He set Bet's chicken sandwich in front of her. Then he knelt and put the paper plate with Schweitzer's dinner on the floor.

"There you go, big guy," Rope said to the dog. "Need anything else?" he asked Bet.

"All set."

Rope returned to his place behind the bar, picking up empty glasses and taking drink orders as he went.

The big dog polished his patty off in two bites, which for him constituted dainty eating. Bet tossed a french fry down to Schweitzer before dosing the rest with vinegar and black pepper. She took a few bites before resuming the conversation.

"I'd like to show you another photograph."

Rob waited, an expectant look on his face. She handed him the photo of Seeley Lander. He gave it a thorough look, but handed it back. "Sorry. Don't recognize him."

She tucked the photo back in her pocket. "What did you study in school?" she asked.

"Which time?"

"Multiple degrees? Or unsuccessful the first time?"

Rob took another drink. "Interests change. What about you? College girl?"

Bet told him a little about her years studying psychology at the university in Ellensburg before attending the police academy in Los Angeles.

"Looks like you went far from home too," he said when she finished. "What brought you back? Had enough of Southern California?"

"My father needed me." It was pointless to hide that her father's cancer brought her back to town. The community knew. If Rob didn't already, he would soon enough.

"I'm sorry for your loss, Elizabeth." The sentiment felt genuine. "And now you're fighting for his seat."

Bet nodded, watching Rope move around behind the bar so she didn't have to meet Rob's gaze. Between his intimidating air and top spot on her suspect list, she didn't want to get into a heart-to-heart. He felt a little too good at reading faces.

"Should I throw my support behind you? The Collier name still means something here."

Now it was Bet's turn to sip her drink while she formulated an answer. What exactly was Rob Collier offering? And why?

"You should do what you think is best for our community."

"You really are your father's daughter," he said, his tone light.

Was he hinting that Robert Collier Senior had tried to bribe Earle at some point in their history? And that Earle had turned him down, just as she was doing now?

Bet started to ask how well Rob had known her father, but he stood and picked his hat up off the bar, his expression shifted into something more serious.

"If you'll excuse me, it's been a long day."

What prompted the quick exit? Something in the conversation? Or did he just not like her company?

"Have a good night," Bet said.

"Elizabeth." Rob tipped his hat to Bet and walked away. Bet watched him cross the length of the bar and lean in to say something to Rope. Then he exited the tavern without a backward glance.

The crowd had grown as they ate. Musicians lined the room, unpacking banjos and fiddles and guitars. She slid around the L-shaped corner of the bar to a now-empty seat so she could lean back, watch the musicians, and keep her back to the wall. Schweitzer shifted around to stay under her feet.

A face caught her attention. Her heart lurched up into her throat as the man pulled his guitar out of its case and began to tune.

Well, isn't this the week for surprises. Wonder how many other specters from my past are going to wander into town.

FIFTEEN

Bet hadn't spoken to Eric Chandler in years. She preferred remembering the boy she and Dylan had looked up to when they were children, not the grad student who broke her heart. He looked much the same as he had in Ellensburg. His wheat-colored hair had thinned a bit, but he still wore his trademark black Levis, Doc Martens, and flannel shirt, sleeves rolled to the elbow. She knew his eyes would still be an icy shade of blue. He looked like he hadn't gained an ounce, a lean one hundred seventy pounds on his six-foot-two frame.

Emotions flooded her the moment she saw him across the room. The joy of seeing him was soon replaced by pain. The final moment as he walked out the door of the apartment they lived in together, slipped into the hot rod he'd owned since high school, and drove away. The bombshell that he wanted someone else was still a fresh crater at her feet.

Two years before that, Bet had walked into English 101 to find Eric standing at the front of the class. A graduate student in English, her childhood friend was the teaching assistant for the semester. One thing had led to another, and after reminiscing over a beer, they ended up making out in the back seat of his car. Halfway through her junior year, she'd moved into his tiny apartment. A week before graduation, she'd come home to find his belongings packed and him waiting on the sofa with the news he'd gotten another woman pregnant and decided to "do the right thing."

Bet moved to Los Angeles and never spoke to him again.

She wondered if she could slip out without Eric noticing her, except she had to walk in front of him to get out the door. Eric's mother had lived in Collier until she died a year ago, and Bet occasionally saw Dylan when the two visited town at the same time. She and Dylan remained friends in that awkward way people have when childhood memories are the only thing left in common. But Bet had managed to avoid Eric. He'd moved back east, and she wished he'd stayed there. He was a successful writer, but Bet refused to read his published works. She didn't want any insights into his emotional life.

Rope's voice broke through her thoughts. "Anything else, Bet?"

"I'd best get home," she said, pulling cash out of her fanny pack.

"Your money's no good tonight," the bartender said. "Rob Collier said I should put your dinner on his tab."

Bet didn't want any favors from Rob Collier. "Oh, he did, did he?"

"Said I should get you anything else you wanted before you left."

Bet contemplated refusing it and buying her own dinner, but common sense told her she had nothing to gain. Rob probably wouldn't even notice when he paid his bar tab, so the gesture would go unnoticed and she'd be out the cash.

"Music is just getting ready to start; you don't want to miss it again," Rope said.

She sat back down on the barstool to listen. "All right, then, I'll take one of your fancy root beers." Rope handcrafted his own.

"Coming up." Rope moved with the grace big men could have in their element.

Bet leaned against the wall, the pressure of the rough wood reassuring against her back. A group of people crowded the bar and blocked Eric from her view. If she waited long enough, the room would have enough bodies in it to allow her to exit unnoticed.

After Rope delivered her root beer, she sat, sipping and listening to the songs learned in childhood. The bluegrass her father played and her mother sung, Fiona's lilt changing the words into something more poignant. Mournful ballads and lively jigs, Bet's mother one generation out of Appalachia. Bet could picture her father there, sitting at the hearth, guitar in his lap. Light glinting off the strings while Bet grew drowsy in her mother's arms.

Earle met Fiona while in boot camp at Fort Benning, Georgia. They'd both said music brought them together and it was love at first sight, but Bet wondered at the price her mother had paid for falling in love with a man who could never stay long from Collier. There would be no return to the soft coves of the Appalachian hills for the future Mrs. Rivers. She'd given up her ties to the South when she married Earle, embracing instead the sharp peaks and hard, rocky ground of the Cascades.

Bet couldn't remember her mother's face, but she remembered her voice and the feel of that voice vibrating against her cheek as she nestled against her. The strangeness of how she'd spoken her words, the elongated vowels and clipped consonants, lingered in Bet's ear. Slang from another culture. A *skift* of snow, a *clever* person being not smart but friendly. Bet had tried to speak like her mother, the burr of Scotland rippling through hundreds of years in the mountains of North Carolina, but she'd never been able to capture the sound. Once her mother died, no model remained and Bet's father rebuked her when she tried on her mother's accent, so she stilled her tongue.

Bet reached the bottom of her glass and, having spent enough time with her mother's ghost, set it down along with a couple dollars' tip. She waved goodbye to Rope and stood to go. The musicians were in lively debate about the next song to play, and Bet moved out among the crush of people standing behind the tables and chairs closer to the fireplace, Schweitzer tight against her side. She felt secure Eric wouldn't notice her cross the room.

"Now, if we could just get my old friend Bet Rivers to join us on this one," she heard his voice say. It pierced her, the timbre of it. The voice that had once said, "I love you," and later, "I'm leaving."

The room took up his cause. "Come on, Bet," and "Let's hear it, Sheriff," echoed around the room. All eyes turned to her. A pathway opened up in front of her until nothing stood between them.

"What do you say, Bet? It's been too long."

Bet looked around at all the faces. Her people. Her town. Not Eric's. She belonged here, not him. These were people she cared for, watched over. Everyone in town expected her to sing. She had ever since she was a child. She couldn't walk out without everyone wondering why.

She nodded and stepped up to take the spot Eric indicated next to him. Sensing Bet's discomfort, Schweitzer placed his body between the two of them. She patted the dog and glanced sideways at Eric. Sitting this close, Bet could see the years did show in his face. Lines had etched their way into the corners of his eyes and grooves had formed around his mouth that might spell unhappiness, or maybe that was just her hope.

Eric started a haunting melody, and she joined her alto voice to his baritone on the old Stephen Foster tune. She released herself to the music and let her mind go blank, the lyrics indelibly burned into her memory so as not to require her attention.

'Tis a sigh that is wafted across the troubled wave.

'Tis a wail that is heard upon the shore.

'Tis a dirge that is murmured around the lowly grave.

Oh, hard times, come again no more.

Images of the body sliding through the broken ice rose unprompted in her imagination. Images that continued to sharpen in her mind, pelting her over and over. Panic swelled in her chest. She couldn't breathe and fought to keep singing the words.

She remembered Eric as a teenage boy. The scraggly beard he'd tried to grow like the grunge band singers he emulated. She looked at his profile, clean-shaven now. The man in the dark with the body at the lake. Eric had been tall as a young man. Her panic grew.

Bet stood at the end of the song and exited as quickly as she could, begging off singing another with excuses of work and Schweitzer needing a walk. When Eric reached out to stop her, his face full of yearning, she slipped easily from his grasp and hit the front door at a near run.

She pretended not to hear him say, "It sure felt good to sing with you again." She didn't want him to know the woman in her agreed, while the sheriff wondered what brought him to town.

SIXTEEN

The following morning, Bet sat at her desk on the phone with Randall Vogel, trying to dismiss another night of tossing and turning haunted by her nightmare. She couldn't let her dreams derail her investigation. No matter what had or hadn't happened seventeen years ago, she had a job to do now. Jane Doe left behind people who loved her. They were Bet's priority, not some long-ago traumatic event. She was tougher than that.

"Sure thing, Rivers," Vogel said, after Bet told him she wanted to go up in his helicopter and fly over the Collier property to look for an access road.

"I can be down to your place around two o'clock," Bet said. "That work for you?"

Vogel and his wife Penny operated a small airfield outside Ellensburg along with their son, Paul. "Long as no one gets themselves lost or hurt in the meantime, that'll be just fine."

Vogel had flown in the area for almost forty years. He and Penny did search and rescue when people went missing in the backwoods, and in the winter they dropped extreme athletes on top of inaccessible peaks so they could ski down. Randall Vogel piloted, while Penny and Paul used their EMT training and nursing skills. They also helped with firefighting and airlifting people out to the hospitals in Seattle when there was a serious medical condition or accident. Bet had flown with the Vogels many times.

After hanging up the phone, she went out to check on Alma, who reported finding three girls who looked vaguely like Jane

Doe in Seeley Lander's friends list on Facebook. She'd tracked two of them down, and neither knew where Seeley lived for the summer.

The third girl wasn't proving easy to find. Her Facebook posts ended a week ago, with no explanation. Carrie Turner was nineteen years old and lived in Seattle, but when Alma tracked down a landline number for the girl, Bet called and it rang without voice mail picking up. Bet's pulse began to quicken.

"Finding this girl Carrie is your top priority," Bet said.

"I'm on it," Alma said, before her attention turned to someone coming up the front steps. "Well, if it isn't Eric Chandler," she exclaimed, getting up out of her chair.

As Alma crossed over to open the door, Bet contemplated bolting to her office and locking herself in. Alma had no reason to know anything of Bet's history with Eric after they both left Collier. Alma only knew they had been friends as children. Bet wanted to keep it that way.

Eric greeted Alma with a hug as he came through the door, a different T-shirt on than last night, the flannel shirt now tied around his waist, too hot for the summer day. Bet picked up the list of names again as if it contained the most important information in the world.

"Good to see you," he said to Alma, towering over the woman.

"Here to stay? Or just a visit? Is Dylan coming too?" Alma peppered him with questions.

"Nope, just me."

"Sorry to hear about your divorce," Alma said.

Bet looked up at Alma's comment.

"Thank you," Eric said, a quick glance at Bet inviting her to ask about his marital status, but Bet remained silent, returning her eyes to the paper in her hand.

"So what brings you to town?" Alma ushered Eric in and led him to the chair next to her desk.

"Before you two get to talking, I need to ask Eric about something."

Eric looked at her, his face expectant. What did he think she'd ask? Bet reached over and picked up copies of Jane Doe and Seeley Lander from Alma's desk.

"Have you seen either of these two since you arrived?"

She watched Eric's face closely. She liked to think she knew him well enough to know if he was lying.

He studied the two pages, wincing as he looked at Jane Doe.

"What happened to her?" His voice held concern.

"Accident."

"Fell?" It wasn't a bad guess. A surprising number of people fell from the nearby trails every year. The advent of the selfie made it even more common. On high ledges, people backed up to get the perfect shot and stepped into space.

"Something like that."

"He's missing?" Eric asked. Bet nodded. "No. I'm sorry. I don't. But I haven't been back long, so there's probably a lot of people living here I don't know."

Bet studied his face. None of the telltale hints of lying appeared. He looked relaxed and met her eyes.

"Okay. Thank you." Bet started back to her office. "Oh, by the way, when *did* you get back to town?"

"Sunday," he said with a laugh. "Then I slept for a full day after driving cross country."

"Don't you want to stay and get caught up?" Alma asked Bet. "You can't have seen Eric in a month of Sundays."

"More than a few," Bet said. "But I need to get some things finished before I head down to Vogel's airfield. Don't chat too long. I need that information we talked about."

"Maybe dinner, Sheriff?" Eric said. "We could get caught up then."

"That's a fine idea," Alma answered, before Bet could say a word.

"There's a lot going on right now."

"Too much going on to have dinner?" Eric asked.

"You still need to eat," Alma said. No one ever won an argument with Alma.

"It would have to be late," Bet said.

"Okay by me." He leaned back in the chair as if he belonged in her station. He pulled a business card out of his pocket and handed it to Bet. "Call me on my cell when you're free."

Bet took the card and had started to leave the room when she heard Alma clear her throat in a loud command. Turning back to her, Bet saw Alma's hand outstretched and one eyebrow raised and realized she still held the list of names. Bet handed the paper over and returned to her office, where she shut the door she usually kept open. Even with the door closed, however, she could hear the low hum of his words.

Determined not to sit and stew about Eric Chandler, she picked up the phone and called the University of Washington, where she tracked down Seeley Lander's academic adviser. Bet explained that Seeley might have witnessed a crime and she needed to find him. School wasn't back in session, but she hoped the adviser might be able to get in touch with him. Bet also described Jane Doe, without reporting her dead, saying she was also a potential witness and a close friend to Seeley. The adviser said she would do what she could.

Hanging up the phone, Bet heard the front door open and close and the outer office fall silent. It surprised her to hear Alma's knock a moment later.

"Just thought you might want your door open again," Alma said, leaning against the doorframe.

"Okay."

"Good to see Eric." She watched Bet like a cat stalking a mouse.

The silence stretched between them. Bet finally caved.

"Anything else, Alma?"

"People make mistakes, when they're young. Maybe you should hear what Eric has to say."

"I'm not sure what you mean."

"Eric did what he thought was right when he left you. He stood by that woman, and he stood by his daughter. But years have gone by. He's different."

"Different how?" Bet asked, shocked to hear Alma knew about her relationship with Eric.

"Eric never knew who he was. He grew up too fast, the oldest child, no real father figure. He made mistakes."

"I grew up without a mother. That didn't make me a cheater." Bet heard the hurt and betrayal in her voice. She hadn't meant to say those words out loud.

"You've always been stronger than most people, Bet. You're just like your father that way. But you're at fault too. Eric strayed because he couldn't fill the empty spot his father left inside him. And look at what his own father did, abandoning his family. He didn't exactly model good behavior. But did you ever really let Eric in? Or did you hold him at arm's length?"

Bet started to respond with angry denial, but Alma cut her off.

"Don't get uppity with me. You know I'm right. You've chosen to be single ever since Eric left. No one gets hurt that bad; you just find it easier to be alone. Just like your dad."

"Time for me to leave for the airfield." Bet rose from behind her desk and headed for the door.

Alma strode toward her desk, irritation sounding in the thump of her heels on the floors. Bet continued to the front door while Alma crossed over and sat down, telling Schweitzer he couldn't go on this trip with Bet.

"Dogs don't belong in helicopters," she said, scratching him behind the ears. Bet paused at the door, looking back at the woman who never ceased to surprise her.

"I know everything," Alma said, as if Bet had asked.

"I guess you do."

"At least dinner with Eric beats dinner with Peter Malone."

Bet laughed, the storm temporarily blown over, and went out the door. She should have known Alma would know about her eating dinner with Peter at the tavern. At least she hadn't commented on her sitting with Rob Collier last night at the bar.

———

Bet left Collier in Dale's hands for the rest of the day, though she hoped he didn't like the view from her chair too much. It was a beautiful afternoon for flying. As the helicopter rose over the valley, Bet could see the town of Ellensburg to the east and the foothills of the Cascades to the west. Mt. Rainier rose in the southwest, with Mt. St. Helens just beyond, the flattened silhouette reminding Bet what happened when a volcano blew its top. The majesty of the Cascades filled her with awe. The endless expanse of wilderness, places where even to this day no person had ever walked. The line of jagged ridgelines that stretched all the way into Canada, a pipeline for wolves and moose, the return of the grizzly bear.

Maybe Bet had returned to these mountains on instinct too, like the animals once pushed out by men invading their territory, as if the soil ran in her veins.

Vogel headed toward Collier. Using the headsets they wore to communicate over the rotor noise, Bet explained that a visitor had found a body in the lake and they needed to locate a missing person and a missing vehicle. She wanted his eyes to help her search.

Twenty minutes later, Lake Collier appeared in front of them. Vogel eased up and their forward motion slowed.

"There's our visiting scientist." Bet pointed to Peter Malone out on the water. Sunlight flashed off his equipment and the silver of his boat. Nothing else was visible on the lake, just a dark expanse of blue rimmed with turquoise. "Let's fly over the Collier place."

Vogel soon circled over the impressive residence, where nothing stirred. Bet couldn't tell if Rob's Bronco was in the garage.

Bet pointed north, and Vogel tilted the aircraft to the right. Bet felt her body shift with the force, like riding a Tilt-a-Whirl at the fair. The agile craft straightened again and flew around the far side of the mountain, and maybe another entrance to the old mine.

"Did you ever notice another road into this area?" Randall Vogel knew the landscape of the Cascades as well as anyone.

"There are a few cutoffs from Ingalls Creek Road," Vogel said. "I've been thinking about it since you told me what we're looking for. I didn't think anything went all the way through, but it's possible. It would have to wind around below Three Brothers."

Bet looked down at the topographical map on her lap. She located the lake, the mine, and Three Brothers peak. There were a few lower valleys along the ridge heading up to the summit. It made sense there might be an old road there.

"This would be the back of the mine," Vogel said, pointing down while hovering in place. In this heavily wooded area, they could see little of the ground, just the tops of trees. But a lighter patch of dirt showed through the canopy half a mile away. Vogel gestured toward it with his chin while he dipped the chopper over for a closer look. A path wound through the evergreens. Bet held up her binoculars and studied the terrain.

"Looks like a trail to me," she said, lowering the binoculars back into her lap. "See anyone down there in the woods?"

"No. But it's dense enough a whole army could hide out in there and we'd never know it."

"Well, I sure hope that's not true."

Vogel chuckled.

"Too bad we can't make all the trees shed their needles and leaves," Bet said. "Just for a little while."

"Trust me," Vogel said. "You don't want that. I saw what Agent Orange could do to a forest in Nam. I pray I never see anything like that again."

Bet looked over at him but couldn't see his face.

"You must have seen a lot of awful things in the war," she said.

Randall shrugged and gave her a look she couldn't decipher. "Not something I usually talk about. Let's see if we can find where the trail comes out."

Bet started to say more, but a memory of her father stopped her. She'd asked him about the wars he'd been in, the battles he'd fought.

Let it go, Bet.

Maybe she should have tried harder to get him to talk.

They moved north, the dirt track appearing and disappearing through the dense mix of evergreens and big-leaf maples. Nothing moved below them except a huge six-point buck they startled out of a thicket with the noise of their rotors. They traveled north until the rapids of Ingalls Creek showed white through the trees. The trail came out at one side of the creek; Ingalls Creek Road ended on the other.

"You'd have to know that trail was there to find it," Vogel said. "But it looks like there is another way onto the back of the Collier property."

"This is part of the Okanogan-Wenatchee National Forest here, right?" Bet asked, pointing to the other side of Ingalls Creek, where the road stretched out to Highway 97.

"Yep. The creek is the dividing line."

"What's that?" Something flashed through a gap in the forest. Vogel maneuvered over for a closer look.

"Probably would be hidden from anyone who drove to the end of Ingalls Creek Road," Vogel said.

"What does that look like to you?"

He squinted at the vehicle.

"Looks like a red Ford Ranger."

SEVENTEEN

Bet wanted to set the helicopter down right away and investigate the truck, or at least read the license plate.

"No can do, Rivers. It's against regulations to land on national forest land without permission. Even if I could find an open spot on private land outside the boundary, I'd need permission from the owner; otherwise I'm guilty of trespassing. Just because a helicopter can land anywhere doesn't mean it should. If you can't see the plate from the air, I'm afraid you're out of luck. I'm not risking my license over this."

Bet trained her binoculars on the truck, but trees blocked the tailgate no matter how low they flew.

"Sorry, Bet," Vogel said. "You're going to have to drive back out here on your own."

Bet understood his position, but a lot could happen in the time it would take her to return. If Seeley Lander remained nearby, he would have seen the helicopter circle. If he was guilty of a crime, it might make him run. If it was Seeley's truck but someone else drove it and left the area after they flew away, she'd never identify the driver. Seeley could also be injured somewhere down there, and it would get harder to find him as daylight faded. She willed Vogel to fly faster as they turned and headed for the airfield.

———

Bet called Alma from her SUV as she raced back to Ingalls Creek. Alma had located seventeen women on Seeley's friends list without profile photos, but Carrie Turner's whereabouts were still unknown.

"I'll keep at it," Alma said. Bet anticipated Alma wouldn't quit that night until she located all the women on the list and Bet returned to Collier safe and sound.

"Good. Anything else?"

"Seeley's adviser replied to your email."

"She have any useful information?"

"Nothing yet. She just wanted you to know she's still trying."

Bet went on to explain she thought they'd located Seeley's missing truck and she would radio in from the scene.

"I may need a tow truck sent out, depending on what I find." Bet couldn't impound the vehicle without evidence of a crime, and nothing they knew so far proved Seeley Lander guilty of anything, even if it was his truck in the woods.

Nothing but static came through from Alma's end.

"You get that, Alma?" Bet asked.

"Just remember some bastard shot that little girl in the back."

"Will do," Bet said. "Over and out."

Bet turned onto Ingalls Creek Road. On either side, dirt tracks disappeared into the trees onto private property that skirted the national forest. Bet could see run-down properties in the woods, ramshackle buildings gone to ruin in the forest. Old trailers and rusted automobiles on blocks glinted through the trunks. The road ended in a small parking lot for the trailhead, which led into wilderness.

She felt her apprehension rise at her own isolation. The SHER-IFF sign painted on the side of her vehicle didn't make her safer in the woods. The denizens of this community could just as easily view her with suspicion and ignore any pleas for help.

Working in isolated areas meant things were often quiet. It also meant she rarely had backup to rely on. She hadn't felt the current situation warranted having either of her deputies meet her here, but the woods were dark and she started having second thoughts. It was human instinct to be wary of the forest at night.

Using photographs she snapped from the helicopter, she identified the dirt track where Seeley had parked his truck. He sat close to the end of the road on private property, not on national forest land. She had no way to know if the owner had given Seeley permission, so she couldn't use him parking illegally as a justification for impound.

She pulled over in her SUV before she reached his vehicle, not wanting to announce her arrival.

Trust your instincts, she could hear her father say. *If you're cautious, that's one thing. If you're afraid, that's another. Fear keeps us from doing something stupid.*

Bet determined she wasn't doing anything stupid. Besides, Earle wouldn't have needed backup, and Bet hated not measuring up.

She slid out of the SUV, strapped on her bulletproof vest, and unsnapped the keeper on her service weapon. She walked down the ruts of a narrow, overgrown side road to where the truck sat. The tall conifers, mostly firs, pines, and cedars, cloaked the area in darkness, and the dense undergrowth of dead trees and bushes made it harder to see if anyone watched from the woods.

She came upon the vehicle, a red Ford Ranger with a black camper shell. The tinted windows of the shell made it impossible to see inside, so she continued her cautious approach. Pulling her flashlight out, she shined the light through the window of the camper.

A cooler, a spare tire, some paper grocery sacks, and a crumpled fast-food bag were all she saw in a quick glance. Moving to the passenger's side door, she played her light through the windows of the extended cab, also tinted. No one, alive or dead, sat in the cab. Two takeout cups from Sandy's coffee cart sat in the cup holders. Other than that, the truck sat empty.

Twigs and pine needles covered the vehicle, and the windshield was dusty as if it had been parked there several days. The forest lay quiet, though the splashing of the rushing stream in the background could mask the sound of someone moving through the woods. Bet looked around for footprints and saw two distinct sets of tracks leading away from both sides of the truck. One set of tracks looked smaller than the other, both with the treads of hiking boots.

After taking photos, she followed the tracks to the creek near where a bridge had once crossed onto private land. The roadbed had fallen away, leaving only footings in place. The water split around the concrete posts, the current swift.

Bet estimated the trail from the end of Ingalls Creek Road to the back of the hillside with the mine to be roughly five miles. A twentysomething in good shape could easily navigate the distance, despite the rugged terrain and rise in elevation.

The question remained, however: why hadn't they both come back out? Were two people out in the woods right now? With no connection to Jane Doe? Or had one of the hikers arrived here in this truck and ended up shot, wrapped in canvas, and abandoned in the lake? Most importantly, if the latter was true, had the other set of footprints been left by a killer or by another victim?

Bet took a look at the license plate and confirmed the truck belonged to the missing Seeley Lander. She decided to get her kit out of the SUV and dust the outside of the truck for prints. They had so little to go on that it would be worth making a mess of a civilian's car if she came up with a set that identified Jane Doe.

She called in her location and situation to Alma, relieved her cell worked so far back in the mountains.

"You want a tow truck?" Alma asked.

"I don't have justification. Let me look for fingerprints and see if I find anything interesting on the trail. I'll call you back before I leave."

Finishing up the call with Alma, Bet pulled out her evidence case. She felt her pulse quicken. The truck was the first solid piece of evidence beyond Jane Doe's body. If Jane Doe's fingerprints were in a database—and since the eighties, a lot of parents had fingerprinted their children—this could give them an ID. Once she had Jane Doe identified, she could track down information about her trip to Collier.

Proof the woman had traveled with Seeley Lander would put him squarely in her sights as perpetrator, second victim, or at least a witness. She felt a spark of hope that the investigation was about to take a turn ahead of her deadline with Jamie Garcia.

She wanted any press on the investigation to put her in a good light and, even more importantly, come out after she notified next of kin.

Bet managed to lift a few good prints on the passenger's side of the vehicle. The prints on the handle were too smudged to be of use, but she found clear prints on the roof, where people put their hands getting in and out or when the window was open. Exterior prints on a car were useless in court, but right now she only wanted an ID.

She had finished up with the prints when movement off to her right caught her eye. Whatever slipped through the woods stood taller than a deer but smaller than an elk, and bears didn't walk on their hind legs. Someone crept around in the woods.

The flashlight must have given her presence away, as the intruder made a beeline toward her. She took a deep breath and went out to meet them.

EIGHTEEN

Bet shined her flashlight into the person's eyes. She'd started to say, "Sheriff Bet Rivers," when she recognized Rob Collier.

"Please keep your hands where I can see them, Mr. Collier."

"That's the second time in two days you've said that to me, Elizabeth," Rob said. "I might start to take offense."

"Can you please tell me what you're doing out here?" Bet rested a hand on her holstered gun.

"Take the flashlight out of my eyes, and I might take more interest in answering."

Bet dropped the light down to the level of his chest.

Rob lowered his hands but kept them visible. Between the high peaks, the dense trees, and the lateness of the day, the remaining light was fading fast. Bet didn't relish being out here alone with Rob Collier, but she didn't have a lot of choice in the matter. She wanted answers from him, and she could hardly handcuff him and throw him into the back of her vehicle without cause.

"My apologies, Mr. Collier. Can I ask what brings you out here this time of night?" she asked again.

"It's not against the law to walk in my own woods."

"You left your woods when you crossed the creek."

"You got me there, Elizabeth. But it's also not against the law to walk on national forest land."

"No, but it is against the law to lie to an officer." Which wasn't true in every circumstance, but it was if the lie obstructed justice.

"You'd catch more bees with honey."

He was right. She didn't want to admit that something about the man put her on edge. He hadn't done anything wrong she could prove and she had questioned him twice in less than two days, the first time in his own garage. She took a step back into a more relaxed position.

"Lovely to see you again, Mr. Collier. Mind telling me what brings you out here?"

"That wasn't so bad, was it?"

Bet didn't reply.

"I wanted to do a little scouting around on my property. The trail over there comes out not far from the house. Thought I'd see where the trail ended."

"That's a long walk."

"Not on a horse." Bet looked back in the direction Rob had come. "I left Figure over there," Rob continued. "No way for him to cross."

It sounded reasonable to Bet, but someone had killed a young woman, most likely less than a week ago, and Rob Collier had arrived back in town at the same time.

"Why'd you bring your horse with you from Arlington?"

"Where I go, he goes."

Bet could appreciate that. She wished Schweitzer were here with her now.

"You still looking for the kid?" Rob asked.

"Find anything besides this trail?"

"I did."

Bet waited.

"Found something you might want to look at in person. I was going to call you after I rode back to the house."

"What did you find?"

"It's near a cave entrance, on the back side of the mountain the old mine is in. Figure can ride us both back."

"Wouldn't it be closer to go from your house?" Bet asked, "I can drive us both around."

"That won't get my horse home."

"Shit," Bet muttered under her breath.

"What is it you think I'm going to—" Rob stopped midsentence. Something flashed across his face, an emotion landing so briefly Bet couldn't read it in the dim light.

"That girl didn't die in an accident, did she?"

Bet said nothing.

"Why didn't you tell me that? That's what we're talking about here, isn't it? Homicide? You wouldn't be spooked like this on account of an accidental death, even with another person missing."

Bet kept her peace, trying to judge Rob's reaction to his own deduction.

"Where did you find her body?"

Bet decided to lay a few cards on the table. If he was guilty of something and he thought she trusted him, he might give himself away. If he was innocent, he might have important information.

"Just her. In the lake."

"In the lake?"

"Is that a surprise?" Had he expected her to be found somewhere else? Had he dumped her in the mine only to have her surface unexpectedly?

"No. But if you found her in the lake, why isn't it all over town? I didn't hear any talk in the tavern."

Bet wondered if he'd gone to the tavern for just that reason, to suss out if the body had been found.

"And the boy?"

Bet shook her head.

"Missing." Rob thought a moment. "Killer or victim?"

When Bet didn't respond, Rob speculated. "Must think he's a killer, or you'd have a search-and-rescue team out looking for him."

"We don't know exactly what his involvement is yet," Bet said. "And we have no idea where to search, so a team would be pointless."

The radio in the SUV sputtered to life, making both of them jump.

"Just do me a favor, Mr. Collier." Bet moved over to open the passenger's side door. "Stay right there where I can see you."

Rob nodded, the humor finally gone from his demeanor.

"Find anything interesting in the Ranger?" Alma asked.

"What Ranger?" Rob asked.

"Who's that?" Alma had the ears of a bat.

"Rob Collier," Bet said.

"What the hell is he doing there?"

"He was out on a little trail ride. I'll fill you in later. Better call Dale to meet me here. I know Clayton had to go back down to Cle Elum."

"There's a little problem with that," Alma said, her voice heavy. "That's part of why I'm calling." She went on to explain that Dale had responded to a fight at a campground fifty miles out of town.

"Doesn't sound like serious injuries, but there were drugs, bikers, and minors involved. Dale is there sorting out the mess. There's also a car the bikers claim isn't theirs abandoned nearby, so we have to track down the owner. It could relate to your case."

Even if Jane Doe had arrived at the trailhead with Seeley Lander in the Ranger, she might have met him first at the campground, so it could still be her car.

"All right," Bet said, leaning against the passenger's seat. She could feel a headache starting behind her eyes.

"Leave the truck until tomorrow," Alma said. "Come on back to town."

"I need to search the area. If Seeley is nearby, he could be hurt. If not, I don't want him driving away."

For a moment, no one said anything.

"Leave the Ranger for now," Rob said. "Ride with me on Figure. I'll show you what I found."

Bet considered her options. She knew Seeley Lander owned the truck, but she didn't know for a fact he'd been the one driving it. If he came out and drove away, they could eventually track Seeley down. But if someone else had borrowed it, the only chance to catch whoever it was might be if that person came back for it now. It could have been abandoned already, however, in which case waiting for the driver to return would be nothing but a waste of time.

She calculated how long it would take her to drive back around the mountains to Collier, meet Rob at his house, then travel back to this mine entrance he mentioned on a three-wheeler or a dirt bike. She estimated least an hour just to drive around the mountain.

"How long will this ride take?"

"Twenty minutes."

He almost had her convinced. She didn't trust the man, so maybe she should keep him where she could see him.

"Besides," Rob said. "This trail goes onto my private property. If you want to follow those footsteps, you need my permission."

"Only if I come close to your house; open land is fair game."

"But you don't know how close to the house I'm taking you. Trust me."

"Sounds so simple when you say it that way."

"It is."

If it's so simple, why do I have the feeling going into the woods with you is a bad idea?

Bet decided following the tracks and seeing whatever Rob wanted to show her took precedence. If Seeley was at the other end of this trail, the fact that he didn't return to the Ranger felt more like he was hurt or lost than guilty. If he'd been the perpetrator, Bet thought, he would have already gotten the hell out of Dodge.

"All right, Mr. Collier," she said, pulling on a backpack she kept stocked with emergency supplies in the SUV. "We'll do it your way."

NINETEEN

With the bridge out and the rushing water so deep, Bet wondered how Rob had crossed the creek. She followed him downstream twenty yards and discovered a fallen tree spanning the banks. The trunk looked sturdy, but with no rail and high above the water, the natural bridge presented a challenge. After watching Rob walk along the narrow crossing, Bet's confidence rose. Trusting years of hiking, rock climbing, and going off-trail to find the best fishing spots, she quickly followed. Not long after they left the creek behind, the silhouette of Rob Collier's horse appeared, a darker patch against the trees.

Rob walked over to Figure, who wore a red halter and stood quietly munching grass. First Rob slid a bit into Figure's mouth that attached to metal rings on the halter; then he clipped on a set of reins.

"Are you sure he can carry both of us?" Bet asked, eyeing the animal. "He's big and all, but the two of us combined are pretty heavy."

Rob swung up into the saddle as he explained, "It's not something I would ordinarily do. It's not good for the horse, but that boy could be in trouble. It's a fair amount of weight, but Figure can handle it." He walked Figure over to a large rock, where he directed Bet to stand so she could swing up behind him.

Once Bet settled in behind the saddle, Rob clicked softly to his horse, and they began to stride away from the creek. It took Bet a moment to adjust to the movement, but she found the horse's walk smoother than she'd expected. Beginning to relax, Bet leaned out to the side to point her flashlight on the ground in front of them, picking up a few footprints like the ones near the Ranger.

"Best not tilt out to the side like that," Rob said. "You'll make it harder for Figure if you keep him off-balance. His footing will be better if his eyes stay acclimated to the dark."

Bet clicked off the flashlight and they continued on in silence, the tall horse's hoofbeats and the creak of leather providing a cadence to their journey. She leaned against Rob's broad back. He wore a windbreaker over his T-shirt, but it wasn't enough to keep the heat of his body from seeping through.

"Why Figure?" Bet asked.

"The very first Morgan horse on record had that name."

"Is that what he is? A Morgan?"

"Mostly."

"What's the rest?"

"Moose. That's why he's so big."

Bet laughed.

They fell silent again. The only sound was the wind in the tops of the trees whispering above their heads.

"I didn't know a horse could walk this fast," Bet said a few moments later.

"Most horses walk three or four miles an hour. A gaited horse can do closer to ten. We're not doing quite that fast with the poor light, but I'd allow we'll cover a couple miles in twenty minutes."

Bet adjusted her hands around Rob's waist.

"I don't have a holster on."

"I wasn't—"

"It's okay. No offense taken. I would have patted me down too, if I were you."

Bet felt herself blush, glad Rob couldn't see her face. She had taken the opportunity of their physical proximity to feel for any kind of weapon Rob might have at his hip or the small of his back.

It didn't take long to reach their destination. Rob dismounted, then reached up to help Bet slide down, her heavy duty belt fighting her descent. Figure was tall—Rob said over sixteen hands—and getting down from where she sat required a little more skill than just slipping from a saddle.

"This way," he said, as he walked toward a sheer granite wall, a pile of loose scree at its base.

Bet pulled her own flashlight out, and the two scrambled up the hillside into a thicket of scrub trees. They pushed their way through the dense tree limbs, and Bet's eyes could just make out an inky black spot on the side of the mountain. A slight cold draft pushed against her from the hole.

A metal bat gate built like an old-time jail cell door, which would have secured the mouth of the tunnel, had been sawn through, bypassing the security.

"I assume you found it this way?" she asked Rob.

"I did. Take a look at that." Rob pointed not far inside the entrance. Bet illuminated something silver and cylindrical. A flashlight.

"We don't know how long that's been there. It might have nothing to do with the current situation," Bet said.

"Get a little closer. What do those smudges look like to you?"

Bet crouched down. What she'd first thought to be dirt on the flashlight had a redder tinge.

Blood.

Bet looked farther down into the mouth of the cave. The opening went forward several feet before it turned hard to the left.

"Did you go back in there?" Bet asked.

"I went back as far as that turn." Rob flashed his light across a few footprints in the entrance to the cave. "Being very careful not to step on those."

Bet inspected the footprints. Two sets resembled the ones Bet had found at the Ranger. Bet pulled her camera out of her backpack and compared them to the photos. The prints were identical. Another set, most likely made from an adult male, judging by the size, appeared to have come before the first two, then returned later going out of the cave. Bet could tell by the direction they pointed and how they overlapped. Bet also saw Rob's carefully placed footprints entering the cave off to the side.

The prints showed only in the soft soil at the mouth of the cave. Outside, the loose rocks showed indentations where people or animals had gone up and down the side of the hill, but individual tracks were impossible to see. Bet took a few photos of the prints in the mouth of the cave.

"What could you see from the bend?" she asked after she finished.

"The trail goes another twenty feet, then turns again. I didn't go any farther."

"You didn't pick this up or touch it in any way?" Bet gestured toward the flashlight.

"No, ma'am."

Bet photographed the flashlight, pulled on gloves, and retrieved an evidence bag, evidence tape, and a permanent marker. She put the flashlight in the evidence bag and labeled it with the date and location. She took photos of the damaged gate. The thought of going down into the cave made her uneasy, but if Seeley was in some kind of trouble, she needed to get to him soon. He could have been down there for days.

"This would be a whole lot easier if the blood on that flashlight didn't look so fresh," Bet said, putting the latex gloves back in her fanny pack to throw away later. Though dry, the blood on the flashlight appeared gummy, not yet fully assuming the flaky, rusty appearance blood took on when it had been exposed to air for an extended period of time.

"I'm guessing you're wondering the same thing I am," Rob said.

"Did someone drop this flashlight going in or coming out?"

"And were they being chased? Or doing some chasing?"

Bet nodded and pulled out her cell phone. No reception. Rob stood silent next to her.

"How did you know this cave was here?" Bet asked. "You can't see it from the trail."

"I learned about it when I was a kid."

"Why didn't you tell me this before?"

"Tell you what? There's an old cave on my property? Why would I tell you that just because you're looking for someone? You said the girl died in an accident. I didn't know we were talking about something more serious."

"You must have thought this was a potential hazard."

"No one knows about this cave; you've lived here your whole life and you didn't know about it. Besides, it's usually locked."

"If it was so unlikely anyone would be out here, what sent you here to look?"

"Something from last night started me thinking."

"What?"

"You are your father's daughter."

"I know that, but what started you thinking?"

"That's not what I meant."

Bet waited as Rob fought an internal battle over what to tell her.

"You're going to think I'm nuts," he said.

"Try me."

Rob pulled a faded sepia photograph out of his pocket. Despite its age, the picture showed a young man very clearly. He leaned against an ore cart, pickax next to him. He sported a huge grin, despite the smudges of coal on his cheek.

"Where did you get this?" Bet asked.

"The photo you showed me looked familiar, but I couldn't place it. Then I said, 'You are your father's daughter.' That turned my attention to family resemblances. I used to look at these old photo albums my grandfather had. That's where I'd seen this face."

"So, that's the original Seeley Lander."

"How'd you know that?" Rob asked.

"The boy I'm looking for is his great-grandson. Same name. Same face."

"I'll be damned."

"You found this old photo and, what, decided to come out here to look for ghosts?"

"The only people who could know about this old cave were my family and someone who worked in the mine."

"And everyone who worked in the mine died in the mine—"

"Except Seeley, who might have told stories to his kids."

Bet thought about that for a moment. "So this really is a back door."

"It is," Rob said. "And now the only way in."

"But," Bet said, thinking about her theory of an underground river into the lake, "it might not be the only way out."

TWENTY

Bet faced a dilemma. Going into the cave alone was foolish. She didn't know what the conditions were like or who might be down there in the dark. But Seeley could be injured. The sheriff's station motto started *To protect all people*, not *To protect oneself.*

If Seeley had killed Jane Doe inside the cave and she floated out into the lake through an underground river, why wouldn't he have left the area in his truck? Bet felt in her gut that if he'd gone into the cave with Jane Doe, he would have come out on his own if he could.

"What's the plan, Sheriff?" Rob asked. "Think your boy Seeley is stuck down in the tunnel?"

"I do."

"We going in after him?"

"We are."

She looked at Rob in the glow of her flashlight. They were a long way from help, but Alma knew Rob was with her. He would be stupid to do her harm.

"I don't want you to do anything you aren't comfortable with."

Rob ignored her. "Do you want me to lead the way?"

She still didn't like the thought of turning her back on him, but he was a civilian, and she wasn't about to let him lead.

"Follow me, Mr. Collier."

Bet kept her flashlight trained on the footprints, but the floor of the cave soon turned from dirt to rock and there were no more prints to see. After they made the first turn, the temperature dropped and Bet's attention turned to finding solid footing. She didn't want to risk spraining an ankle.

The only sound Bet could hear was a slight drip of water and Rob's steady breathing behind her.

Fifteen minutes later they reached a fork in the rough-hewn tunnel. The split to the right led downhill at a gentle angle. The split to the left went ten feet and disappeared around another corner.

"Hear anything?" Bet asked, her voice low. Rob stood in silence for a moment before he shook his head.

"What do you think?" he whispered, as he inspected the ground. "I don't see evidence of anyone going either way."

"Let's go as far as that turn and see what happens." Bet scraped an arrow into the hard-packed dirt floor to mark the direction to the outside. It was easy to get turned around in the claustrophobic dark. They followed the left split and went around the turn. The tunnel narrowed and dropped away at their feet. A rocky staircase cut into the earth.

"What do you think? We could flip a coin," Rob said. "Or split up."

"I don't want to split up." Bet couldn't risk him getting lost on his own. She was responsible for his safety too, even though he accompanied her willingly. She also didn't trust him and preferred knowing what he was up to. "Let's go twenty minutes the other way and reassess. All things being equal, I don't know why someone would choose the harder route down."

Turning around in the narrow tunnel, Rob stood tall enough he had to stoop. Bet's head was mere inches from the ceiling.

Coming back out to the split, Bet made sure her arrow was still visible before they went the other way. The two continued down the trail to the right. A few minutes later, they reached a spot where the ceiling rose above them. Bet noticed that the floor turned white under their feet. Shining her flashlight up, she saw eyes and heard the rustle of leathery wings. A bat dropped off and flew out over her head toward the exit.

"I hope that's the only colony we stumble across," she said. She also hoped the rest of them exited the cave before she and Rob came back to this section of tunnel. She liked bats fine, but from a distance.

At the twenty-minute mark, the trail continued in front of them.

Bet pulled the compass out of her backpack.

"What's our heading?" Rob asked.

"South and slightly west," she said. That meant the heart of the mine should be in front of them.

"Twenty more minutes," Bet said. "Let's go twenty more minutes in this direction and see what it brings."

The two set off again. The path continued to be traversable, the ceiling high enough that even Rob stood upright. Bet began to believe their route would intersect with the mine and the lake. Fifteen minutes later, however, the trail ended at a tumble of fallen rock.

"Any way to tell how long ago this happened?" Bet asked.

Rob shook his head. "No idea. Are you wondering if Seeley is trapped on the other side?" He poked around in the rocks while he spoke. "Look at this." He held up a cylinder made of brass or copper. It was misshapen and dented.

"What is that?" she asked, reaching out.

"A lantern."

"Looks like it might be from back when the mine was in use," Bet said, taking a closer look.

"We could take it out and give it to George," Rob said. "He knows a lot about the history of this area. I'll carry it."

She didn't argue. "If this cave-in happened that long ago, I think we can assume Seeley isn't stuck behind it."

"Agreed," Rob said. "What about the other tunnel, the one with the stairs?"

"If he's still down here, it's the only way he could go."

They retraced their steps to the stone staircase and started to descend. Chipped into the stone, the steps were far enough apart to be a big drop, even with Bet's long legs. The steps were narrower than typical stairs, making it hard to balance. Keeping one hand on the wall, Bet could feel the backs of her legs start to complain.

Just when she thought she couldn't take any more, her flashlight picked up the bottom of the stairs. She couldn't see what lay beyond the last step, but she could see the trail flattened out. The low ceiling forced her to crouch moving forward. She focused on finding Seeley Lander as a way to keep the walls from closing in. Reaching the last step down, she discovered the mouth of a small tunnel. Taking a deep breath, she crawled into the space, wondering what, or more importantly who, would be waiting on the other side.

TWENTY-ONE

The sheer size of the cavern that opened at the base of the stairs would have been impressive even without the magnificent rock formations.

Rob let out a low whistle as he stood next to Bet. "I can't believe I never knew this was here."

The bright LED light from Bet's flashlight barely made a dent in the black void in front of them. A group of stalagmites stood a few feet away, rising like fossilized trees from the cave floor. They glittered, throwing off light like a disco ball at a roller rink. Bet clicked her light off and Rob did the same.

Complete and utter darkness.

Bet waited to see if her eyes adjusted to any tiny spark of light in the cave.

Nothing.

The darkness pressed against her eyes. Beside her, Rob breathed slowly and evenly, which allowed her to fight the impulse to scream as loud as she could, anything to break the overwhelming, permanent night.

"I don't see any light at all, do you?" Bet whispered.

"Not a thing," Rob agreed. "We could try this again during daylight. There might be an opening to the surface, but I don't see any manmade light sources, that's for sure."

"Do you hear what I hear?"

"Running water. There's a river down here?"

"Sounds that way."

"You don't seem surprised."

Without replying, Bet clicked her light back on and lit up the ground in front of them. Some parts of the cavern floor were softer than the rocky pathway they'd followed down. Footsteps disappeared into the dark in front of them.

"Someone has been down here," Bet said.

"Looks like two or three different shoe sizes." Rob scanned his light over the marks. "Hard to tell in this footing."

"We have no way of knowing how long those prints have been here," Bet said as she snapped a few photos. "Could be days, weeks . . ."

"Even years."

Bet pulled her compass back out. "I think we can go partway into the cave without getting turned around. Last thing I want is for us to get lost down here."

Rob nodded. "If we're careful, we should be all right."

Standing with her back to the tunnel, Bet took a heading due south and carefully made her way toward the sound of the river. The footprints in front of them disappeared, but Bet had the compass and the river noise to guide her. With no direct path through the rocky formations, they wound around through a garden of stalagmites and stalactites, which occasionally grew together to form a column.

Even with their circuitous route, it didn't take long to reach the river. Bet played her flashlight across the surface of the water to the other side roughly fifty feet from where they stood. The water roared by, and Bet couldn't guess at the depth.

"Hate to get sucked into that and pulled to wherever it ends up," Rob said. Bet sent her light in the direction the water flowed, but it continued far beyond the beam. Rob pointed his light on the other side of the water, and something white flashed and disappeared. Bet felt a frisson of fear spread through her body at who else might be down in the cave. Her childhood fear of the miners' ghosts competed with her adult knowledge that whoever had shot Jane Doe might still be around.

"Yeah, I saw it too," Rob whispered in Bet's ear before she could say anything.

"Any idea what that was?"

"Nope. Shouldn't be anything moving down here. We're way too deep for any animals. I doubt if that was the ghost of a miner. Looked too substantial to me."

"Could be Seeley."

With their lights off, they stood silent again, waiting to see if they could hear anything over the sound of the river. Bet weighed their options. She hadn't come this far to turn back at the first sign they'd found someone.

Bet clicked her flashlight back on and looked upriver. A short distance upstream, she could make out rocks scattered through the water like giant stepping-stones.

"I think I can cross there," Bet said.

"We don't know how deep that is," Rob said. "One slip and you could be in trouble. Even with me here to catch you."

"Guess I better not slip," Bet said, with more confidence than she felt.

"Are you sure you don't want me to make the crossing?"

"No. I'm not sure at all." Bet started taking off her backpack. "Sit here and keep your flashlight off. That way you can track my progress without giving away your location. If I run into trouble, I'll yell. If my light goes out or you hear a big splash, you know what to do."

"Run like hell?"

"You're a funny man, Mr. Collier."

Setting her backpack at the base of a stalagmite, Bet tried not to think about all the things that could go wrong. Standing at the river's edge, Bet assessed the steps she needed to take. She liked what she saw. The rocks in front of her were situated close enough together that she could reach each step, though the one in the middle would be more of a leap. The rocks looked solid, though that could be deceptive.

Bet started her way across the water, step by careful step. She paused before the largest gap between rocks. Not only was it wider than she'd thought from shore, but the surface of the rock she would land on slanted steeper than she expected. Adjusting her launch position, Bet gripped her flashlight and leaped out toward the next rock as someone simultaneously blinded her with a light.

Landing but unable to see, Bet felt herself continuing forward with the momentum of her jump. She dropped down onto the edge of the rock before the trajectory could send her tumbling into the water in her heavy bulletproof vest.

"Stop. I've got a gun," a voice said out of the darkness.

Bet felt her heart jump into her throat.

Rob remained silent. She knew he could hear the voice from the other side too, and see the light pointed in her face. She hoped he stayed quiet until they knew more about the situation.

"I know you have a gun too," the voice said. "I want to see you drop it in the water."

"My name is Sheriff Rivers. I think you know I'm not going to toss my weapon in the river," Bet said, relieved her voice remained steady. She pointed her flashlight in the direction the threat came from. At least she'd managed to hang on to it during her leap. "Now we're both blinded by the light."

"I will shoot you," the voice said.

"I'm just as likely to shoot you," Bet said, pulling her gun from its holster. "I don't think you want to take that chance."

Bet waited to see what he would do. Had she really come this far just to end up like Jane Doe?

TWENTY-TWO

Time stopped. Bet's legs went numb from the awkward stance she held on the rock.

"I'm almost across the water. How about you let me finish coming over to your side?" Bet said.

"You aren't the sheriff."

"I am. My name is Sheriff Rivers," Bet said. "But you can call me Bet."

"You're lying. Sheriff Rivers is a man. His name is Earle."

"That was my dad. I'm the sheriff now. Elizabeth Rivers. I have ID on me. I can come over and show it to you. Plus I'm wearing the uniform, right? Who am I talking to?"

"I'm asking the questions here." For the first time, Bet heard hesitation. The voice wavered. She doubted this person was a hardened criminal, though that didn't mean he couldn't be dangerous.

Amateurs with guns are just as dangerous as career criminals, Bet. Her father's voice cut through her fear. *But you're more likely to talk them down.*

"No problem." Bet spoke again to the voice in the dark. "I won't ask a thing. Sure would be good to get off this rock, though." Bet squinted her eyes against the light and looked down. Although the flashlight shined in her face, it also lit the edge of the stone in front of her.

Nothing came back but silence. Bet decided to keep going.

"I'm going to step onto the next rock. I need to get better footing." Bet took another step forward onto a flat rock closer to the bank. "You don't want me to fall into the river and drown."

Step by step, she moved toward the dry land in front of her, trying to keep her gaze averted enough to keep her eyesight. She kept up her litany, hoping her voice would keep him calm.

"I think you need some help. I can get you out of this cave."

Bet reached the edge of the water and was preparing to make the final leap when the light shining in her face fell away.

The flashlight clunked on the floor of the cave a half second before the sound of a falling body followed. Focusing her light, Bet saw an inert form sticking out from behind a group of columns.

"Hold up, Rob," Bet called out. "I think he's injured." Bet flashed her light around the area, spotting no one but the unconscious figure in a heap on the ground.

Kneeling down next to him, Bet could see the young man from the photo Alma had found. The sprinkle of acne in the picture was gone, replaced by a few scars. His features were fine, a slim nose, high cheekbones, an almost feminine face to match his slight form.

Pulling on a pair of latex gloves, Bet began to assess the young man's condition. She put her fingertips on the boy's neck and found a pulse, faint and rapid. He undoubtedly suffered from shock and hypothermia. Taking off his backpack, she discovered a makeshift bandage fashioned from his torn shirt that covered a bloody wound on his side.

He could have been down in the cave for as long as four days. Wondering what the bandage covered, she turned him to see if she could get a better look. She felt something hard and cold underneath his body, and recovered an ancient revolver.

"Okay, Rob," Bet called, wondering if he was still there or if he'd taken off at the sound of an armed standoff. "He was armed, but I have it now and he's unconscious. No sign of anyone else here. We better get him out of the cave." Bet checked the weapon and found three cartridges left from the five it carried. She unloaded the gun and tucked the ammunition into her pocket.

Did the boy shoot at Jane Doe twice? And only hit her once? Or did he fire at someone else, potentially in self-defense?

"Coming over," Rob said. At least he hadn't bolted. His flashlight illuminated his path across the rocks. As confident as he'd been crossing the downed tree, she didn't doubt his steadiness.

"Think we can carry him out of here?" Bet asked as Rob arrived. "He's injured, but I don't dare take off the bandage to check. It might just make things worse."

"It'll be tough to cross the rocks, but I think I can manage. I'm not going to be able to get him up that stone staircase, though, and there isn't enough room for both of us to try to carry him."

"I was afraid of that." Bet thought for a moment. "Can we at least get him to the tunnel?"

"That we can do."

"What do you think he weighs?" Bet asked.

"No more than one hundred fifty pounds," Rob guessed as he crouched down. "We'll have to get him up on my back. If we pull his arms around my neck, I can hang on to him like a giant backpack."

Bet pulled the unconscious man's arms over Rob's shoulders as he grabbed hold of Seeley's forearms.

Rob stood, and they set off for the water. Bet was prepared to help Rob keep his balance, but he moved across the water sure-footed as a cat on a porch rail. Once they reached the other side, Bet picked up her backpack and stuck Seeley's almost empty backpack into her own. She hoped it had started out full of food when the boy arrived in the cave. Last, she picked up the lantern Rob had carried and stuffed it in as well.

Pulling out the compass, she took the lead back to the tunnel. "Let me know if you need me to spell you," she said as Rob's breathing became labored, but his trudging footsteps remained unflagging behind her. Once they reached the tunnel, Rob lowered Seeley to the ground before he and Bet pushed him carefully through the entrance.

"I need to go for help," Bet said.

"I'm not letting you ride my horse."

"I'll jog until I get back into cell phone range."

Rob looked unhappy with the arrangement, but that could be a ruse. What if he wanted her out of the way so he could finish what he'd started with Seeley? Bet could return with help only to find the young man had "succumbed" to his wounds, and it might be impossible to prove Rob had helped him along.

"Are you concerned there's a third party down here in the cave?" she asked. Someone had shot Seeley. If it wasn't Rob, he could be a target.

"I can take care of myself."

Bet pictured all the places people concealed weapons. Rob might still be armed. It didn't make her feel better to know he could have a gun. Sending Rob for help didn't guarantee anything either. He could lock the gate behind him somehow, and she and Seeley would never be found. It would be easy enough for him to report the two of them had parted ways. Bet tried to remember if she had mentioned to Alma that Rob had found a cave, but she wasn't sure. Regardless, it was her responsibility to get assistance for Seeley.

"I'll be back with help as fast as I can."

He clicked off his flashlight. "Probably best if I wait in the dark. We don't know who else might be down here waiting for you to leave."

Bet reconsidered her decision. Maybe she *should* send Rob out to get help. Situations in Los Angeles always had support nearby; she wasn't used to being so on her own. She started to have a new respect for her father and what he'd faced as sheriff. She wondered what choice he'd make.

"I'll be fine, Elizabeth," Rob said, the warmth she'd come to expect returned to his voice. "Let's get this boy out of here."

It didn't matter what Earle would do. Bet was in charge now.

"Just keep Seeley alive, Mr. Collier. I'm counting on you."

TWENTY-THREE

Bet kept herself in strong physical condition. Even with her height, her strength couldn't match that of some men, but her endurance made her competitive in these kinds of situations. She climbed the stairs as fast as she could and, once she reached the top, broke into a respectable jog. She easily retraced their steps, and it wasn't long before she could see a paler area in front of her, signifying the outside entrance to the cave.

Picking up speed, she flew out of the mouth of the tunnel and started to scramble down the hillside toward the trail to civilization. The moon stood near full and blanketed the area with the surreal luminescence of a pearl. While the trees remained dark, lighter objects stood out as bright as bones against the background of dark evergreens.

Bet caught movement out of the corner of her eye, and her instincts kicked in. She dropped to the ground mere seconds before the hiss of a bullet sliced the air above her head. The round pinged against the granite hillside, ricocheted off a large rock, and continued its trajectory away from her.

Rolling down the incline, Bet pulled her own weapon and returned fire. She heard a startled cry, then silence.

"If you're injured, I can help you," Bet called out, before she settled into the trees a safe distance from Figure and listened. Figure had his ears up, his focus intent on a spot in the trees, but she couldn't hear anyone moving nearby. She pulled her cell phone out, hoping for a few bars.

Useless. She stuffed her cell phone back in her pocket, picked up a rock, and tossed it as far away from her as she could. It hit a tree trunk some distance away, sounding almost as loud as the gunfire had, but no one shot again.

Figure relaxed again, looking at her quizzically, as if expecting her to mount up and ride him out of there. She hoped that was a sign no one else stood nearby.

Seeley Lander needed immediate medical attention. That was her priority. She wasn't sure if it was safe to move, but she couldn't stand there forever.

Don't let fear paralyze you, she remembered her father telling her more than once. *You get paralyzed and all your decisions become someone else's.*

He was right.

Bet started down the trail, checking her cell phone periodically for service. Once a few bars appeared, she stopped and called Randall Vogel. Luckily for Bet, the Vogels had already flown two injured people to Seattle from a wreck on Interstate 90 and were back at the hanger refueling.

She explained the situation and how challenging it would be to get Seeley out of the cave.

"I'll drop Paul down with the rescue litter to take into the cave," Vogel said. "It will be easier to haul the boy out in that."

Bet described someone taking a shot at her as she exited the cave. "It's possible the shooter is still around."

"Wouldn't be the first time someone took shots at us," Vogel said. "Don't worry, we can handle it."

Ending the call with Vogel, Bet contacted Clayton, hoping he wasn't in Cle Elum. She wanted him to fly out with Seeley. Luckily, she caught him still in town. She asked him to call Dale and request that he meet her at Rob Collier's house and bring a padlock and chain. Then Clayton would follow her directions to the cave entrance, wearing his bulletproof vest. Bet raced back to the tunnel. She knew it wouldn't take long for the Vogels to arrive on the scene. She reached the open area in front of the cave entrance and waited, ears straining for someone skulking around in the woods.

She stood with her flashlight off, waiting for the sound of rotors. No sense giving her spot away to anyone hiding in the trees. But other than Figure shifting his weight, the forest lay still. She wondered how the horse would react to the helicopter, but Rob hadn't seemed worried about leaving him alone.

As she waited by herself in the dark, peering into the trees, images from her dream rose in her mind. The man she saw on the lake in the dark, struggling under the weight of a canvas-wrapped figure. The hole he bored through the frozen lake. The long hair visible out of the top of the bundle before it slid, silently, through the ice.

Her heart rate pounded. This wasn't just the fragmented pieces of dreams anymore. She knew these images were memories, if only she had external evidence to prove it. Why had she gone out into the cold? Why was she alone by the lake? She let her mind go where it wanted.

Another memory surfaced. A dare. Trek to the lake alone. Dylan laughing and holding out a coffee cup. "Bring back water so I know you went all the way." The feel of the three-wheeler Eric taught her to drive, speeding alone through town. Everyone knew the lake water tasted different, the tang of a copper penny. Where was Eric? Why did she only remember Dylan?

Just when she thought she couldn't handle one more minute in the dark, she heard the sound of the helicopter above her.

She turned on her flashlight and signaled. Despite its small size, the Vogels should see the light against the dark trees.

While Randall Vogel hovered, Paul came down with the litter. Vogel's son had spent a few years training in the military before returning to the area to work with his parents. With medical experience like his mother and pilot training like his father, he planned to run the business one day.

Bet helped him unclip the litter from the cable. Paul wore a light on his helmet to keep his hands free. Bet could carry the front of the empty litter with one hand, her flashlight in the other.

"You okay with this?" she asked Paul, just before they plunged into the darkness of the tunnel.

He gave her a thumbs-up, his boyish grin backing up his confidence. The two sped through the tunnel, the route starting to feel familiar to Bet. They soon arrived at the top of the stairs. She called down to Rob, who clicked on his light in response.

At least the man hadn't fled.

"I brought reinforcements," Bet said, as she and Paul reached the bottom with the litter. "How's he doing?"

"He hasn't regained consciousness, but he hasn't stopped breathing either."

Nor had Rob finished off Seeley while the two were alone in the dark. Bet wished she had more insight into Collier's motivations. Was he a Good Samaritan? Or a bold killer inserting himself in her investigation?

Paul did a quick check of Seeley's airway before the three lifted him onto the rescue litter and Paul strapped him in.

"Had a little excitement," Bet told Rob as Paul worked.

"What was that?"

"Somebody shot at me."

"What? Where?"

"As I came out of the cave."

"Figure okay?"

"He's fine. Wasn't even bothered by the helicopter circling overhead."

"He's spent a fair amount of time in urban settings. Did you shoot back?"

"I did. Just wanted you to know what we might be walking into when we head outside."

"Let's get going," Paul said with a final adjustment to Seeley. "The sooner we get him out of here, the sooner Mom and I can start tending to him."

"I'm a little taller," Rob said to Paul as he reached for the foot of the litter. The men lifted the backboard and Bet fell in behind them, her light all Rob had to see by. The climb up the stairs was slow but steady. Once they were on mostly level ground, it didn't take long to reach the mouth of the cave.

"I'm going out first to see if anyone makes me a target," Bet said.

She edged her way around the men and the litter and stepped outside. If anyone lay in wait, they would see her dark shape against the light-colored stone of the mountainside. She walked a few paces from the mouth of the tunnel.

When nothing happened, she went back in and waved for the guys to follow and signaled Penny to drop the cable.

Paul hooked the cable to the litter while Bet stood guard. The litter rose up to the helicopter and disappeared as Penny swung the boom inside. At the same time, Clayton arrived on a dirt bike. A moment later, Penny dropped the cable over and Paul helped Clayton into the rigging.

She and Rob stood guard while Penny hauled Paul up last. Paul gave Bet an all-clear signal, which Bet returned, before the helicopter tilted away.

Bet moved over to Clayton's dirt bike, pulling on the helmet he'd left behind. Rob walked over to Figure, who appeared remarkably calm despite all the commotion.

"I'll lead. Don't follow too close," was all Rob said as he swung into the saddle and started up the trail.

Bet stayed a safe distance behind, but it didn't take long before the big house of the Collier estate rose in front of them and she parked in the driveway.

Dale stood near his truck waiting for them, an ATV on a small trailer behind his vehicle.

"Tell me about this mine entrance," Dale said by way of greeting.

Bet described the events of the night. "I think someone shot Seeley in the cave," she said, after she'd filled him in. "And I'm betting our Jane Doe died down there too."

"Think Seeley shot Jane Doe with the gun you found?" Dale asked.

"I don't know right now. But we know there's more than just the two kids involved, since a third person shot at me."

Rob stood nearby, and Dale turned to give him a look that was hard to read. Bet thought he might be questioning why she'd let a civilian participate in hauling Seeley out of the tunnel.

"I used the people I had at hand," she said, with a nod toward Rob, though she didn't owe Dale an explanation.

"What now?" Dale asked.

"We have to get back down into that cave soon and do a more thorough search. But no one goes down there alone. It's too dangerous."

"We need a few more deputies," Dale said.

"Too bad the budget only covers you and Clayton," Bet said. "For now, just hide yourself nearby and watch the entrance. If anyone else is down there, I don't think they have another way out."

She described the road back and how to find the cave. Dale agreed, letting her know he brought the lock and chain she'd requested should they decide to bar the entrance and leave it unattended.

"Good," Bet said. "Though the killer could be the person who shot at me, which means they're aboveground. Unless they snuck back in after we left, they might be halfway to Canada by now."

"What about the Ranger?" Dale asked.

"It's not going anywhere. Seeley probably has the key with him. We'll deal with that later."

"So Seeley might be guilty of killing Jane Doe," Dale said. "But he's also a victim, probably of the guy who shot at you."

"That's what it looks like," Bet said. "Though Jane Doe could have shot him first, then ran, and he shot her in the back. We can't assume the shooter tonight was involved until we have proof."

Dale nodded. "You sound like your dad."

Bet took that as a compliment.

"If Seeley pulls through, he should be able to ID Jane Doe for us. She used his phone, and she bought two coffees from Sandy.

There's two cups in the truck with her logo on them. He'll have a tough time denying he interacted with her. For now, we just need to protect the crime scene in the cave and see if whoever shot at me left any evidence or tracks behind."

Dale left for the cave entrance, and Bet gave Rob a long, appraising look. He returned her gaze without expression.

"I don't want to leave Dale without his vehicle here or use the dirt bike to go to the station. Can I borrow your Bronco?"

Rob handed over his keys. "You know where to find me."

Exhausted but wired from the night's activities, Bet drove over to the office, where she found Alma and Schweitzer waiting for her.

"You look like crap," Alma said, eyeing Bet as she came through the front door.

"I missed you too, Schweitzer," Bet greeted the dog. He bounced around a few times at her appearance. His obvious pleasure at seeing her filled her with an emotion she couldn't name.

Alma snorted and handed Bet a stack of messages. The top one was from Eric.

"I told him business tied you up," Alma said, referencing Bet's forgotten dinner date.

"Thanks," Bet said, as she pulled on a pair of gloves and retrieved two evidence bags before she took the vintage revolver out of the backpack. Labeling the evidence bags, she put the weapon in one and the cartridges in another.

"Where'd you get the antique?" Alma had an affinity for vintage weapons.

"Found it on Seeley. What is it?" Bet handed the revolver over to Alma in its clear plastic bag. Alma pulled her desk lamp closer to get a better look. She peered at the weapon through its protective cover, turning it over under the light.

"Looks like a Remington number three, five-shot revolver."

"Valuable?"

"Not nearly as valuable as a number one or number two; a lot more of these were made. Maybe seven or eight hundred dollars."

"Strange gun for a kid to have. When were these manufactured?"

"Late 1800s. I'll have to check the exact dates. Could have been something the first Seeley Lander owned."

Bet nodded; the age of the revolver made that a reasonable guess. She gave Alma the lantern to look at too. They set it on a table in the back of the room to pass on to George.

"I'm going to take Schweitzer home and get some food," Bet said, the dog hopping to his feet at the word *food*, but the ring of her cell phone interrupted her. Clayton's number showed on the screen. Bet answered, getting an earful of noise from the rotors of the helicopter.

"How's Seeley?"

"What?" Clayton yelled.

Bet repeated herself louder and just barely made out his response.

"Still alive."

"What's up?" Bet yelled again.

"Seeley came to . . ." Bet lost Clayton in the noise, but she made out the rest. "He said, 'What about Katie?'"

"Katie? That must be our Jane Doe."

"Not Jane Doe," Bet made out. "'Emma's dead. I . . . kill her, but what about Katie?'"

Jane Doe was Emma? And Seeley had killed Emma? Had it been with that revolver? Without a bullet to match, there were no ballistics to compare.

"Emma is our dead girl? Then who is Katie?"

"What?" Clayton yelled back.

"Who is Katie!"

Bet heard his next line loud and clear.

"I think there's another girl down in that cave."

TWENTY-FOUR

Bet took a moment to assess the situation. One of the challenges of her new position was that sometimes she worked as a patrol officer and sometimes in the role of detective. Patrol officers made quick decisions, acting fast in difficult, often complex situations. As a detective, her actions must be methodical, the work slow and exacting. Her instinct was to rush back down in the cave, but she needed a plan before chasing another girl based on nothing but the ramblings of a semiconscious college kid.

"Working faster isn't always better," her father would say when Bet wanted immediate results. "If you're investigating a crime, you can't afford stupid mistakes. Unless someone is in immediate danger, choose precision over speed."

Sitting in her office, Bet leaned her chair against the wall and looked out at the tiny sliver of Lake Collier visible through her window. The water was as flat and still as a pewter tray in the moonlight. She cleared her mind of everything except what she'd just learned, trying to decide how best to proceed.

Was there another girl in the cave? Or was this Katie the person who shot at her when she exited the cave? Could Seeley have been saying Carrie, not Katie? They still hadn't located Carrie Turner.

Bet wished Seeley had provided more information before he slipped back into unconsciousness. All Clayton could say was he didn't think this Katie had been the one to shoot Seeley, as he appeared concerned about her welfare. Bet wanted to go back down in the tunnels looking for this second girl. But what if she didn't exist? And if she did, was she the one who'd killed Jane Doe? Seeley had also mentioned an Emma. Was Emma Jane Doe?

Full identification of Jane Doe still remained one of the most important things on her to-do list. Now she had a possible first name: Emma. She thought back to Seeley's friends list on Facebook. Thumping her chair back down on all four legs, she woke her computer up, found his page, and scanned down his list of friends.

No Emma on the list, but there were several Katies, Katherines, and Catherines, any of which could be "Katie." Or, since Clayton had said Seeley was hard to understand, he could have referenced this Carrie after all. She thought about searching other social media, except with nothing but a first name, it felt pointless.

She pulled out the phone number they believed belonged to Seeley's parents in Jaxon and put in another call. She'd rather meet them in person, but they needed to know their son's life hung in the balance in a hospital in Seattle. She also needed to gauge what they knew about their son's activities. They might also have last names for Emma and "Katie" or have information about Carrie Turner.

Once again, an answering machine picked up on the other end. Bet hung up and contemplated a drive to Jaxon.

Bet called Clayton, who reported that Seeley was in surgery. Bet gave Clayton the Landerses' phone number. She asked him to keep trying to contact them, verify that they were Seeley's parents, and tell them their son had been injured.

"I think you need to stay in Seattle and talk to them in person. They might know Emma and have information we need. They are more likely to be helpful if you're there in person. They might also know something about why these kids were out here to begin with. Maybe we can get a handle on this Katie person and ask about Carrie Turner."

"It could be a long wait."

"Leave your number; tell them it's urgent. Hopefully they'll get back to you soon. If I don't hear back from you, I'll call in a few hours after I see if Schweitzer can find anyone else in the cave. By that time it should also be getting light."

Bet grabbed her cell phone, which she'd put on the fast charger, and double-checked her emergency backpack, loaded with items like a first aid kit, bottled water, power bars, matches, a candle lantern, a compass, a flashlight, and extra batteries. She kept it ready for when hikers went missing in the mountains. She hadn't bothered to take off her Kevlar vest and still had Seeley's backpack from the cave. She could use that to give Schweitzer a scent to follow. Alma had fed him dinner earlier, so they were ready to go.

Heading out of the office, she stopped at Alma's desk and explained what she planned to do with the possibility that another girl might be in danger.

"Schweitzer and I have to go back in to look for her," Bet said.

"Not by yourself."

"Dale is at the mine entrance. I'll take him in with me."

She called to Schweitzer, who bolted upright, ready for action.

"Don't let anything happen to my dog," Alma said, turning back to her computer.

Bet headed back out the door. She and Schweitzer piled into Rob's Bronco. Once they were on the Colliers' private road, George heard her coming and met her out front. She rolled her window down as he stepped to the edge of the road.

"You're in a hurry, Younger." He eyed the vehicle, no doubt recognizing Rob's car. "Awful late to be out driving around. Something wrong?"

"Just following up on something. You sure you haven't seen anyone in these woods recently? Someone a little more substantial than a ghost?"

George said he hadn't, and Bet suggested he stay out of the forest for the next couple of days.

"This is more than an accidental death, isn't it Younger?"

"I can't get into it now."

"You go do what you do. I'll keep an eye out on the woods."

Bet continued forward and pulled up to the front door. Rob opened up while Bet let Schweitzer out of the Bronco. The dog walked over and sat at Rob's feet, looking up at him as if waiting for something.

"I appreciate the use of your vehicle."

"Anytime, Elizabeth."

Rob squatted down next to the dog and held out his hand. Schweitzer solemnly reached out his paw for a shake. "Nice to see you again, Schweitzer," Rob said.

"I've never seen him do that before," she said, amused. Rob gave her a look of curiosity. "We're still getting to know each other. He was my father's dog."

Rob turned back to Schweitzer. "Looks like you're going to work, big guy."

Rob stood and watched as she pulled Seeley's backpack out and started toward Clayton's dirt bike, Schweitzer on her heels.

She wondered if there was any chance Collier's prodigal son planned to follow her back to the mine entrance. It didn't make sense for him to be involved in Jane Doe's homicide and then take her to the mine entrance and help her find Seeley. But something had brought him back to town the same week Jane Doe died.

TWENTY-FIVE

Bet started up the bike. Schweitzer's eyes gleamed with the thought of a race. Even though her dog could move faster than her across the rutted terrain, Bet still kept an eye on him. He loped along without flagging all the way to the tunnel. Dale came out of the woods as Bet pulled up.

"What's up?" Dale asked.

Bet explained what Seeley told Clayton in the helicopter. "We need to go back down with Schweitzer to look for this other girl."

Dale looked around in the woods. "It's been quiet. Think it's safe to leave this unguarded?"

"Let's lock the bat gate behind us with the chain you brought so no one can follow us in."

"Your call, Sheriff." Dale went into the woods to where he'd stashed his belongings and came back with a length of chain and a padlock.

The two climbed the shale hillside and stepped into the tunnel before Bet gave Schweitzer a sniff of Seeley's pack. Dale ran the chain around the squares of the metal gate and locked it behind them.

"Remember the combination?"

"I do," Bet said. "Though the plan is for us to come out together." With that, Bet pointed Schweitzer at the footsteps she believed Seeley Lander had left. Though they had crossed them returning with the boy on the backboard, the scent would remain. Schweitzer could help them backtrack Seeley's route through the cave.

With Schweitzer in the lead, Bet and Dale followed as fast as they could in the dark, rough passage. Even with flashlights, they could see only a few feet in front of them and hear nothing except the drip, drip, drip of water seeping through the porous limestone rock. No surprise to Bet, Schweitzer led them directly to the stairs.

They reached the bottom, and Bet crawled through the low opening into the cavern beyond. She splashed her flashlight around the space, the structures glittering and shimmering, throwing starlight patterns of iridescence onto the cave walls.

"Wow," Dale said.

Bet turned her attention to Schweitzer, who started to follow different scent trails. He'd move forward, then fall back, move forward and fall back again.

"What's he doing?" Dale asked.

"He's losing the scent."

"What now?"

"I can take us back to where Collier and I found Seeley and see if we can work our way backward from there."

Bet pulled out her compass and led the way. Arriving at the water, Bet turned her light onto the rocks. She made Schweitzer sit/stay while she navigated the stepping stones. Turning back to Dale she asked if he felt confident crossing.

Without saying a word, Dale made his way across. Once he was safe on the other side, she called to Schweitzer and he leapt across in three huge bounds.

Bet and Dale examined the spot where Seeley had fallen unconscious but found nothing useful. Schweitzer nosed around, then sat and whined low in his chest. He had found the scent again.

Bet sent Schweitzer ahead to follow the trail. The dog moved boldly forward, nose twitching. The trek he took wound around stalactite and stalagmite formations. An occasional bloody hand-print showed where Seeley had paused to catch his breath or regain his balance. The sound of the river took on a different note, and Bet could see they'd reached the far side of the cavern. The water vanished into a wall.

"Seeley must have crossed here," Bet said, shining her light on the other side of the water. Schweitzer sniffed around the face of the mountain where the river disappeared.

"Look," Dale said, illuminating another bloody handprint above the hole where the river swept into the side of the mountain. A lip stuck out along the edge of the wall. Moving slowly, first Bet and then Dale arrived safely on the other side. Once more, Bet called to Schweitzer, who made the scramble and picked up the trail on the other side.

Schweitzer stopped at a dark spot on the ground, where he laid down and whined. Bet rewarded him with a biscuit, then flashed her light around in front of them. The spot on the ground looked like blood, and a second, even larger bloodstain darkened a patch of gray stone a few feet away.

"That's far more blood than one body could lose and live," Dale said with a gesture toward the larger stain.

"I'm guessing Jane Doe died here," Bet said. "Unless this Katie person is dead too and we have another crime scene elsewhere."

Before they searched further, Bet took a couple of blood samples from both patches to compare to Seeley Lander and Jane Doe. They found no other blood or evidence of a crime scene. Schweitzer picked up the trail heading back toward the original entrance.

"They must have come in this way from the tunnel," Bet said. "Then Jane Doe was killed and Seeley was injured, but made it to the other side of the river."

"And the mysterious Katie?"

"Here's what's bothering me," Bet said. "What brought these kids down here to begin with? How did they even know this cave was here?"

Neither of them had an answer for that.

Nothing indicated that either the missing "Katie" or the shooter remained below. As much as Bet felt in her gut that whoever had targeted her at the mouth of the cave was involved in Jane Doe's murder, she didn't have proof of that either. It could have been someone hunting illegally on Rob's land making a poor shot in bad light.

If there had been a Katie or a Carrie with Seeley in the cave, either she'd vanished, or she was the one with the gun.

"We have no way of knowing how many other tunnels or accesses to the outside might exist down here," Bet said.

"What now?"

"Let's go up and see if we can assess which direction I was shot from. I don't want to be out of cell range too much longer. Alma might need to reach us."

Back at the mouth of the tunnel, Dale removed the lock and chain, then asked if she wanted it locked behind them.

"Leave it unlocked for now. You stand guard again. I'll go investigate the woods."

It was starting to get light as Dale melted back into the trees and Bet headed in the direction she thought the shots had come from. After searching around in the forest for several minutes, she had almost given up finding anything useful when something caught her attention. Schweitzer started to move forward, but Bet caught his collar and asked him to sit.

The structure, built of materials from the surrounding woods, slender logs and branches, covered a space just large enough to park a dirt bike underneath. A set of tire tracks led in and out. She hadn't heard a dirt bike start up after the shots were fired, but she'd left the area fairly quickly. Maybe the shooter had waited until she did.

Bet pulled out her camera to take a few shots of the lean-to, wondering why someone had shot at her in the first place. Perhaps the shooter hadn't expected anyone coming out of the cave to exchange fire with them, so once it happened they'd slunk away in the dark. Maybe they'd thought she was Seeley and, once they heard her voice, slipped away. Or it was an unrelated incident, a poacher sneaking through the woods, not expecting to find anything tall moving around except elk and deer.

Bet decided to bring a crime scene tech out from Ellensburg to process the lean-to and the cave. She could do the basics—fingerprints, casts of tire tracks—but a cave and a lean-to were way beyond her abilities.

Rob Collier knew the geography and knew about the cave. He might know something about this lean-to. Or at least who might be using it. Though if he did, why keep it quiet? Maybe there was more than one person involved in all this and Rob knew exactly who'd shot at her and why. He could be involved in whatever had brought Seeley out to the cave in the first place, even if he wasn't Jane Doe's killer.

TWENTY-SIX

Bet described the lean-to location to Dale, warning him to keep an ear out for someone coming from that direction. Then she returned to Rob Collier's house, Schweitzer loping along beside her.

Back in cell range, Bet stood on Rob's driveway and called Alma to find out if anything required her attention in town, but all was quiet.

She reached Clayton. He'd managed to wake the Landers with his repeated calls. They arrived in Seattle, stunned and confused about their son's condition.

"They had no idea he wasn't in Seattle, and they don't know who either Katie or Carrie Turner might be," Clayton said. "But I do have information regarding Jane Doe. Seeley's girlfriend is Emma Hunter; their description of her matches Jane Doe. They didn't have a phone number, but her parents live in Spokane. I tracked down contact information for them."

Clayton relayed the phone number for the Hunters, assuring Bet he'd given the Landerses no information about her condition. He also had the keys to the Ford Ranger; they'd been on Seeley when they reached the hospital in Seattle. Clayton had arrived back in Cle Elum not long ago, after he caught a ride with a highway patrol officer.

"Want me to coordinate getting the Ranger?" he asked. "I could get out there and drive it to the station."

"I want to have a crime scene tech process in place first. Besides, at this point we have a possible ID for Jane Doe. I think if there is a Katie, she arrived in a different vehicle. There're no signs of her getting out of the Ranger; there're only two sets of footprints."

Was it possible Katie had come in on the dirt bike? Was she the person who shot at her from the woods? Seeley and Emma were so young. Maybe Katie was older?

Young people commit acts of violence too, Bet could hear Earle say.

She finished her conversation with Clayton, telling him to get some sleep. Rob stood in his doorway. He gestured to her and she followed him into the kitchen, where he stood at a range big enough to serve a small army.

"They teach you to cook when you played for the Crimson Tide?" she asked, leaning against a kitchen island large enough to seat six people comfortably on tall, leather barstools.

"Mock me and you don't get eggs the way you want them," he said, without turning around. "That coffee there is for you."

Bet picked up the cup sitting on the island and took a sip. "Not bad," she said.

"Not bad? That's the best coffee you ever had."

Bet had to admit it was true. "Over easy," she said instead, "Got toast?"

Rob dropped two slices of wheat into the toaster and turned around to look at Bet. "What did you learn?"

Was that his intention? To find out what she knew?

"Can't talk about an ongoing investigation," she said. Rob snorted. "Even if you did help me get Seeley out of the cave."

Rob remained silent, serving up the food. Schweitzer ate a slice of bacon in a single bite, then curled up on the floor under Bet's feet.

Bet noticed a manila file folder on the counter not far from where they sat. A photo had slid partway out. She reached over and pulled out the photo of a woman.

"Who is this?"

Rob turned from the coffee machine, where he'd poured himself another cup. A look of annoyance crossed his face, but it vanished so fast Bet wasn't sure what she'd seen.

"That would be my mother."

"Why do you have a photo of your mother in a file folder?"

"Not that it's any of your business." He took the photo from Bet and returned it to the file. "But I'm here, in part, to track her down."

"You don't know where she is?"

"If I did, I wouldn't have to track her down, would I?"

Bet recognized the new emotion that settled on Rob's features. Sorrow. She understood a little something about loss. If Rob was innocent, his return to Collier could be a painful one.

"When I'm finished with all this, perhaps I can help you find her."

Rob appraised Bet for a moment. "That would be appreciated."

Finishing her breakfast, Bet stood. "Just what the doctor ordered, Mr. Collier."

"Aren't we on a first-name basis yet, Elizabeth?" Rob said, picking dishes up.

"If that were true, I'd feel the need to stay and help you clean up," Bet said, getting ready to leave.

"Am I ever getting my Bronco back?"

"It's on my list of things to do." Bet headed out the door with Schweitzer hot on her heels.

Bet turned Rob's Bronco onto the dirt road leading to Peter Malone's campsite. The DMV photo Alma had found proved Jane Doe was Emma Hunter. Local law enforcement in Spokane notified Emma's parents.

The Hunters were on their way to Ellensburg. Bet anticipated a call from them once they formally identified their daughter at the morgue. She wished she had more to tell them. She couldn't verify where Emma had died until they matched her blood with the patch they found down in the cave or Seeley regained consciousness. Bet's theory about the underground river wasn't something she felt compelled to share with the girl's parents until it could be proven beyond a shadow of a doubt.

The wrapped corpse sliding through the dark passage to find its way to the surface was a grim parallel to the mythological River Styx. Bet pictured the ancient boatman, Charon, paddling Emma's corpse down through the chasm into the earth and out into the lake. Or worse, without the coin to pay for her passage into Hades, the river spat Emma's body out, dooming her to wander the requisite one hundred years before her soul could rest.

She considered dropping something into the river down in the cave and waiting for it to appear in the lake, but dismissed the experiment. She had more pressing issues, and if it snagged on something underwater, it wouldn't prove anything anyway. Investigating the underground river could wait.

The CSI from Ellensburg, Todd Jones, promised to process the blood samples Bet had collected and visit the lean-to and the mine, with Clayton to escort him to both scenes.

Clayton would use the ATV they kept at the station to take Todd to the lean-to and the mine and down the trail to the Ford Ranger so he could process that as well. For Todd to drive all the way back down to Highway 97 and up Ingalls Creek Road would take too long, and Bet didn't want him in the woods alone.

After the two men left, Bet drove back out to the lake. From Peter's campsite, Bet could see the professor in his canoe. She stood on the shore and called to him, her voice traveling over the cold water, breaking through his intense concentration. He waved and gestured that he would bring up his equipment and row to shore.

Bet waited to meet him.

"How goes the investigation?" Peter asked as he hauled his craft above the waterline.

"Ongoing."

"Meaning you can't talk about it."

"Find anything in the lake?"

"Nothing of note." He didn't quite meet her eyes. Nor did he say no. Bet stood quiet for a moment, wondering if he'd fill the silence with a little more information, but this time the professor kept his mouth shut.

"I've another question for you," Bet said, when it became clear he had nothing else to say.

Bet explained what she wanted. Peter thought about it, looked out at the lake, and nodded.

"Sure. If you think you know where the body went in, even that long ago, it's conceivable it's still near the same spot. We can look for it. How do you know where it went in?"

"That's what they pay me for," Bet replied, deflecting any further questions. "Any chance you could look today?"

Bet walked through the trees. Mother Nature had long since reclaimed the path she'd traveled that cold night. No one used the old trail through the woods anymore; another path had been cut and paved a little closer to the road. Bet never went on the original path again. Until now, she'd never thought about why she stayed away.

She pushed her way through the remaining trees. Much of the surrounding woods had been cut down to make way for the larger parking lot and the expansion of the picnic area, but the heart of it still remained. She moved down the remnants of the path and found the spot where she'd hid and watched the body being sent into the depths of the lake. She touched a tree, thicker now and taller than she remembered, but the view matched the one in her mind.

She leaned against it. Her heart beat against her rib cage and her breath grew ragged. She felt like a child again. At the base of the tree something glinted white, like bone. She reached down and pulled up a long-forgotten coffee mug. The one she'd carried to bring water back.

Physical evidence her memories were real.

Time and weather had broken the mug into several pieces. She pushed the shards back into the ground. Some things were best left buried.

Looking up, she could see Peter in his canoe, waiting for a signal from her. She took a bead on where he should start looking, the place where the man had hacked through the ice and sent a body tumbling into the depths. She let herself feel the fear and the cold and the dark from all those years ago. Then she stepped back out into the sunlight of the September day, leaving history behind.

She gestured to Peter, and he moved over to the spot to drop his camera. Walking over to the picnic tables, Bet sat down on top of one to wait, glad she had the place to herself. After a while she called out across the water.

"See anything?"

"Rock," Peter said. "So far, nothing but rocks."

"Keep looking, Professor. You'll find her."

TWENTY-SEVEN

Half an hour later, Peter looked up and Bet knew. He waved her over, and she met him at the water's edge. The rocky side of the lake dropped off immediately into nothing but a dark void. Unable to beach his canoe, Peter swung as close to shore as he could, giving her a view of his monitor.

Bet leaned out over the water. At first she wasn't sure what the camera caught, and then Peter did something with the controls and what had been a gray smudge took on eerie details. The screen showed the camera hovering at the three-hundred-and-fifty-foot mark and focused on an image. Something white and wrapped with ropes.

"What are those?" Bet pointed to several large black circles attached to the figure on the screen.

"I think they're weights."

"Crap."

"The knots look familiar, don't they?"

Bet nodded, unable to tear her eyes from what she saw. "Can you get a look at the top of . . ." Bet trailed off, not wanting to say the word *her.*

Peter moved the camera around, focusing in on a dark mass that undulated in the water like reeds near a shore.

Long black hair.

"How do we bring something up from that deep?" Bet asked.

Peter shook his head. "It's going to be a big job. That's a very long way down. We have to get a hook onto . . . her"—Peter struggled with the word—"or grab her with pinchers and reel her up. She's in a crevice of rock and it looks like she's wedged in, but I can't tell how tightly. We don't want her to tumble farther down. I have access to that kind of equipment, but it's nothing I brought with me."

"I have to get her up to the surface. Can you go out to Seattle and bring back what you need?"

"Better if I have some colleagues join me and bring the equipment with them. I can't do this alone, and I'll have better luck with people versed in deepwater recovery rather than using you or one of your deputies."

"This isn't something I want made public," Bet said, thinking about the reporter waiting for her exclusive. Did she have a spy in Collier who would contact her when the professor raised the dead?

"Is this connected to what I found?" Peter asked. "You said this happened almost twenty years ago."

Bet said nothing. Peter started to ask more, but stopped himself. "Seems like an awfully big coincidence."

Bet couldn't have agreed more.

———

Todd Jones arrived at Bet's office with a report of his findings at the lean-to. His mournful features and liquid black eyes always appeared like he was on the edge of tears. Todd also looked like he'd just struggled out of bed, his black hair mussed, clothes askew, but she knew his work to be impeccable. He immediately apologized for the paucity of evidence.

"I made casts of the tire tracks on the missing dirt bike. We might be able to figure out the brand, though I'm not sure it will help you any."

"It could be useful," Bet said in encouragement. Todd shook his head, face drooping even more than usual.

"That's about as useful as I can get. I hoped to find some fingerprints on the wood of the lean-to. I went over the whole thing, but alas, nothing." His words trailed off at the end of the sentence, and Bet thought how relieved she was she didn't have to spend a lot of time with Todd. "I was hoping I would have more for you."

"You lifted a fingerprint off a carpet for me a few months ago," Bet reminded him. "If there's anything to find, you'll find it."

Todd perked up. "That was pretty cool, wasn't it? The Path-Finder is a lifesaver," he said, referencing the wireless handheld device that could identify fingerprints in dust.

"What about the Ranger?" Bet asked.

"I didn't do a very thorough job," Todd reminded her. "You didn't want me to spend a lot of time at it."

"I know. I think the cave's more important."

"So I just went over the obvious places, and I have the prints you took from it as well. I did the parts of the interior that were easily reached and fingerprinted the coffee cups. Checked the interior and the bed for blood. No signs. I really should take the seats out and everything, get all the possible info for you I can."

"We have to prioritize your time," Bet reminded him. "I know the girl didn't die in the truck, and we've identified her."

"I might get luckier down in the cave."

Bet replied she hoped so, and the CSI said he was going to head over to the tavern for food before he went underground.

"Oh, by the way, can you process this for me?" Bet handed him the sealed envelope with the flashlight Rob had found at the cave.

"Looks like blood," Todd said, turning the flashlight in his hands and squinting at it through the plastic bag.

"Hoping for a fingerprint off that, along with the blood info," Bet said.

"I'll do what I can."

No sooner had Todd left than Bet heard the door open again. She could tell by Alma's greeting Eric had returned. Bet steeled herself as his footsteps come down the hall. Eric stopped in the doorway with Schweitzer standing at his side.

"What's up, Schweitz?" Bet asked, watching her dog to avoid making eye contact with the man who'd broken her heart.

"Hello to you too," Eric said.

"Sorry about last night," Bet said. "I'm in the middle of something."

"Alma told me. Anything a semi-successful writer in the middle of a divorce and midlife crisis can help you with?"

Bet chuckled, feeling her tension about Eric ease slightly. "I can't talk about it," Bet said.

"Intriguing. Is this about the photos you showed me? Have you figured out what happened to the kid?"

"I still can't talk about it."

"Maybe we could get a quick bite or a beer?"

"I'm still on duty."

"Yeah, I get that. I just thought you might be able to take a break."

"Why don't you tell me what it is you want?"

Eric looked at the picture of Bet's father. "Hard to believe your old man is gone," Eric said. "He was such an institution around here."

Bet stayed quiet, wondering what he really wanted to talk about. Clearly something was on his mind.

"I always thought my mom and your dad would hook up, what with them both alone and raising kids."

"I don't know if my life would have been easier or harder if you'd ended up as my stepbrother."

Eric laughed. "I know what you mean. You know my mother never asked for a divorce."

"I did."

"I remember them together, your dad and mine, I mean. They had such a strong bond, I guess from the wars."

"Yeah. They were members of a tiny club the rest of us couldn't join. It always surprised me when your father left that he didn't stay in touch with my dad. I know Dad was disappointed, about the Lillian business, but he would have stayed his friend. Do you ever hear from him?"

Eric shrugged. "No. He made a clean break . . ." Eric's voice trailed off. "To be honest, I don't think all of him came back from Afghanistan on that last tour."

"I'm sorry about your mother," Bet said.

"I thought I'd see you at the funeral."

"I saw you. You had your hands full with your family. I wasn't interested in meeting your wife."

Eric winced. "I've wanted to apologize."

"It was a long time ago." Bet did not want to take a trip down memory lane with her ex.

"I've wanted to talk to you for so long. I tried calling a few times, but . . ."

Bet had never returned any of his phone calls. She didn't owe him anything.

"Growing up like that," Eric continued, "without a father. I didn't want to be like my dad."

"Funny," Bet said.

"What?"

"Here we are, a lot more like our fathers than we ever bargained for. I'm sorry about your divorce." He started to speak again, but Bet cut him off. "Look, Eric. I appreciate you want to make things right, or get some kind of redemption from me. But now is not a good time. I really am in the middle of something that has nothing to do with you. I've barely slept and there's a lot more work to do. It's not that I don't want to catch up or hear how your life is, but I can't." It was close enough to the truth. "I'm not mad at you anymore. Can we just call it good and move on?"

"I'll be around. When you can, we'll talk."

Bet sighed. It seemed to be the best she could hope for. If she avoided him long enough, maybe he'd go back to where he lived.

Bet stood and went to walk Eric out. "Okay. We'll get together next week sometime." She put her hand on his shoulder and was surprised to feel him flinch.

"What's wrong?" she asked.

"Oh, nothing. I hurt my arm is all."

"Something serious?"

"No. It's nothing. See you later, Bet."

"See you." Bet stood in her doorway and watched Eric walk down the hall. Schweitzer stayed, pressed against Bet's leg.

Bet couldn't picture Eric as the shooter at the cave entrance, winged by her shot in the woods, but his appearance in Collier did coincide with Emma's death.

Just like Rob Collier's reappearance in town.

She knew what her father would say.

Do we ever really know anyone at all?

TWENTY-EIGHT

Bet and Todd stared at his laptop where it perched on Bet's desk. The computer spat out matches for the fingerprints Todd uploaded. Seeley's were on the truck and in the cave. The only prints from the cave and the bat gate that came back with a match to anything were from Rob and Dale. This left Todd with two sets of fingerprints that didn't come back with a match. One set on the coffee cup in the truck, and one from the cave.

"Sorry, Bet," Todd said, his voice returned to its usual dirge-like tone. "I really thought I might have something for you."

Bet shrugged. Not much they could do about the fact that the last two sets of prints weren't registered in the most common databases. The prints on the coffee cup were most likely Emma's, so they wouldn't help them identify the third person involved. As for the strange set from inside the cave, Bet wasn't going to hold her breath.

"What about the print off the flashlight?" Bet asked.

"Still searching. Nothing came up right away, so not someone with a police record. I put it through a few other databases, which will take longer to run. I'll do the same with these two sets."

Bet helped Todd carry the rest of his equipment out to his van while they let his laptop continue to scan. Todd went to get a cup of coffee before he started his long trek back down to E'burg. A dark-blue minivan pulled up in front of the station. A middle-aged man drove, with a woman in the passenger seat and a teenage girl in the back.

"Excuse me," the woman called from the passenger window. "Are you Sheriff Rivers?"

Bet introduced herself, guessing correctly this would be the Hunters. They'd positively identified their daughter in the morgue. Now they came to Bet wanting answers. She'd tried to encourage them over the phone to stay the night in E'burg. There wasn't a lot to tell them yet. But they didn't want to wait.

Once in her office, Stanley Hunter, a lean, sharp-faced man wearing work boots, jeans, and a western shirt, and his wife, Rosemarie, a rail-thin woman in a print dress, who had trouble sitting still, sat across from Bet with expectant expressions. The teenage girl, an awkward blending of her father's sharp features and her mother's anxiety, went immediately to Schweitzer on his dog bed and curled up with him.

"Be careful, Meredith," her mother cautioned. "That's an awfully big dog."

Bet assured the grieving woman that Schweitzer was very gentle. Bet knew firsthand how comforting a dog could be, and the girl looked like she could use it.

"I'm very sorry for your loss," Bet said. "I know how hard it must have been to see your daughter like that."

"It was," Stanley said. "We just want to know what happened to our little girl."

"The investigation is ongoing. I don't have all the answers yet."

"But you'll catch the man who did this? Whoever shot my daughter in the back?" Stanley's body looked relaxed, but Bet could hear the tension in his voice. Rosemarie muffled a sob.

Look past the grief when you're dealing with a victim's family. Bet remembered her father's words before she observed him conduct an interview. *They know more than they think they do, and it's your job to find out what it is.*

"It would be helpful for me if I could ask you a few questions," Bet said.

"Anything we can do," Stanley said.

"What can you tell me about your daughter's relationship to Seeley Lander?"

"Seeley is her boyfriend," Rosemarie answered.

"No, he's not," Meredith said from her spot on the floor.

"He is, Meredith. They've been dating since high school." Rosemarie's fingers worked the handles of the purse she balanced on her lap.

"They broke up." Meredith tucked her face into Schweitzer's neck, making it impossible to read her expression.

"Are you sure that's safe?" Rosemarie's eyes darted between the sheriff and the giant dog.

"Perfectly safe."

"Don't argue with your mother," Stanley said to Meredith.

"I'm not arguing, Dad. I just know they broke up." Meredith turned to her father with a look of defiance, eyes bright with a film of tears that didn't fall.

Stanley's tone grew sharp. "Meredith, don't interrupt the adults."

Meredith curled herself around Schweitzer again.

"Mrs. Hunter? Is it possible Emma and Seeley broke up, but you didn't know about it?"

Rosemarie looked back and forth between her husband and her daughter. Finally she crumpled. "I'm not sure. Maybe. We haven't seen as much of her since she started college."

Rosemarie began to cry in earnest, and Bet handed her a box of tissues. Out of the corner of her eye, Bet saw Meredith watching her mother with a look of irritation on her face.

Interesting family dynamic.

"How did they get to know each other in high school?" Bet asked. "Didn't Seeley live in Jaxon? And you live in Spokane?"

Rosemarie regained her composure. "We only moved to Spokane a year ago."

"Had you ever been here before? To Collier?"

The two adults looked at each other, unspoken communication passing between them.

"Go on and tell her, Dad."

"Tell me what, Meredith?" Bet looked at the girl, her face still hidden.

"Nothing that matters now," Stanley said, his voice a warning to Meredith.

"Let me be the judge of that," Bet said, still looking at the girl. She seemed the most likely to talk.

"My big brother started doing drugs."

Stanley and Rosemarie both looked away, not just from Bet but also from each other.

"We were here once before," Meredith said. "When they sent my brother to that farm."

"You mean Pearson's Ranch?" Bet asked.

"Our son straightened out after that." Rosemarie still avoided her husband's eyes.

"How long ago did he come here?" Bet asked.

"Six years. He graduated from college back east a year ago. He's working a good job now, out there." Rosemarie glanced at her husband then, but he didn't look her way. Bet wondered what it said that the boy had moved so far from home.

This could be the connection to her father, though. The brother might have talked about Collier and he would likely have met Earle, who had volunteered with Pearson just like Bet did now.

"They went to the same high school," Stanley said, and it took Bet a moment to realize he meant Emma and Seeley. "Did that boy have anything to do with this? Is he why she was here?"

"We aren't sure of anything right now. Seeley was also injured."

Bet watched Meredith's face finally show a true emotion: fear. She thought she knew why the girl was so sure Emma and Seeley had split up.

"But they're still friends?" Bet asked the teenager. Parents often knew little about the private lives of their children, even before they left home.

"Yeah," Meredith said, her voice catching as she finally started to shed the tears Bet saw in her eyes.

Tears for her sister? Or Seeley?

Bet handed Meredith a tissue too, but decided to let that go for the moment. "Does the name Katie mean anything to you?"

Both Stanley and Rosemarie shook their heads. The look on Meredith's face telegraphed that she again knew more than her parents did. Bet asked a few more questions but learned nothing helpful. Before they wrapped up, Bet explained that she preferred to have their daughter's death remain confidential.

"Aren't you putting other young women in danger by not advertising a killer is out there?" Stanley asked. Bet hoped he didn't get a call from Jamie Garcia, who would be all too eager to let the Hunters talk.

"We don't believe this was a random killing."

"This was someone my daughter knew?" Rosemarie spoke through her tears.

"We believe your daughter was in the wrong place at the wrong time. I will tell you more when I can, but for now, no, I don't believe the community is in any danger."

The Hunters agreed not to divulge the cause of their daughter's death on social media or to the press.

"We want to go to where her body was found," Stanley said, not noticing his wife wince when he said the words *her body*.

"It's going to be dark."

"We still need to go," Stanley said. Bet looked to Rosemarie, who was shaking with silent tears. Stanley reached out and put a steadying hand on his wife's shoulder. She leaned into him and took a deep breath, her body becoming still for the first time since they'd entered her office. She looked at Bet with pleading eyes.

"I have flowers for her. She should get that at least, right? Flowers to mark the spot?"

"Absolutely, Mrs. Hunter. We can do that for Emma." Bet stood up to lead them out to the lake.

Schweitzer followed, ready to go along for the ride, and Bet saw an opportunity to get Meredith alone.

"Maybe Meredith would like to ride with me and Schweitzer over to the lake? She seems to have made a friend."

"Can I, Mom?" the girl pleaded, never taking her arm off the dog. "He's so cool. He makes me feel better."

Mrs. Hunter looked to her husband, who nodded. "That would be fine, Meredith," Rosemarie said.

Todd stood waiting near Alma's desk when the four walked out of Bet's office.

"I didn't want to intrude," Todd said, with a gesture toward the Hunters as they went out the front door.

"This is Meredith," Bet said, introducing the girl to Todd. "Todd is helping us find who hurt your sister."

"You mean killed her," Meredith said, her voice husky from crying.

"You're right, Meredith. I'm sorry."

"It's all right. Lots of people think I'm just a dumb kid."

Bet started to speak again, but Todd beat her to it, soothing the young girl.

"Well, I, for one, think you are a very brave young woman," Todd said, surprising Bet with his gentle tone. "I think Schweitzer weighs more than you do, and here you are, not scared of him a bit."

"I wish we could have a dog like this," she said, her mind taken off her sister and the injured Seeley. "I'd take good care of a dog, but Dad doesn't think I'm responsible enough."

"I think you'd do just fine. I know you're going to have a dog of your own one day."

Bet smiled to Todd in thanks. "We're going to go over to the lake," she explained as she started out the front door with Meredith and Schweitzer behind her.

"I'll leave any information I find on your desk," Todd said. Bet thanked him, and she and Meredith left.

After getting Meredith and Schweitzer loaded into her SUV, which Bet and Alma had rescued earlier from the Ingalls Creek parking lot, Bet slid into the driver's seat and pulled out onto the road with the Hunters behind her. Alone with the girl, Bet brought their conversation back to Seeley.

"So you and Seeley are close?" Bet asked.

The girl nodded, tears in her eyes again. "Is he gonna die too?"

"He survived his surgery. I'm sorry I can't tell you more. Is he your boyfriend now?" Bet asked.

"Well . . . not exactly."

"But you'd like him to be?"

"Emma is a dork. She doesn't know what an awesome guy Seeley is. Not like I do."

Bet looked over at the girl, who seemed much younger than sixteen. Her anxious face looked out the window at the silhouettes of the granite cliffs lining the road. She appeared more concerned about the injured Seeley than her dead sister, whom she still spoke of in present tense. Grief, however, did funny things, and Bet knew she had yet to take in the reality of what had happened to Emma.

"Who is Katie?"

"Not who, what."

"I don't understand," Bet said.

"KD. It's not a who, it's a what. Killer diary."

"A killer's diary?"

"No, killer, like as in cool."

"Whose diary are we talking about?"

"Seeley's great-great-great-great-great-grandfather, the man Seeley's named after. Don't you think that's like the best name ever? Seeley?" The girl clearly enjoyed saying the name. "Seeley let me see it once. The diary, I mean."

"KD is a book?"

"That's what I'm saying. It's full of all kinds of stuff Seeley's great-whatever-grandfather knew. About this place, I guess. And some old mine."

"What about the old mine?"

"Seeley—the old one, that is—helped the owner kill a bunch of people."

"What do you mean, kill a bunch of people?"

"That's why Seeley called it that. It's a—whatchamacallit—a play on words. Killer, like as in awesome, but it's also about people getting killed. Killer diary. But that was like a million years ago, right?"

"The diary talked about the explosion at the mine?"

"Yep."

"Do you remember anything else?"

"Not really."

"Nothing at all?"

"No. Well, except about the gold, but you already know about that, right?"

TWENTY-NINE

Mr. and Mrs. Hunter followed Bet to the edge of the water in the fading light, while Meredith—escorted by Schweitzer—picked her way along the shore to their left. Finding a flat-topped rock, Meredith sat with her legs tucked up against her, half woman, half child, Schweitzer close beside her. Mrs. Hunter sent a bouquet of white daisies out onto the dark surface of the lake.

"Daisies are Emma's favorite," Mrs. Hunter explained, unable to speak in the past tense of her daughter's life.

The lacy flowers floated away on the water. A gentle breeze came up and took them on a path to the point where Peter had found the body.

"Look at that," Mrs. Hunter said as the flowers continued on their way to the scree-covered hillside jutting into the lake. "Almost like they know where to go."

Rosemarie bowed her head, and Stanley said a prayer for their daughter as the flowers started to sink into the dark. Bet stood a respectful distance away, watching Meredith. The girl hadn't been able to tell Bet anything else about the diary or the gold. If there was gold, surely the original Robert Collier would have wanted to mine it, not bury it under tons of rock. Perhaps Seeley had built up the reality of the situation to make his hunt for gold more exciting. It was also possible the original Seeley had made the story up and there had never been any gold in the mine.

It crossed her mind that the diary could be hidden in the Ranger. Todd's inspection had been cursory.

The Hunters finished their prayer and called for Meredith to join them again. The family piled into their minivan, and Bet led them back to where the road dropped down to Highway 97. She waved as they started down the mountain and Bet returned to town. Schweitzer gave a whine and looked out the back window to watch the other vehicle slip out of sight.

Once back at the station, Bet called down to the hospital, only to learn that Seeley remained unconscious. Knowing there was no missing Katie, Bet felt better. If they found a suspect, they had fingerprints to compare to the set Todd had found in the cave, but at this point Bet had no reason to believe another murder would take place.

Bet made arrangements among herself, Dale, and Clayton to keep watch again at the mine entrance. She thought it most likely the shooter would return after dark, if at all. Dale went home at ten to get some sleep; Clayton was on from ten PM to four AM. A tough shift, but he would have the rest of the morning off. Bet's shift went from four to eight AM so she could be back in the office at nine.

All three had an uneventful night, and when Dale showed back up to relieve her, Bet thought about calling off the watch on the cave entrance, but decided to give it one more day. If the person who had parked a dirt bike at the lean-to was the person who shot at her and Seeley and killed Emma, something down in that cave was important enough to keep them around after Emma died. She didn't want to risk missing them if they decided to come back for one final visit.

Bet arrived at the station, feeling a little more human after a shower and a fresh uniform, to find Alma peeling an orange.

"I found something online today that might interest you," Alma said. She gestured for Bet to come around and look at her computer screen. Carrie Turner's Facebook page was open.

The girl had posted a photo of herself in a bikini on a beach in Mexico.

Been off the grid, just coming up for air! her post read.

"That's that, then," Bet said. "Carrie is not the person Seeley mentioned to Clayton during the helicopter ride. I think he had to be saying KD." Bet thought about the diary that might be hidden in the truck. "I'd like to pick up the Ranger."

"Let's go get it." Alma pulled the key Clayton had retrieved from Seeley out of the lockup. "Todd left this for you." Alma handed her an envelope. "I'll forward the phone to your cell and come with you to pick up the Ranger."

Bet had pulled the sheet of paper out of the envelope and started to unfold it when Rob Collier walked through the front door.

"Thought I'd come by and see how you're all doing."

"You're with me, Mr. Collier," Alma said. She handed him a slice of orange. "You drive."

Bet shrugged her shoulders at Rob's questioning look. "Can't argue with Alma," she said.

Rob took the slice of orange and held the door open. "Thank you, ma'am. It'd be a pleasure to serve you."

"Silver-tongued devil." Alma gave him a poke in the ribs as she sailed out past him.

Bet walked back to her office, returning her attention to the information Todd had left her about the flashlight. The paper listed the blood type on the flashlight and a positive match for the fingerprint in the blood. Todd had also printed out the name and a copy of the driver's license issued to the person with the best match. The picture was a few years old, but Bet would have recognized Eric anywhere.

———

The Chandler house, which now belonged to Eric and Dylan, looked dark and still as Bet drove up. She walked to the front door, as she had so many times as a child when Tracy Chandler had taken on the role of surrogate mother as best she could. Not a particularly warm woman, she'd still helped Bet navigate the confusing waters of young womanhood when her father balked at having to talk about tampons and birth control with his only child.

The house was a simple, white two-story with three bed-rooms upstairs and a living room, kitchen, and den downstairs. Years ago, Michael Chandler had turned the basement into a game room for the boys, and Bet spent a lot of time there playing board games, darts, and foosball. Now it showed the neglect of a house no one lived in full-time. The windows were dirty and the front yard needed attention.

Compared to her own home, the Chandlers' house felt like a happy place, even after Michael left. Looking back now as an adult, she wasn't so sure.

Despite the fingerprint on the flashlight putting Eric at the cave, Bet couldn't know if he'd shot at her or parked a dirt bike at the lean-to, but he did need to explain his presence at the tunnel.

Bet knocked, though she didn't think anyone was home. She made a circuit of the house. It looked like Eric had moved furni-ture around inside as if he planned to stay for a while. The back room, once a guest room, was now an office. Bookshelves that had been in the living room now lined the walls. She arrived at the garage and peered inside—empty.

She thought about leaving a note, something benign, like she'd found time for lunch and stopped by to see if he was free, but she didn't want to spook him. If Eric was involved in this mess, she didn't want him to think he was a suspect. Anything that felt out of char-acter, like her sudden willingness to get together, might tip him off.

Before she could make a decision, she heard a voice call to her from the neighbor's house on the left. Mrs. Villiard had lived next door to the Chandlers for as long as Bet could remember. She'd babysat, so that often included Bet. She was now well into her nineties and osteoporosis turned her once strong, straight back into a question mark, but nothing was wrong with her lungs.

"Looking for Eric?" Mrs. Villiard asked, raising her voice in the way people do who are hard of hearing and believe the rest of the world is too.

"I am," Bet said, thinking how much the floral muumuu looked like a sofa cover.

"What's that?"

"I am looking for Eric," Bet yelled a little louder.

"Eric?" Mrs. Villiard peered up at Bet from her hunched position.

"Yes!" Bet moved closer to the old woman so she wouldn't alert half the neighborhood to her presence.

"He's gone," Mrs. Villiard hollered, even with Bet standing next to her.

"Do you know where?"

"What?"

"Do you know where!"

"Down to Ellensburg. Said he'd be back in a couple hours."

Bet nodded her thanks, hoping they'd finished their loud exchange.

"Want me to tell him you came by?" Mrs. Villiard announced at the top of her lungs.

"Don't worry about it. I'll catch him later."

"What?"

"I said"—Bet took Mrs. Villiard's hand in hers, and shook her head to signify no—"I'll catch him later."

"Sometimes it's nice to surprise a young man, isn't it?" Mrs. Villiard laughed in a throaty way Mae West would have been proud of.

"Nice to see you, Mrs. Villiard," Bet said, her mouth close to the old woman's ear.

"You too, dear," she said, patting Bet on the shoulder. She reached up awkwardly to do so, but the hand she laid on Bet felt strong and sure. A flash of memory—the old woman putting up peaches in the summer. Bet helping her prepare the glass jars, lifting them out of the boiling water with the big metal tongs. Mrs. Villiard listening to Elvis Presley and dancing in the kitchen, using her tongs for a microphone. Bet could recall the satisfying sound when the jars popped as they cooled, signaling a good seal.

"Nice to have Eric back, isn't it?" Mrs. Villiard said, as Bet walked to her SUV parked in the driveway.

"I hope so," Bet said under her breath, but she smiled at the old woman just the same. As she drove away, she noticed the *BET RIVERS FOR SHERIFF* sign in the front yard. At least she could take Mrs. Villiard off the list of people who might have left her notes that she no longer belonged in Collier.

Rob and Alma drove out to Ingalls Creek Road and back in record time. Now, with the Ranger parked in the secured lot behind the station, Bet started searching. The hot pavement burned through the knees of her uniform as she knelt next to the open door to look.

A few moments later, Bet found a package wrapped in plastic wedged underneath the driver's seat. Bet stood and unwrapped it to find a black leather volume. The killer diary.

Bet opened the first page. She wondered how a boy one hundred years ago in Seeley's financial situation could have afforded such a nice journal, but the opening entry described how he'd stolen it during his trip west. He believed he would one day come to greatness and wanted to record his travels for posterity. Though some of the words were blurred from age, Bet could read enough.

Seeley had been born to a mining family back in West Virginia. He'd migrated west looking for adventure and heard Collier needed men for his mines. At fifteen, Seeley knew enough about the industry to talk his way into a job.

Bet skipped forward to where a red ribbon marked a page; she could go back later and read about the rest of Seeley's early days.

"I'll be damned," Bet said out loud after reading the passage. "I guess I have to go back down in that cave."

THIRTY

Accompanied by Schweitzer, Bet rode back out to the mine entrance. Dale came out of hiding to let her know he hadn't seen anyone else in the area. Bet explained what she'd found in the diary.

"You really believe there's gold down there?" Dale asked.

"I do. More importantly, it's what Emma and Seeley believed, and it could be why protecting the cave was worth killing for."

"What do you want to do?" Dale asked.

"Let's head down together. Lock the gate behind us."

"If our shooter returns and sees the lock, we might lose our only chance to grab him."

"We might. But we might also find evidence down there of who it is."

Dale got out the lock and chain and followed Bet to the gate.

They arrived at the naturally occurring stairs Bet now knew the first Robert Collier had enlarged in his attempt to reach the trapped miners. With Schweitzer on her heels, Bet started to climb down while contemplating the events of her town's past.

After the explosion closed the front of the mine, Collier went immediately to the back entrance, trying to rescue his men. Finding the back tunnel blocked as well, by the same cave-in Bet and Rob had found, Collier, Amos Stand, and the original Seeley Lander tried to find another way into the cavern. They worked to make the steep tunnel more accessible, realizing they would never get through the original tunnel buried under the jumble of rocks.

Since the mine was unstable, Collier didn't want the help of anyone else in town. He couldn't bear the thought of more men buried inside the caves. No one else knew the back entrance existed. Collier, Seeley, and Amos Stand had just broken through to the cavern and a possible entrance from there into the mine when Collier suffered a heart attack and died. Not wanting to continue working in the dangerous caves, Amos and Seeley hauled Collier out of the cave, cleaned him up, and reported that he'd died at home.

Seeley wrote in his diary that Amos Stand reassured him the miners would all be dead by this time anyway, and Amos wanted to respect Collier's decision to keep other men out. The two agreed to stop the search and never speak of it again.

When Collier's son—Rob's grandfather, Robert the Second—returned to town after his father's death, Amos and Seeley reported that nothing could be done except keep the mine closed. There was no way to get through the cave-in at the front entrance, and they told him the back entrance didn't lead into the mine.

Disinterested in a mine that no longer produced much any-way, Rob's grandfather placed the bat gate on the back tunnel, and that was the end of the search.

Seeley's life, on the other hand, was saved by greed.

The miners had found a rich vein of gold. The workers' strike, though legitimate, covered their real reason for wanting to hole up in the mine. They wanted to explore the magnitude of the gold deposit before it came to light. One thing they demanded in their strike was partial ownership of the mine. They knew if Collier learned about the gold, he'd never give in to their demands. As it was they had a chance, because the mine's days were numbered with the coal almost gone, and Collier would likely give in to their request, not realizing the true value of what he was giving up until it was too late.

The night of the explosion, the miners planned to blow a sec-tion of the mine to see what more they could find. Seeley, aware of the scheme, set an extra charge in another tunnel. He wanted to distract the other men while he slipped out to Collier's place and told him the truth about what they'd found in exchange for a stake in the gold. As the youngest, most recent addition to the workers, he guessed he would earn little from the mine even if the strike went their way.

But he misjudged the amount of dynamite, and combined with what the miners set off, it collapsed the entire front entrance to the mine and inadvertently blocked the back entrance as well.

Seeley snuck out front just before the charges blew. With the fiery comet streaking overhead, Seeley witnessed the entire side of the mountain sliding down into the lake, the twisted black ties of the railroad stretching into the boiling waters like a path to hell. The locomotive, half buried, carried a man—the miner who had actually been guarding the train that night—screaming with it into the depths.

Realizing what he'd done, Seeley made up the story that he'd been the one to guard the train that night and had seen someone race out of the cave and take the train down the mountain. Seeley ran to Collier's house for help, but he never told a soul about the gold.

After Collier's death, Seeley left town as soon as he could and made a life for himself elsewhere. The events ate at him, however, and he founded a church in Jaxon, repenting every day for the rest of his life.

Maybe the Colliers knew about the gold. That would put My-friends-call-me-Rob on the top of the suspect list. Maybe that was the personal reason that brought him home and looking for his mother was a cover.

But why would he help me if that's true? Why show me the mine to begin with?

That question weighed heavily on Bet's mind as they descended into the cavern. Was Rob being helpful to insert himself into the murder investigation? Criminals did that from time to time out of a need to be involved. Or maybe to guide her away from evidence? Or to get rid of her if the need arose?

Then there was Jamie Garcia. Someone had tipped the girl off. Who would benefit from the investigation going public?

They arrived at the mouth of the cavern. Schweitzer leaned against her leg, waiting for a command. She pointed to their right. "Let's go this direction," Bet said, indicating a lane between boulders to the right of the return path from the crime scene.

Dale fell in behind her.

Flashlight to the ground, Bet looked for footprints or a trail, but the slick rock surface of the cave floor gave nothing away. They wound between the stalactites and stalagmites, like hikers navigating a forest of rock. Bet was considering trying another direction when Schweitzer caught a whiff of something. He growled once, a noise that echoed around the cavern and increased in volume to sound like a pack of hellhounds on the loose, then looked to Bet for approval.

"Good boy," Bet said, though she hoped he wouldn't do it again. The sound sent shivers down her spine.

"Find something?" Dale asked.

"It looks that way," Bet said, following her dog as he moved away from them.

No evidence of a trail appeared in front of her, but a glimmer on the wall in the darkness caught Bet by surprise. She passed her flashlight over the area where she saw it, and nothing showed up, but once her flashlight moved on, a green glow appeared at the edge of her vision. Moving over to the cave wall, she could see a pale mark.

"Glow-in-the-dark-paint," Bet said.

"What good's that do down here?" Dale asked. "There's no light source to charge it."

"Probably a fail-safe. If someone charges the marks with their flashlight as they walk by and they have to get out without turning on a light, they can follow these marks."

"How long would the charge last?"

Bet shrugged. "An hour, maybe an hour and a half." She played her flashlight across the area where the mark appeared. She touched a hole drilled into the stone nearby. "Looks like a hole for dynamite. Maybe the paint is a way to locate these easier."

"Huh." Dale leaned in to look closer. "Left over from the miners?"

"Maybe." Bet signaled to Schweitzer that he could continue.

The big dog stepped forward with confidence. Bet and Dale followed, flashlights moving side to side. They each found additional glow marks, strategically placed to be hard to find unless a person knew where to look, and each with a hole drilled nearby.

A few minutes later, Schweitzer turned a corner and sat down at the entrance to another tunnel. A generator sat just outside, with cables twisting away into the darkness of the next cave. Schweitzer growled once, then whined and looked at Bet for reassurance.

"There's something in there he doesn't like," Bet said, putting her hand on her weapon and stepping around the dog. She gestured to Schweitzer to fall in behind her. If anyone inside the tunnel came out shooting, she didn't want Schweitzer in front. Her bulletproof vest reassured her, but only a little. The vest couldn't prevent a direct shot to her head.

Dale followed her into the new tunnel. A few feet in and the tunnel opened into a large room, at least forty feet on a side. White cloth covered various shapes on the floor. Other objects were stashed in niches chipped into the wall. Bet pulled back the edge of the canvas to uncover toys, clothes, and small household items. It was like an underground Goodwill Store.

Dale's voice finally broke the silence. "What the hell?"

Black snakes of electrical cords twined around to several work lights, mounted high on orange tripods.

Bet's flashlight illuminated another opening at the far end. Bet made Schweitzer sit/stay outside so he wouldn't leave hairs behind or disturb evidence before they brought Todd down to process the scene. Pulling on latex gloves, Bet and Dale tread carefully down the pathway between the piles. Flashing her light inside the opening, she found a much smaller room, roughly ten by ten, set up like a primitive campsite. A cot with a sleeping bag sat against one wall, while bottles of water, a camp stove, and canned food filled a shelf chipped into the wall.

"Is someone living down here?" Bet asked.

"Looks that way, but what's with all that crap in the other room?"

Returning to the larger room, she and Dale began looking through the items piled up. Bet peered into a dark cavity. A set of kitschy salt and pepper shakers sat in the space.

"What the hell is this?" Bet asked, with a gesture. Dale came over to see what she'd found. "Salt and pepper shakers? Who hauls decorative salt and pepper shakers all the way down into a cave?"

Dale shook his head without a word.

Bet moved down to the next niche and shined her light in. "It's not just tableware," she said, as her light found a porcelain doll.

At the next niche, adrenaline surged through her veins. She reached in to pull out an exquisite bracelet. Silver filigree with red and blue stones. As if it burned her fingers, she dropped the jewelry onto the stone floor.

"What?" Dale asked, as Bet stumbled backward.

"That belonged to my mother." The bracelet was like a viper that would raise its round head and strike her.

"You sure?" he asked.

"Dad brought it back from Kosovo. It's handmade. Totally unique." Bet knelt and picked it up, carefully setting it back in place. "I remember looking for it a few years ago, but I couldn't find it. I thought Dad packed it up somewhere, or threw it away. I didn't want to ask him about it."

"Think your dad did this?"

Bet shrugged. Her father had lived a double life before, when he served overseas and simultaneously had a life and a family back home.

Bet turned and looked across the pile in the stone room.

"Those shakers, that doll—I think these are all things stolen from people in town. You know when things go missing around here, we just blame the ghosts of the miners. I think this has been going on for years."

"Why?"

"Maybe it's a memorial of some kind," Bet said. "Or a tribute, or an altar."

"Someone killed Emma over this?"

"It's possible." At least she knew her father hadn't killed the girl.

"If someone killed to protect this stuff, they're likely to come back if they think it's safe," Dale said, echoing Bet's thoughts.

"Agreed. If I go public with Emma's death and say we're done with our investigation, and don't mention these two caves at all, they might think it's safe to return. They might think we never found this."\

"When, though?"

"We'd have no way to know. It could mean watching the cave twenty-four/seven for weeks." Bet considered the best course of action. "This must be where our shooter holes up. They found Emma and Seeley in the cave, killed her, and tried to kill him."

Schweitzer whined from the entrance of the room.

"I'm with you, buddy. Let's get out of here." Bet rubbed the dog's head as she stepped out. "I need to decide what to do first— try to find evidence here or hope to lure the killer back. I don't want to jeopardize anything by letting them know we found this part of the cave. They might take off for good."

Once back in the larger cavern, Bet turned her flashlight off. Dale did the same and Bet moved slowly forward, finding one glow-in-the-dark mark after another. They followed the trail back to where Bet had found the first one. She clicked her flashlight back on.

"I don't know what to think," she said. "This could be someone who lived in the community for years, our ghost a real person. Maybe that's who George has been seeing in the woods."

"Never killed anyone before," Dale pointed out. "Maybe your dad shared this with someone else? Who would he be that close to? Besides you?"

"And is it someone who lives in Collier?" Bet asked. "Or visits once in a while?"

Or shows up out of the blue. After being gone for years.

THIRTY-ONE

Bet left Dale at the cave entrance and returned to the station. She couldn't believe her father had been "the ghost" of the miners. But if he had, did that mean he was involved with the event coming back to her in memories? If so, that might have increased the trauma preceding the dissociative fugue she'd experienced.

She walked across the street for coffee while waiting for Clayton to arrive, and was surprised to see Sandy manning the coffee cart.

"Working late today," Bet said as she came in.

"I lost my afternoon barista to Central Washington University," Sandy said, mentioning Bet's alma mater. "Want a part-time job?"

"Have you lost faith in me winning the election?" Bet pictured working the coffee stand if she lost and couldn't face returning to LA defeated.

"You still have time to pull it off. The community would rather have you. The election is yours to lose."

Bet thought about the notes and her missing fly, and she wasn't as confident.

"I'll take coffee for me, Clayton, and Alma instead."

Sandy started fixing everyone's drinks from habit. Bet picked up a blueberry muffin.

"I've been worried about you," Sandy said. "You look so serious. Are you the one having doubts?"

Los Angeles continued to recede. Did that mean she was giving up on a dream? Or evolving as an adult? Bet thought how nice it would be to share her insecurities with someone. Sandy would understand her situation.

"Just a lot going on."

Clayton arrived in the station parking lot across the street, and Sandy pulled out a carry case for the drinks.

"Don't ignore the campaign forever," Sandy said before Bet left. "Just because it's yours to lose doesn't mean you're guaranteed a win."

Bet tried to imagine losing to Dale. "I won't," she promised.

And this time she meant it.

Back at the station, everyone sat around Alma's desk, and Bet described what she and Dale had found.

"Is everything you found from Collier?" Clayton asked, his blond eyebrows knitted together in concentration.

"What are you thinking?" Bet asked.

"If it is, it would show a connection to this community," Clayton said. "Otherwise, why steal things from just here? If there's stuff from other communities, he might be someone with no connections here other than it's a good place to hide things."

"Like who?" Alma asked.

Clayton shrugged. "Maybe the stuff will tell us more."

"Should I call Todd?" Alma peeled the top off her muffin.

"Yes," Bet said. "We can slip him in. Those objects are likely to be covered in fingerprints. He has his work cut out for him. He'll have to figure out whose fingerprints are common to all the items."

Bet glanced at her cell phone to check the time. She noticed a text had come in from a strange number.

"For now, we stay hidden and do surveillance at the mouth of the cave twenty-four hours a day. Dale's there now; we'll need to spell him in a few hours."

"I could take a shift at the cave," Alma said. "I can still plug a bull's-eye at one hundred yards at the range."

Bet had no doubt of Alma's ability to shoot her gun, but she wasn't sure she trusted her judgment or her ability to stay quiet while she watched.

"There's something else I need you to do, Alma. Go back through the stolen-item reports over the last several years. That might give us a pattern." Alma agreed, even though the idea of surveillance no doubt intrigued her more. "Include break-ins where people thought nothing was stolen; these are the kind of items that might have gone missing without notice. If this person is the same one who killed Emma, it may be our best shot to find evidence of the culprit."

"Okay. I'll get right on it after I call Todd."

"Clayton, I want you to go talk to George again. See if you can get any details about the 'ghost' he keeps seeing in the woods. We've always discounted him seeing anyone, but maybe that was a mistake. Find out if George saw anything about how he was dressed or a physical description—age, height, race, anything."

"What if George is the ghost?" Clayton asked. "He might tell the story just to keep people on edge. He could be hiding things in the cave. He works for the Colliers. Amos Stand was his ancestor. Maybe he knew something about the gold too and George has been looking for it all these years."

"That's an interesting thought," Bet said. "He would have access to lye, which was dumped on Emma's fingers, and we know he owns plenty of firearms and ties those kind of knots."

"And he lives closest to the lake," Alma said.

Bet took a deep breath. She tried to imagine George hauling stuff down into the cave. Had his relationship with her father been closer than she realized? Could they have done it together?

"Okay. We have to consider him a suspect, but if he's not, he may be the only person to have seen our hoarder. Tell him we're following up on his report. Don't connect it to the other events. If he's not making it up, it could give us useful information. Especially if his description is anything like Rob Collier, Eric Chandler, or even Peter Malone."

Clayton said he'd try.

"There's one more thing," Bet said before they wrapped up. "There may be something in the lake that can help us."

Bet went on to explain she believed there was a second body in the lake, submerged for twenty years.

"If Professor Malone just found it, how do you know it's a woman?" Alma looked at Bet with suspicion.

"Or how long it's been in the water?" Clayton asked.

"I don't know for sure, but I could see long dark hair on the monitor. As for the timing . . ." Bet paused. How much could she share? "There may have been a witness who saw a man dump her in the lake. A child."

"Who?" Alma asked.

"Let's not get ahead of ourselves. I want to get it raised first and confirm it's truly a person. If it is, after Dr. Pak does an autopsy and report, I'll bring in the witness."

If she was right about what she'd seen and how long she'd blocked it out, she would come clean to the community before the election. It would be their choice whether to keep her or not. She only wanted to win if it was a fair fight.

Alma started to ask another question, but Bet cut her off. "I know we all want to be more proactive about this, but I think we need to proceed carefully." She looked each of them in the eye. "This man has been moving among us for years and leaving no trace. He must be someone who lives here or has reason to visit regularly. He's been very careful so far. We aren't going to find him overnight. "

Clayton and Alma were nodding, agreeing with her assessment. She liked that they were all on the same page.

"History makes me think it's not Peter Malone, but it's also possible we're talking about more than one person involved, so he's not off the list. A geomorphologist could come in handy looking for gold in a cave."

She didn't say her father could be on the list too.

The group dispersed, and Bet headed out to check in with Peter Malone and the lady in the lake.

Once back in her SUV, she remembered the text that had come in and clicked on her phone to read it.

Why are you still here?

The number was blocked. The phone would no doubt be a burner, impossible to trace. Bet started up her engine. All she could do was focus on the investigation. Maybe solving it would demonstrate that she'd earned the title of sheriff of Collier, and her secret "admirer" would change their mind about where she belonged.

———

Peter introduced Bet to Professors Winter and Lacey, both vigorous-looking men in their early sixties. She sensed the excitement tingling among the three men.

"How deep is this object we're bringing up?" Winter asked Peter. He must be the *Ed* who'd loaned Peter the trailer.

Winter had a gray ponytail, in contrast to Lacey's shaved head. If it hadn't been for the different hairstyles, Bet wasn't sure she could have told them apart.

"Three hundred fifty feet," Peter said.

"We brought quite a lot of equipment with us since we weren't sure what we're going after. You were very vague on the phone," Lacey said.

"Downright mysterious," Winter said with a gleam in his eye.

"So what is it? Something valuable? Or just interesting?" Lacey sounded as excited as a kid on Christmas.

"Maybe we should tell them what they're really here for." Bet gave Peter a pointed look. He winced, realizing the callousness of his excitement over bringing up a body.

"Sorry, Sheriff. You're right." Peter turned solemn, and the visiting scientists picked up on the change in mood.

"It's a body."

"A body!" Winter said. "Recent?"

"She's been in the lake roughly twenty years," Bet said. "So we have no idea what condition she'll be in."

"She?" Lacey repeated.

"Most likely," Bet said. The two men exchanged looks Bet found hard to read. "I hope you're still willing to help me."

"Absolutely, Sheriff," Lacey said. "We just had no idea this would be so—"

"We have to keep this low-key." Peter stepped in. "It seemed better to tell you in person."

Bet wondered what the other scientist was going to say.

"Where we couldn't brag to the grad students." Winter and Lacey shared a laugh.

"Exactly," Peter said.

"Well, let's go see what we're dealing with." Winter rubbed his hands together in delight. "You said you have the . . . object located?"

Bet noticed his enthusiasm hadn't changed with the knowledge of what was in the water. In fact, if anything, his interest was further piqued.

Peter and Winter launched Peter's canoe, while Bet and Lacey brought his rowboat down to the water's edge. Peter and Winter floated just offshore as she and Lacey launched into the water, settling in to paddle to the far side of the lake. They would lower Peter's camera and assess the situation. The other professors had brought a submersible camera with them too, so they would have more than one view when they prepared to bring the body up.

When they arrived at the location Peter had identified the previous day, he tuned in his controls and sent the camera to where the corpse waited patiently on her rocky ledge. Peter moved the camera from side to side after he dropped it down to depth, and it wasn't long before his "I found it" signaled success in relocating the body.

Winter whistled low under his breath as he took in the image lit by Peter's camera.

"Let me see," Lacey said from his perch in the rear of the canoe. He and Bet maneuvered around for an unobstructed view of the canvas-wrapped shape on the monitor.

The three men went into a lively discussion of various methods for bringing her up. They finally decided on a plan, and Peter pulled his camera to the surface. They turned their boats around to get their equipment together and leave Bet on dry land.

"How long will this take?" Bet asked, after they'd beached the canoes.

"Could take hours," Lacey said. "We can't rush this. We don't know how well she'll do as we bring her up from depth. We don't want to risk dropping her and having her fall deeper into the lake."

"We might want to tow her back to my campsite before we pull her out of the water," Peter said. "That way no one driving by will see us hoisting a body out of the water."

"Can you do that without risk of losing her?"

"Once she's close to the surface, we can secure her to one of the canoes and bring her in."

Bet thought for a moment. She knew that if anyone saw them haul the woman into the canoe, it would be all over town. And she'd lose control of how the public learned about events. Jamie Garcia would know she'd been holding out on her, and that could blow up in Bet's face.

"It's what I did with the other body," Peter said out of earshot of the other men, already unloading equipment from Lacey's van. "I couldn't pull her dead weight into my canoe by myself." Bet saw him swallow hard, as he had when he spoke of seeing Emma's hair. "I promise I'll take care of her." Bet knew Malone had secrets, but on this she believed him.

With that, Bet climbed into her SUV, leaving the scientists to work their magic and raise the dead. If she identified the corpse and solved her murder, would she put her childhood nightmare to rest? And somehow prove her father wasn't involved? At least to herself?

The scientists brought the corpse to the surface without mishap and she now lay on a table in the morgue in E'burg, just as Emma Hunter had a few days before. Solid, tangible evidence to support Bet's memories.

Carolyn prepared to remove the ropes that bound the figure, to unwrap her from the shroud.

"Shall we?" Carolyn asked, as she pointed at the ropes with the scalpel in her hand. The knots were the same as the ones that had bound Emma.

"Go ahead," Bet said. Carolyn cut through the bindings. It took a few minutes, but they soon had the ropes free and the weights removed, and began to unwrap the corpse. The long dark hair flowed out across the coroner's table. Bet drew her breath in with a sharp intake at the preservation of the dead woman. She looked like she was sleeping. With her features so intact, Bet knew her identity immediately.

"What's the problem?" Carolyn asked. "This isn't who you expected her to be?"

"I didn't have any expectations," Bet said. "But yeah, this is a shock. I also know who to bring in to make a formal identification."

THIRTY-TWO

Bet arrived at Rob's house to find him waiting for her after her cryptic call. She sat him down in the living room and told him who Peter Malone had pulled out of the lake.

"How could I not have seen this coming?" Rob's voice shook with emotion. "How could I have believed all these years she just walked away?"

He agreed to go with her to the morgue to confirm the ID. On the drive back down she took a chance and told him about her own recovered memories. She felt she owed him that. And she might as well do a practice run before she told the whole town.

Now they stood in the hallway outside the morgue while Rob caught his breath. It had been difficult for him to see his mother looking eerily suspended in time.

"Your father told you she abandoned you. Why would you think otherwise?"

"But still, all these years. I never looked for her." He laughed, though the sound held little mirth. "Until now."

Whatever else might be true about Rob Collier, she believed his shock and grief were real. She wasn't sure what she could do to comfort the man. She reached out and touched his arm.

"You believed she left you. You didn't want to be rejected again. And you thought she never tried to reach you. You had no way to know she couldn't."

Rob rested his head in his hands, but no tears came. His shoulders sagged, and Bet felt the sadness and regret coming off him in waves.

"Who did this?" Rob finally spoke. "My father? You saw the person who pushed her through the ice. Are you sure you didn't recognize him?"

"It was dark and I was looking through the trees. Apparently I was terrified enough for that to put me into a fugue state," Bet reminded him. "You said you believed me about that."

"But you remember now. Was he a big man? Like my father?"

"Rob," Bet said, keeping her voice even. "It was freezing out. Whoever it was had on winter clothes, a parka, a knit cap." Bet shrugged helplessly, feeling like a failure for not having more to tell him. "I was a kid. Everyone looked big to me then." She didn't add that she might not have recognized her own father under those conditions.

Rob took a deep, steadying breath. "I know. I'm sorry." He straightened up and began to walk back into the autopsy room.

"Rob, you can't be in the room for this."

"I'm not going to watch the autopsy, but I need to see her again."

Carolyn looked up as they entered, concern on her face.

"It's okay," Rob said. "I'm just going to be a few minutes; then we'll leave you to do your job."

Carolyn nodded, and the three of them moved around Lillian's body. Carolyn had covered her with a sheet, but she clearly lay naked underneath it. Only her face, neck, and upper shoulders remained visible for the moment.

"She could be sleeping," Bet murmured.

"Incorruptibility," Carolyn said.

"What?" Bet asked.

"The Roman Catholic Church believes that supernatural interference prevents decomposition in certain bodies," Rob said.

"I've never seen it before, myself," Carolyn said. "Catholics believe the body should exude an odor of sanctity."

Rob leaned over his mother and breathed in deeply. "I don't smell anything floral. Maybe . . . metallic. Like copper."

"We'll have to assume, then," Carolyn said, "that your mother is not a saint."

"You two don't really think this is supernatural, do you?" Bet looked back and forth between them.

"No, of course not. I didn't mean that," Carolyn said. "I just meant that's the name the church gives this phenomenon. There's going to be a scientific reason for it. Probably the cold. Human remains have been found preserved in ice, even cold peat bogs in Ireland. In those cases a combination of highly acidic water, cold, and low oxygen preserved the skin and organs."

"But not the bones," Rob said.

"Correct again, Mr. Collier." Carolyn watched Rob closely. "Bones eventually dissolve from the acid in the peat; it attacks the calcium phosphate."

"But this preserved after almost twenty years?" Bet wouldn't have believed it if she hadn't seen Lillian with her own eyes.

"One of the most famous cases of mummification is that of Lady Dai," Carolyn said. "She died in China in 163 BC. When she was found in 1971, she still had hair, skin, even blood in her veins."

"That's incredible." Bet shook her head. "She'd be almost two thousand years old?"

Carolyn nodded. "That makes your find here seem a lot more possible, doesn't it?"

"Why was she preserved in our lake, though? It's not a peat bog." Bet kept her eyes on Rob. She couldn't imagine what was going through his head as they looked at his mother's corpse.

"Besides the cold," Carolyn said, "she was wrapped up pretty tight. Without anaerobic activity, the decomposition process would slow. It would keep fish from eating her."

"There are no fish in the lake."

"What?" Carolyn's face showed her surprise.

"In Lake Collier. There are no fish."

"Seriously?"

Bet laughed at her incredulity. "How can you not know that? You've lived here in E'burg how long?"

"I've never been up to Lake Collier, though." Carolyn stood quiet for a long moment, deep in thought. "No fish at all?"

"Nothing. Not a fish, not a tadpole. No signs of life."

"Ever?"

"Not as long as I can remember." Rob rejoined the conversation, and Bet nodded in agreement.

"Why is that?" The medical examiner looked at the two of them as if they could explain the vagaries of the lake in detail.

"I always assumed it was the cold or the altitude." Bet thought about Peter Malone. "The scientist studying the lake right now thinks it was formed from a glacier. Maybe nothing ever started growing."

Carolyn rejected the thought. "That doesn't make sense. Lots of fish and amphibians can survive in cold water, and at higher elevations. You should have something. Is there plant life? Anything?"

"No, nothing," Bet said.

"Anyone ever tested the water?"

"Tested?" Rob looked troubled. "Tested for what?"

"That would be the question," Carolyn said. "What could be in the water that keeps anything from growing and preserves the dead?"

"You have something in mind?" Bet felt a sense of dread creeping up her spine.

"You do have an old mine up there, right? Lots of stuff can ooze out of an old coal mine."

Bet had never heard anyone speculate about why Lake Collier was dead. It had just always been that way.

The medical examiner returned to the case at hand. "You sound very certain about the year your lady went into the lake."

"I have no doubt," Bet said.

"How can you be so sure?"

"Eyewitness account," Bet said.

"Reliable?"

"Very." Rob didn't look at Bet as he answered.

"Odd. Coming so many years later." Carolyn gave Bet a searching look.

Bet shrugged. "People keep secrets for all kinds of reasons."

"True." Carolyn turned and pulled her light down closer, inspecting Lillian's face. "But secrets have a way of coming out, don't they?"

"Did you see anything that would indicate cause of death before you covered her?" Bet asked.

"Nothing obvious, but I'll have to do a full autopsy. Keep in mind, after all this time it may be difficult to ascertain for certain. She's incredibly well preserved, but time has still taken its toll. I should get started. Exposure to oxygen may start breaking things down."

Bet asked one last question. "Is she missing any hair?"

Carolyn took a thin metal instrument and carefully separated the long strands of Lillian's hair. She looked up at Bet, eyes wide.

Bet didn't need her to say yes to know the answer.

THIRTY-THREE

Carolyn promised to call as soon as she had any information. Bet and Rob left E'burg soon after. As they drove home in Bet's SUV, Rob remained lost in thought. They drove west up the valley toward the mountains and Collier. Hayfields and small ranches ranged alongside the freeway as they crossed back and forth over the Yakima River. The crystal-clear water raced across stones and reflected the blue sky in the slower, deeper pools.

"So," Bet finally said to break the silence. "I have to ask. Do you have any idea who might have killed your mother?"

"I was just contemplating that myself," Rob said.

Bet sped up and changed lanes to get around a truck towing a horse trailer. She passed the rig and moved to the right lane again. The mountains rose in front of them like a wall of granite that split Eastern Washington from the west side. Snow-capped peaks showed where glaciers survived, despite raising global temperatures.

"Something is wrong with my timeline, though." Bet settled back at seventy miles an hour. "Didn't your mother disappear before I was even born? How would I have seen her put in the lake?"

"I don't know. She must have come back into town and I didn't know about it."

"That puts your dad—"

"Top of the list. I get it," Rob said.

"Or, if Lillian and Michael Chandler did have an affair," Bet said, thinking about the information she had, and how it could possibly form an answer to her questions, "she could have been coming back to Collier, to you and your dad, and Michael killed her. That would explain why Michael finally left for good. If I killed someone I abandoned my family for, I'd never come back either. Maybe Michael snapped."

Rob closed his eyes for a moment, leaning back against the headrest. "When did you last see Michael Chandler?"

"It's been years. And I can't imagine he would be in town and I wouldn't know about it."

Unless he just comes and goes late at night sometimes, without any-one seeing him. Like a ghost. Bet thought of the collection of things left in the cave. *Someone who is a part of our community, and yet not?* Could Michael and her father have set up the cave together? George said military people would know the knots too. Maybe her father had continued to see Michael even after Michael left.

"You're going to have to talk to his sons," Rob said. "I heard Eric was in town. Maybe he's seen his dad recently."

"He said he hadn't," Bet said.

"Are you sure he's telling the truth?"

Eric was capable of great deception.

"I'll call Dylan and talk to him first, then go out and see Eric in person," she said. "Are you going to contact your father?"

"I don't know. I'd rather be with him in person to see his reaction when I tell him."

Bet thought about the new case Lillian Collier represented. Bet would have to open a case file on her. Even if she was connected to Emma Hunter's murder, her death and disposal were separate crimes.

"I'd like to talk to your father before you do," she said. "Where is he now?"

"I thought you knew," Rob said, looking over at Bet.

"Nope. I don't keep track of your father."

"He lives in Vietnam."

A country with no extradition treaty with the United States.

"Why did he go so far away?"

"He visited there regularly for business. I guess he fell in love with the country. It wasn't like he had anything left here."

––––––––––––––––

Once they arrived in Collier, Rob drove back to his place. Bet sent Alma home, overriding her argument that she should put in a few more hours. Then Bet went to her office and sat at her desk. She had a short conversation with Dylan, asking if he'd had any contact with his father. Bet explained she found something of Michael's in her father's effects she wanted to give him, and Dylan appeared to believe her story. He said he'd lost all contact with him and had no interest in helping Bet track him down.

"Whatever it is you have of my father's, Bet, you can keep it," Dylan said, before he hung up the phone. "I don't even want to know what it is."

Todd Jones wouldn't be able to get back to Collier for a few days; too many other cases kept him busy elsewhere. Bet assured him they could wait. Dale would be on call tonight. Clayton was at the mine entrance, so for now, there was nothing to be done.

As she stared blankly at the computer screen, the search bar mocked her. "There's nothing to search for," she said to the machine. "I don't know what direction to look anymore, and I can't force my memories to show me any more than they already have about the man who dumped Lillian into the lake."

"Thank God," she said when her cell phone rang, grateful for the distraction. She looked down to see Eric's number. She started to send it to voice mail, but changed her mind. She had to talk to Eric; it might as well be now.

His surprise came through the phone when Bet answered.

"I grew accustomed to hearing your voice mail," he said, his voice intimate in her ear.

"Sorry," Bet said. "It's been a bit . . ." She let her words drift off, hoping Eric would fill the silence.

"How about a drink?" Eric asked. Bet surprised him further by agreeing.

They arranged to meet at "the Bar," as it was so creatively named, a place that tended to the more serious drinkers in the community. They didn't serve food, unless you counted pretzels and peanuts. No kids or dogs allowed.

Bet drove home and gave Schweitzer a quick walk. Once again she ignored her father's voice telling her to clean out the gutters, but she did pause long enough to pull the garden hose out and water the bright, cheerful daisies before they wilted even more from the hot sunlight that would return tomorrow. She felt relief there were no new notes on her door.

Thinking of how neglected the Chandlers' house felt, she assessed her own windows and decided she'd have to get the Windex out soon.

Bet sighed and entered the house. Walking through the quiet rooms, she made her way to the kitchen in the back. The scarred and marked rose-colored linoleum she'd helped her father put down when she was six still covered the floor. The cream-colored walls showed the scuff marks of a house well lived in. Pencil marks along one doorframe marked Bet's continual progress in height, ending her first year of high school at five feet eight inches. After that, she didn't want to know how tall she became.

Stooping to pick up Schweitzer's food bowl, she put in two scoops from the bin on the floor in the pantry. After giving him fresh water, Bet went upstairs.

She went all the way into the master bedroom's walk-in closet before she finally clicked on a light to find something to wear. She pulled a canvas jacket over a T-shirt and jeans and let her hair down, releasing her curls from the various pins that had anchored them all day. She stood for a moment, peering at her wavy image in the antique mirror, wondering what Eric saw when he looked at her now.

Mostly, she looked tired. Dark circles painted the fragile skin under her eyes, eyes the color of milk chocolate in the dim light. She thought briefly about putting on a little makeup but talked herself out of it. "It doesn't matter what Eric sees," she said to her reflection. "Not anymore."

Eric had been back in the area off and on over the years. He could have been stealing items and stashing them down in the caves, but Bet couldn't find any reason for it.

The one thing Eric had going for him, besides history, was that he hadn't killed Lillian. His beard was too thin to be the man Bet remembered. And she did believe the same person killed Emma.

Bet shut off the lights and went back downstairs in the dark.

"Sorry, Schweitz," Bet said as she got ready to leave. "You can't come with me this time."

The dog crawled up into his favorite chair and lay his head on the back, solemnly watching Bet through the window as she exited the house. It gave her heart a tug to leave him behind.

She arrived at the bar to find Eric holding down a table in the back. As she made her way through the murky darkness, which looked to be full of smoke even though smoking had been banned for years, her boots crunched on the concrete floor covered with peanut shells. The spots of light over the bar illuminated the bottles far more than the patrons or the bartender.

Eric sat in a corner of the room, a knit cap pulled low on his head despite the residual warmth of summer outside. He must have bought a pitcher before she arrived, as one sat in front of him along with an extra glass, so Bet walked over and settled in. They both pressed their backs against the wall, their shoulders almost touching.

"I didn't know if you still liked dark beer. I hope you don't mind." Eric leaned forward. More light fell onto his features, and Bet could see the ice blue of his eyes. The lines around his mouth appeared etched deeper than when she'd last seen him, and she wondered if being home aged him or something else weighed on his mind.

She reached out to pour herself a glass, but Eric beat her to it, taking the ice-cold mug from her hand. "I'll take that as a yes."

"You wanted to talk?" Bet asked.

"Finish everything that had you so busy?" Eric asked, instead of answering her question. He set the glass in front of her.

"No. But a little time away might be exactly what I need."

They fell silent, the easy camaraderie of their early years a strained memory.

"How well do you remember my father?" She could tell by his expression that the question was a surprise. She hadn't planned to ask; it just came out.

"I didn't see him much after I moved away. Is that what you mean?"

"No. When we were kids. How well do you remember him from when we were kids?"

"I remember I wished he was my dad. My dad was so . . . absent, even before he left for good. Earle was quiet, but at least he was always here."

"Funny," Bet said.

"What's that?" Eric asked, one side of his mouth turning up in a smile while the other didn't. Bet remembered that expression well. Eric wore that half smile when he truly listened. She could always tell when his mind was far away because both sides of his mouth would tilt up if he faked it.

"I remember wishing I had your dad. Your father wasn't always around, but when he was, he was so much more fun. Earle always felt gone even when he was here."

"I never thought about my dad that way," Eric said.

"Michael saw things differently than the rest of us. One time we went fly-fishing over in Idaho. You remember that trip?"

"Sure, we were fishing the Clark." There'd been only one trip to Idaho before Michael abandoned his family.

"Me and your dad went upstream while the rest of you went down."

"Seems to me we caught a big string of fish, but you and my dad came back with squat."

"We did catch a fish. We caught the biggest fish I'd ever seen. A rainbow." Bet held her hands two feet apart. "Had to be this big."

"You lost it?"

"Nope. Your dad, he held it through the gills so he wouldn't damage it and pulled the hook out. He had us using barbless. He said, 'Come here, Lizzie.' Remember how he called me that?" Eric nodded. "He said, 'Look real close at this one.' I did. I mean, I really looked at a fish for the first time. How the light played on the colors of its sides, the big dark circle of its eye. Then he slipped it back into the water and we watched it swim away."

"I don't believe you. Why would he do that?"

"He said, 'Some things, Lizzie, they're just too pretty to kill. Best to leave him here in his pool. We know exactly where he is if we want to see him again. If we kill him, he's gone for good.'"

Eric sat quiet.

"Do you remember my mom?" Bet asked.

"I remember she was beautiful. You look a lot like her, you know."

"Do I? I thought I looked more like Dad."

"You have her incredible hair." Eric reached out for a curl and wrapped it around his finger, the way he used to. He tugged and watched it spring back into place. Bet froze. The gesture felt good. Bet had lived with loneliness for so long, she'd forgotten what it felt like when she wasn't alone.

"Why do you think she killed herself?"

"This isn't what I thought we'd be talking about tonight," Eric said.

"I know, I just . . ." Bet wanted to tell the man who'd meant so much to her all those years ago about the doubts she had around her father's "accident." How she believed he'd taken his own life rather than fight his cancer. That he'd brought her back to town so he could leave it in her hands, which meant she should have seen what he planned and prevented it. What kind of sheriff didn't know her own father was going to commit suicide?

She longed to tell Eric everything, like she used to, back when they were the only two people in the world. Like how her mother's bracelet sat inside the cave and Bet wondered if her father had put it there or disposed of Lillian Collier in the lake. Bet reminded herself that Eric was still hiding things. It was his fingerprint on the flashlight Rob had found in the cave.

"Well, you know about the affair." Eric broke the silence.

"Affair?"

Discomfort flashed across Eric's face, then embarrassment. "Ah. You didn't know. I'm sorry, I—"

Bet cut him off. "What affair are we talking about? There's been so many."

Eric didn't rise to the bait, but continued. "Your mother. I don't know why I thought you knew."

Bet took a long swallow of beer, her thoughts whirling. "Who with? And why do you know about it?"

"I overheard your mom talking about it with my mom. They didn't know I was home, I guess. They were both a little drunk.""

"What did you hear?"

"Just that. Your mother slept with someone else and she felt guilty about it, even though it had been over for a long time. Believe me, I understand the feeling."

Bet ignored Eric's reference to their own history. "Who? Who was it with?"

Eric shrugged and took a drink from his mug. "Why does it matter now?"

"My mother had an affair? I thought *your* mother had the affair."

Had all the adults in Collier been cheating? Or was Lillian's affair with Michael a lie? She had been dead all these years, so she wasn't off living somewhere with him. "What do you remember from their conversation? You must have heard more than that."

"I remember my mom saying something about how money wasn't everything but it sure beat nothing. I'm not sure how that fit in, except maybe . . ."

"The other man had money." Bet finished Eric's thought.

"Maybe."

"Like Robert Collier?"

"Robert Collier!" Eric's response came out louder than Bet thought the name warranted.

"Why is that so hard to believe?" She didn't remember Rob's father well, but he was a handsome man in his own right.

"It's not that." Eric paused. "I guess it's possible. Maybe that's what she meant. I didn't think about it at the time. I was too busy hoping to hear about sex."

Bet punched him in the shoulder.

"Ow! What? I was a curious kid. It wasn't like *my* mother was the one talking about screwing around." Eric rubbed his shoulder.

"What happened?" Bet asked, curious how he would explain his injury.

"You can't laugh."

Bet held up two fingers in the Boy Scout salute. "Scout's honor."

"I was moving furniture around and a bookcase fell on me."

"Seriously?"

"Seriously."

Bet started to laugh.

"You promised not to do that," Eric said.

"I didn't know it would be such a dumb story."

"Thanks a lot. I'm being honest with you, and you make fun."

"I hope it pinned you down for a while. How'd you get out from underneath it?"

Bet continued to chuckle at the image of Eric stuck under a mountain of books with one of the old, solid walnut bookshelves of his mother's stretched across his fallen form like a tree down in a storm. The story had a ring of truth. She'd seen the furniture he'd moved around.

"I'm lucky I didn't get seriously hurt."

"Should I write the bookcase up? Assault as a deadly weapon?"

Eric took another drink of his beer, then started to laugh himself. "I can imagine how it looked. I'd taken all the books out, and it turned out it was a lot more top heavy than I anticipated. It started to go over and I threw myself under it, thinking I could stop it, and . . ." He shrugged. Their laughter died down, and with it the tension that crackled between them since Bet had first laid eyes on him a few days ago.

"They were all friends, you know. Years ago."

"Who were?" Bet asked, confused.

"My parents and your parents and the Colliers. Before everything turned so . . . wrong."

"My parents were friends with the Colliers?"

"That's what I was told. It was a long time ago, before we were born."

Bet looked at Eric, wondering what he really knew.

"When is the last time you saw your dad?"

"You asked me that already." He dodged her eyes.

"Remind me."

"We don't stay in touch." He evaded her question again.

Bet let it go for the moment; she couldn't force him to tell her anything. She thought instead about how to bring up the flashlight.

"Did you know there's another entrance to the Collier mine?" Bet hoped the element of surprise might cause Eric to say something he wouldn't otherwise.

Eric looked at Bet with an intensity she hadn't seen before. "You know?" he asked, his voice dropped low.

"Know? Know what?"

"About the mine, about . . ."

"What Eric? What about the mine? What is it you think I know?"

Eric looked down into his beer as if it held answers.

"If you're in some kind of trouble, I can help you," Bet said softly, trying not to break the intimacy of the moment.

Eric looked at Bet. "I was going to say the same thing to you."

"I don't understand."

"I hear you've been spending time with Robert Collier. If you're . . . involved in some way."

"Involved with what?" Bet couldn't believe Eric thought she had anything to do with the murders, and had no idea how he knew about them. She'd only told him Emma died in an accident and asked if he recognized Seeley's photo. "Are *you* involved in some way?"

Eric sat back for a moment while the two glared at each other, neither wanting to give anything away. Finally, Eric put his hands up. "Wait a minute. Just, wait. Are we talking about the same thing?"

"Since I don't know what you're talking about, how can I answer that?"

"What do you know about the old mine?" Eric asked.

"Why did I find a flashlight with your bloody fingerprint on it in the tunnel?"

"My flashlight?" Eric's voice trailed off. "So that's what happened to it. I knew I dropped it somewhere."

"Want to explain what you were doing there?" Bet was surprised he was so quick to admit he'd left something at the scene of Emma's murder and the attempted murder of Seeley.

"Research."

"Research into what?" Bet's mind spun. Did Eric know about the gold? If he was involved in some way with the bodies down there, he wouldn't say research or admit so quickly he'd been there.

"How well do you know Robert Collier?" Eric asked.

"Junior or Senior?"

"Either."

"I don't know Senior at all. Junior, just a few days."

Eric struggled with himself, but talking to Bet finally won out. "I guess I should tell you what happened."

"That would be a very good idea."

"Relax, Bet. You look like you're ready to bolt out the door. I just want answers about my mother's death."

"*Your* mother?" Bet had not expected this turn in the conversation.

Eric leaned into her, dropping his voice. "I want to believe I can trust you. I want to believe you aren't in on this."

"What is the *this* you're referring to?"

"It's the water, Bet. The water in the lake killed my mom."

THIRTY-FOUR

Bet felt confident Seeley and Emma had gone into the mine on Friday and been shot the same day. Before Eric continued talking about the water, she had asked him when he found the cave entrance.

"Monday morning." Eric looked Bet in the eye, though that didn't prove he wasn't lying.

"Okay." Bet would ask Mrs. Villiard what day she'd first noticed Eric home. "Tell me more about your mother."

Eric described the progression of his mother's illness. Tracy Chandler had always been an introvert, but she became downright reclusive in the last years of her life. Though she continued to live in Collier, Bet only knew she'd deteriorated; she hadn't been privy to the specifics. Tracy began having neurological problems. The doctor diagnosed her with Parkinson's disease because she demonstrated the slowing of movements, lack of facial expressions, and dystonia that often accompanied Parkinson's.

"Dystonia," Eric explained, "is basically a sustained muscle cramp. They can show up in various places on the body, but for Mom it focused on her hands."

"But she didn't have Parkinson's?"

"Ultimately, no."

"Didn't they test her for it?"

"There is no test for Parkinson's. If it's suspected, the patient is given Parkinson's meds. If they improve, they're given a diagnosis; if they don't, the doctor figures it's something else."

"Doesn't sound very scientific."

Eric went on to explain that his mother hated her medications and refused to take them on a regular basis. Her doctor continued to believe it was a correct diagnosis and that her lack of consistent improvement stemmed from her own unwillingness to stick to her regimen of drugs.

Tracy had lived alone. She'd never dated anyone seriously after Michael left. She'd downplayed her illness to Eric and Dylan. No one had observed her worsening symptoms.

"By the time the illness infiltrated her liver, it was too late."

"What did she actually have?"

"Wilson's disease."

Bet gave Eric a blank look, which launched him into an explanation of the rare disorder. Wilson's disease had caused Tracy's body to store unwanted copper, impacting her liver and her brain. When her liver started to fail, her doctor found cirrhosis and believed her to be a drinker. Despite her protestations that she didn't drink, her doctor remained convinced she had Parkinson's and was a closet alcoholic.

"If she hadn't collapsed during a rare trip down to E'burg, I'm not sure I would have ever known the truth." Eric's voice caught as he held back tears.

An emergency room nurse had noticed the brown ring around the irises in Tracy's eyes, a distinctive characteristic of her disease, but by that time it was too late. She died from complete system failure.

"You must be furious at her doctor."

"I believe she didn't receive good care from him. But it wasn't solely his responsibility. Mom became difficult over the years. Even phone calls with her were problematic. I should have come out here and checked on her more, been more proactive in her care. Dylan, too; neither one of us visited much."

"You feel guilty about what happened to her? It's not your fault."

"I should have been paying attention."

Bet considered the responsibilities of children for their parents. She never delved into her own father's demons. She never felt she had the right.

Or maybe you just didn't want to know.

Bet shook off her father's voice and returned to Tracy's story.

"How did she get so much copper in her system?"

"That's what I wanted to know," Eric said. He went on to explain her diet couldn't be the culprit. "It's possible to live with Wilson's by cutting out any source of copper in your food. I know most of what Mom ate on a regular basis. She was allergic to nuts and seafood, didn't eat chocolate, and ate all her fruit fresh, so none of the usual culprits made sense."

"So if it wasn't her food . . ."

"She had to be getting it some other way."

"And you think it's in the water?"

"Groundwater. I think it's seeping into the water table from the old mine."

"So that's why you were in the tunnel? You're, what? Snooping around? Playing detective scientist?"

Eric dropped his gaze. "Yeah, I know, it's stupid. I'm not some Erin Brockovich, but I felt like I had to do something. My life fell apart; I thought I'd come out here and see what I could learn."

"Lots of people get divorced. You'll survive."

"It wasn't just that. My work, my future, everything feels like a bad fit right now. Like I have made a long series of bad choices. I hate living in Manhattan. I don't even know my own kids. I was denied tenure." He paused as if something might be even worse. "I can't write anymore." His voice became so quiet Bet could barely hear him.

"Did you contact anyone about your suspicions?" Bet asked, to keep Eric from talking further about his personal problems.

"I wrote to Collier. I thought he'd want to know if his mine was leaching toxins into the groundwater, but all I heard back was a vaguely threatening letter from his attorney."

"You mean Robert Senior, correct? Rob's father?" Eric nodded. "So you what? Moved across the country? To research your mother's death?"

"I thought a change of pace might get me writing again."

Why had she never wondered about the water in the lake?

She brought her attention back to Eric. "It never occurred to me your mother was poisoned. I'm so sorry."

"It's not your fault."

"Why not go public with what you believe? We should do a study if people are in danger."

"It's not as if people drop like flies from unexplained illness around here. Lakers are a hardy bunch. I don't think the copper is dangerous to anyone if they don't have a condition like Wilson's."

"But it might be why nothing lives in the lake."

Eric grimaced. "I didn't want to start a panic until I knew more."

Bet thought about how much that echoed her own position on Emma's death. She didn't want her investigation public until she had more answers. Her anxiety about Jamie Garcia writing about events was personal as well as professional. But she needed to keep Eric from poking around in the tunnels and didn't want to tell him the truth about the murders and someone stashing stolen property in the cave.

"How did you find the back entrance to the mine?" she asked, to give herself time to think.

"Sheer dumb luck," Eric said. "I was hiking on the back side of the mountain just trying to get a look around and found it. I went partway down, but my flashlight gave out. I was—well, to be honest, when my flashlight started to give out down there, I panicked. I ran out of the entrance so fast, I must have dropped the flashlight when it happened. I wasn't paying any attention to it at that point because it wasn't working. I didn't notice until later it wasn't in my pocket."

Something felt off about Eric's story.

"You did get lucky," Bet said. "That entrance is hard to find."

"It was near dusk. A bat came out of the bushes. I knew there had to be some kind of opening." Eric leaned back against the wall again, shadows obscuring his features.

"Why didn't you come to me sooner?"

"If you recall, I've been trying to talk to you since I returned."

"You said you wanted to catch up. You didn't say you thought your mother died from toxic groundwater."

Eric squirmed, bringing his face into the light again, and she could see his cheeks flush pink. "When I first arrived, I wanted to come to you, but then I heard about you hanging out with Rob Collier at the tavern and I wondered if you were the right person to talk to. It was already going to be hard enough."

Bet sighed. She hadn't made it any easier for Eric to come to her. She could hardly blame him for his suspicions. After all, she considered him a suspect in the murder of Emma Hunter.

"Wasn't the bat gate locked when you found the tunnel?"

"No. Someone had sawn through it already."

Eric sat looking at Bet, the wide-eyed boy from his youth appearing briefly on his adult face. Bet wanted to believe him. She wanted to believe he wasn't lying to her face, convincing her he hadn't done anything wrong, again.

Bet set her glass back down on the table. She told Eric in no uncertain terms to stay away from the tunnel. He told her he'd have test results on the water soon; a friend of his who worked in a lab back east was doing it for him.

"The bat gate is locked now, so just keep away from that area, okay? It's Collier's land, and you're trespassing to be there."

Eric promised to stay away.

Bet picked up her beer glass and finished her final sip.

"Pour you another?" Eric said, his voice hopeful. "We could talk about other things for a while. Not just business and my mother's death."

"No, I better get home. I have a full plate right now, Eric. But it's been nice to see you."

"I hope you mean that," he said, as his smile reached his eyes.

"I do. But now I need to go."

"I'll walk you out."

The two stepped out into the soft air of the summer night. Eric stepped closer, as if he might hug her or kiss her good-night, but Bet stuck her hand out, stopping his forward momentum.

"See you," she said.

He shook her hand, and Bet headed home for the night. It was only when she reached her front door that she remembered she should have asked Eric how he'd cut himself, leaving blood on the flashlight. Opening her door, she went in to find Schweitzer waiting and, for the first time in her life, locked the door behind her.

THIRTY-FIVE

Bet wandered through the empty rooms of her house and thought about history. Rob and all the Colliers, Eric and the rest of the Chandlers, the Riverses. Generations entwined in the story she'd started to unravel. Eric had said they used to all be friends. And then there was her mother. Bet's mind balked at the idea of her mother sexually involved with another man.

Had all the adults in her life been adulterous? Her mother and Robert Senior? Lillian Collier and Michael Chandler? She couldn't remember anything to lead her to believe her parents had been close to Robert Collier. Had her mother's infidelity gone on longer than even Eric knew about? Was that why Lillian turned to Michael?

Though Lillian's body in the lake could point to something else. Had Michael killed her because she planned to go back to Robert Collier? Or had Robert Collier killed her because she stayed with Michael? What brought her back to town?

Bet's cell phone rang, shattering her reverie, and she pulled it out to see Rob's number. Answering the phone, she realized it wasn't just a break from thinking about the past that she looked forward to.

"I thought I'd check in," Rob said.

"All is quiet on the western front." Bet debated what to tell him regarding Eric's speculations that copper seeped into the water supply from the mine. He'd just learned his estranged mother had been dead for years. He didn't really deserve another blow tonight.

"Nothing new?"

When Bet didn't respond immediately, Rob filled the silence. "What? What is it?"

"Something I learned about the lake—or the groundwater, anyway."

"Are you all right?"

Bet didn't know how to respond. It was, after all, his family's mine.

"I can come over," Rob said, after another moment of silence from Bet. "If you want to talk it through."

"Do you know where I live?"

Rob arrived on her doorstep twenty minutes later. He carried a bottle of single-malt scotch and a brown paper bag that smelled a lot like short ribs from the tavern.

"I don't know if you want a drink, but I could use one," he said, following Bet into the living room. Bet gestured to the sofa while she went into the kitchen and came back with two glasses.

"I've never had the good stuff," Bet commented as she watched him splash the amber liquid into the glass.

Handing one to her, he raised his in a toast.

"What should we drink to?" Bet asked.

"To good dogs and the people who love them," he said, as Schweitzer plopped down on the floor, stretched between Rob on the sofa and Bet in the chair.

"To good dogs," Bet echoed. She sipped the liquid and felt it slide down her throat, none of the usual burn from drinking hard liquor straight.

Glad she'd drunk little of the beer with Eric, Bet decided she could get used to expensive scotch.

"I wasn't sure if you were hungry or not, but I thought you might have skipped dinner."

Rob pulled out takeout boxes of short ribs, coleslaw, baked beans, and corn bread while Bet went to the kitchen for a roll of paper towels.

"I guess we could sit at the dining room table like civilized people," Bet said. "I do own real plates and silverware."

"Then we'd just have to wash them. This works fine." He finished laying the meal out on the coffee table, and the two dug into the food. Schweitzer stayed sprawled out on the floor, but Bet could tell his eyes never wavered from the bones piling up.

"What's on your mind, Elizabeth?"

She started with the story of Eric's mother.

"Our mine might have caused her death?" Rob said after Bet finished, his face tight and drawn. "This just keeps getting better, doesn't it?"

"It's not your fault, even if it's true."

"It may not be my fault, but it is my responsibility."

Bet couldn't argue with that; someone had to be accountable. She thought for a moment about her own father and the dead man he'd never been able to identify, about her questions surrounding her father's death. The guilt of things that weren't a person's doing but remained a person's to keep.

"There's more."

Rob looked at Bet with trepidation. "Go on," he said.

Bet went on to recount Eric's story about Bet's mother having an affair.

"I think it might have been with your dad," she finished up, uncomfortable in meeting Rob's gaze. "Maybe that's part of why Lillian did what she did. We don't know which affair happened first. Or if Lillian even had an affair with Michael. We don't know for a fact that's true, right?"

Rob stood and paced the room. Bet could see the agitation in his actions.

"I remember your mother," Rob said.

"You do?"

"You look like her."

Bet could hear Eric's voice saying the same thing.

"It's the hair." Rob sat down and brushed Bet's hair back, catching a curl on his finger. It was so different than the gesture Eric had made at the bar. Eric stretched her curls out, bending her hair to his whim. Rob coiled her hair around his finger as if to catch himself in her, not the other way around. His hand rested on her cheek. It was an intimate gesture, not something she'd expected.

"What do you think?" she asked, barely breathing.

"Anything is possible." Rob released Bet's hair and started to pick up the dirty paper plates and empty takeout boxes.

He stuffed the paper sack with the debris and stood. "I'd best get home." He started for the door.

Bet wondered at his abrupt departure. "Is there something else you're not telling me?"

Rob turned to look at her, weighing his thoughts before he spoke. "We'll talk more tomorrow. I need to sort out a few things on my own."

"If any of this relates to the case at hand—"

"Don't worry, Elizabeth." Rob clapped his hat back on his head, plunging his features into shadow. "I'll tell you everything I think you need to know."

With a last pat for Schweitzer, Rob went out the front door, taking his secrets with him.

THIRTY-SIX

Early the next morning, before sunlight crept over the mountain peaks to light the dark water, Bet headed to Peter's campsite. She knew Peter wouldn't start work with the lake still in shadow. She drove out the main road without passing a single car. Things were definitely quiet now that summer was over and the tourists were gone. The surface of the lake was smooth, the air still.

If Peter felt surprise at seeing the sheriff appear on his doorstep first thing in the morning, he didn't let it show.

"Coffee?" he asked. "I was just making myself a cup."

"Sounds good." Bet headed over to one of the chairs to wait for him.

"I have some questions about the water in the lake," Bet said, after he came out with two cups of the strong brew.

"What do you mean, the water in the lake?"

"What could be in the water that would prevent any life from growing?"

"What brings this up?" Peter shifted in his chair.

"Curiosity." Bet watched Peter closely.

He sipped at his coffee, taking extra time to blow on the surface as if it was far too hot to drink, though Bet found the temperature perfect. People often took too long to answer questions if they were making up a lie.

"Could be a lot of things."

"Hazard a few guesses."

"What is it you know? About why I'm here?"

"Is it about Tracy Chandler?"

An expression that looked like pain shot across Peter's features. "That's her name? Tracy?"

"It was."

"This Tracy Chandler. Someone claimed she died from copper poisoning?"

"Her son. She had Wilson's disease."

Peter looked as if he'd been slapped. "I didn't think about that."

Bet waited for the scientist to explain himself. She knew when a man had had enough of hiding the truth.

"Robert Collier hired me to look into the water here, into what might be in the lake."

"Senior," Bet clarified.

"Senior."

"It's the mine, isn't it?"

Peter looked uneasy, but this time he used silence as an answer.

"It's leaching heavy metals into the water." Bet thought out loud. "Or some other chemical compounds."

"You were right the first time," Peter said. "Copper, mercury, a few other metals."

"Why would that kill the lake?"

"Heavy metals attack living organisms."

"Why aren't more of us sick?"

"Polluted groundwater is a very complicated process." Even now, Peter sounded like a college professor. "The water table is fluid. Just because one area is polluted doesn't mean another area will be. Runoff from the glaciers also provides water around here; your wells are fed by a lot more than just the lake. The fact there was only one isolated death made me think there couldn't be serious contamination out here. I didn't think about Wilson's. Tracy couldn't handle copper levels that wouldn't bother the rest of you."

"So Senior wanted you to find out if he's liable? Were you supposed to cover it up for him? How did he even know there was something to investigate?"

"Someone contacted him, probably the son you mentioned. But I think he always thought about it. Apparently he has other closed mines that have caused problems around the state; this one was in the back of his mind."

Bet wondered what Rob already knew. He could be in touch with his father more than he let on.

"I'm a scientist first." Peter defended himself. "I jumped at the opportunity to investigate the lake. Collier agreed I could do my own research while I tested for his contamination and tried to isolate where the seepage might be taking place."

"But he paid you well."

"I didn't agree to cover anything up." Peter tried to climb out of the situation. "And researching glaciers and glacial lakes are important aspects of studying climate change." His words appeared to ring hollow even to his own ears.

"But you didn't plan on making your findings public, did you, no matter what health hazards might be posed for the rest of us living here?"

Peter fell silent.

"You've racked up a lot of debt over the last couple years."

For the first time, Bet saw anger on Peter's features. "You looked into my financial situation?"

"You were a person of interest in a homicide as soon as you found the body. Of course I did."

"I haven't broken any laws."

"But Senior knew about your debt, right?"

Peter shrugged. "He hinted at it. I didn't want to find out what he knew or how; it just felt like a way out."

Bet handed her mug over and thanked Peter for the coffee. She walked over to her SUV, where Schweitzer waited patiently in the back.

"You knew this Tracy?" Peter asked Bet's retreating back.

"I spent a lot of time with her when I was a kid. After my mother died." She could see her comment had hit home. "Please

don't leave town anytime soon without telling me, Professor
Malone. We both know I can find you if I need to."

"I haven't done anything wrong." Peter's voice held a pleading
note. "And I helped you pull that corpse out without broadcasting
what I was doing. That ought to count for something."

"I appreciate your help on that." Bet meant what she said. "As
for the rest, we'll just have to see how it all plays out."

———

Alma was still putting together all the stolen-item reports from
over the years and the office was quiet, so Bet headed out to the
cave. Now familiar with the journey, she traded her duty belt for
her bulletproof vest. The external vest provided pockets for her
handcuffs and extra magazines and was a lot more comfortable
for the ride on the ATV. She wore her Glock in a holster on her
belt along with her flashlight and brought a backpack with crime
scene investigation materials.

After stashing the ATV in the woods, she waited for Dale to
appear. He came out of the trees crunching on a carrot stick.

"I'm going back down," Bet said. "We've given him time
to reappear; I'm not sure it's going to happen. Unless we make
everything public and announce we're done investigating, I have
to start working another angle." She wanted to be able to tell
Jamie Garcia that she honestly had a solid lead. "With Todd tied
up other places, I'm going to start fingerprinting down there."

"Want company?" Dale asked.

"I'm okay solo. Stay up here and keep watch. When I come
back up, we'll lock up the gate and pack in the surveillance until
we do the public announcement."

"Whatever you think . . . boss." Dale smoothed his hair and
moved to step back into the woods.

Bet decided to take a chance. "There's something I want to
talk to you about."

Dale turned around, his eyes veiled.

"Stop leaving notes."

"What notes?"

Bet kept eye contact with him, and he did his best to stare her down. But unlike Alma, she didn't give in. He finally dropped his gaze.

"I'm not going anywhere, Dale. I'm going to win this election and stay sheriff of Collier. If you want to remain my deputy, you better rethink your attitude and your messages."

Bet turned back toward the tunnel, wondering if she had just made a tactical error leaving her safety in Dale's hands. His voice stopped her.

"How'd you know it was me?"

She faced him again. "The fact you're asking that question just shows I'm the right person for the job." She wasn't going to admit it had just been a stab in the dark. "Did you really think a few notes would scare me off?"

Dale's expression turned sheepish. "To be honest, I didn't think your heart was in it to begin with. I thought if you believed you didn't have the community's support, you'd throw in the towel and go back to LA. You've had one foot out the door since you arrived."

Bet wished she could argue, but he was right. She thought she'd hidden her feelings better. "If you told me that a month ago, I might have agreed with you. But things have changed. I've changed. But since we're laying our cards on the table, let me tell you what I see." Bet knew trepidation when she saw it. "You aren't ready to be sheriff if you're compromising your integrity to advance your own position."

Dale looked ashamed. "So what now?" he asked. "If you win, I lose my job?"

"Starting now. Clean slate. We let the voters decide. What do you say?"

"And may the best man win?" Dale chuckled as she shot him a look. "Best . . . candidate."

"Fair enough." Bet laughed as she walked into the cave. Maybe she and Dale could find a way to work together, no matter the outcome of the election.

Bet started down into the cave by herself. Schweitzer would have been welcome company, but Bet didn't want him transferring hair to the hidden items. She'd left him safely tucked in under Alma's desk back at the station, being fed all manner of baked goods.

Once she arrived outside the room with the objects piled up inside, Bet went directly to the generator. The first thing she did was pull rubber gloves out from her backpack and fingerprint the machine. When she finished that, she started it up, bringing the lights in the cave on, throwing everything into sharp relief.

Bet walked into the tunnel, stepping over the black lines of cables crossing the floor to the various lights mounted on the stone walls, and moved into the room with all the stolen items.

Next, she pulled a clipboard out of her backpack and began making a list of what she found. Leaving her backpack near the door, she set her bulletproof vest next to it and started counting the number of niches chipped into the walls. There were thirty-two.

While she worked, she allowed her mind to consider the two cases, the old and the new. There didn't appear to be any way the bodies of the two women found in the lake weren't connected, even with almost twenty years between them. The fact that both women had been wrapped in similar material and tied with similar knots was enough to connect them.

Thinking about the fabric, Bet took a closer look at the heavy canvas covering the piles of stuff in the middle of the room. It looked exactly like the material the two women had been wrapped in. Bet cut a sample off and placed it in an evidence bag to take to the lab.

Returning to the niches, Bet let her subconscious continue to puzzle over events. She took pictures of the items inside each niche and made notes on her clipboard. She began to see the organization to everything piled in the room. There was a clear walkway around the outside, allowing her to stand in front of each niche. Larger things were piled in the center of the room and could be reached from a trail through the middle.

Rob Collier's face arrived in her mind as she moved from niche to niche. She didn't believe he'd killed his own mother; his reaction to her had felt too real. But that didn't mean he wasn't involved in the other shootings.

He certainly acted strange last night.

Bet walked to another niche and started taking pictures again. The next niche held a child's tea set. Tiny pink flowers on bone-white china.

Collier Senior? Bet's mind continued to sift through the possibilities. He was a likely suspect for the first murder, but unlikely for the second. Alma had researched Senior's whereabouts, and as far as she could discover, he lived in Ho Chi Minh City, as Saigon had been renamed after the war.

"I'd forgotten he had business interests over there," Alma had said when she confirmed Rob's story. "He married a Vietnamese woman and settled down with a new family."

Bet wondered why Rob hadn't mentioned that. Surely he knew about it. How estranged were they?

Senior had worn a beard at the time of Lillian's death. Beards had been in style; almost every man she knew grew one back then, even her father. Rob had one as a high school student too, his more successful than Eric's.

Stepping up to the next niche, Bet looked in and felt her stomach heave. Reaching in, she gently pulled out two hunks of hair, one blond, one dark.

That answers whether or not they're connected.

Sociopaths can also be hoarders.

Bet put the hair back into the niche, snapped a few shots, and turned to look across the strange collection of stuff piled in the middle of the room. An old wooden crate stood off to one side.

Bet could see partial words stenciled on it in black: *ER MIN.*
Collier Mine. Bet wandered over to look inside.

For a moment, Bet's mind didn't compute the cylindrical
shapes lying in neat rows, the lengths of twine attached to each
one.

That would be dynamite, Bet.

I can see that, Dad.

Don't touch that box. Old dynamite can be very unstable.

Wasn't planning on it.

Bet's mind returned to the smooth round holes she and Dale
had found in the walls of the cave. Maybe they weren't left over
from the miners' days. Maybe whoever hid out down here wanted
to be able to blow the place.

Just then, the generator stumbled; the lights flickered, plunging Bet into darkness.

Bet waited.

The generator caught and the lights returned. Even with a
flashlight on her belt, Bet didn't like the idea of the lights going
out. In that half second of darkness, she became aware of the
sheer weight of earth above her and how alone she really was.
She walked out of the stone room and over to the generator to
recheck the fuel level. Once she verified that wasn't the problem,
she moved on to inspect the connections between the generator
and the cables.

Electricity arced between the back of the generator and one of
the cords running to the work lights. The intensity of the shock
caused Bet to stumble and fall to the ground. The sound of a shot
rang out, echoing loudly in the cavern.

Bet continued to roll away, going for her own gun. Another
shot pinged off the rock near where she'd stood a moment before.
She lunged to her right to get behind a set of limestone columns.
She wanted to douse the work lights rigged to the generator, but
she couldn't risk being out in the open. She breathed slowly to
calm her pounding heart.

Where was the shooter now? And how had he gotten past Dale?

Unless Dale . . . her mind refused to think he would shoot at her. She could picture him leaving notes and sending a text to try to shake her confidence, but that was a far cry from trying to kill her.

From her estimate, the shooter must be behind a clump of stalagmites forty feet away. She heard nothing except the hum of the generator and the faint rush of water in the background.

Something flashed between two of the stalagmites. The shooter was on the move. Bet tensed, ready to edge around the column she stood behind, wondering where the shooter would appear next.

Another shot pierced the air, turning a chunk of stalagmite to dust near Bet's head. She saw the sweep of an arm as she ducked around another column and returned fire.

Since the shooter knew where she was, Bet decided trying to talk couldn't hurt. Maybe she could learn something to help herself.

"Not nice to shoot at a person," she called out.

Laughter floated from behind the stalagmites.

"Funny, Sheriff Rivers." The voice sounded strange, almost muffled.

"How do you know my name?" Bet hoped she would recognize the shooter if she kept them talking.

The voice came again. "I've kept my eye on you over the years." Bet sensed she should know who it was.

"To what do I owe that pleasure?"

"Your father would have wanted me to."

"I don't think Earle would like you shooting at me."

"Probably not, but then, your father isn't around to save you, is he? He's not around to save anyone."

The voice was nasal, like someone with a cold.

"Do you know something about my father's death?" Bet wasn't sure what made her ask the question. It was hardly the time or place to get into her family history, but curiosity always did get the best of her.

"I heard he took a very nasty fall."

"What would you know about it?"

"I know all kinds of things, Lizzie."

The sound of the endearment brought Bet up short. There was only one person who had ever called her that. Michael Chandler. Had he hid out all these years, coming in and out of Collier unseen? Had he killed Lillian? And now Emma?

Maybe Lillian decided to reconcile with Robert's father and Michael followed her and killed her here. It would explain why she died years after she first left town.

"Where's Lillian?" Bet asked.

"Clever, Lizzie. You've figured out who I am?"

"The *Lizzie* gave you away, Michael," she said.

The man paused for a moment. Sorry he slipped up?

"We're at a bit of a stalemate, aren't we?" Bet asked.

"Why's that?"

"We're both good shots and there's nowhere to run."

"I guess we learn which one of us is better." He leapt from behind the stalagmites and shot off a few rounds. Bet had anticipated his move and dropped down to the base of the column, firing her own shots in his direction.

The bullets cascaded shards of rocks down on Bet's head, while hers went too far to the left to catch him before he dove behind a new set of stalagmites, bringing himself closer to Bet.

She'd said there was nowhere to run, but the reality was *she* had nowhere to run. Michael's back was to the rest of the cave and the paths to daylight, while she stood with her back to the wall.

If you think you have a way out, take it. There's nothing worse than being paralyzed by fear. If you're going to go out, at least go out moving.

"I hope you're right, Dad," she said under her breath, just before she made a break for another series of limestone shapes. The ground dropped off not far from her and she flung herself across the lip with the hope it wasn't too far to fall. Bullets flew over her; one ricocheted off a rock formation and winged her arm before she managed to clear the edge.

Landing heavily on her right shoulder, Bet moved sideways as fast as she could in case Michael followed her. She plummeted a few feet, breath knocked out of her as she landed, but the wall she rolled off protected her.

"I think that last one drew blood," he said.

"Nope, I'm just fine."

Dodging behind another set of rocks, Bet assessed the damage to her arm as fast as she could. It didn't appear to be a deep wound—the ricochet had minimized the bullet's velocity—but it bled more than she liked. Tearing a strip off her shirttail, Bet set her gun down for a few terrifying moments while she tied up her arm. Once she assured herself she wasn't going to bleed to death, she leaned against the rock and listened for sounds from above.

Something bad had happened to Dale. That much Bet could guess. The two of them weren't due to check in with anyone else for a few hours. There was no way she could hold off someone this aggressive for very long. Bet had to save herself. She went for her extra ammunition, then realized her extra mags were in her vest, which sat back in the room full of junk.

"My deputy is coming down here soon," Bet called out, trying to track the shooter by the sound of his voice.

"I don't think so, Lizzie."

Bet's heart sank at his words. The thought of what Michael might have done to Dale cut her to the bone.

"Not Dale, Clayton." Bet kept her voice steady.

"No he's not. We both know you're understaffed. I'm sure Clayton is tucked into his bed right now and not coming on duty for hours."

"You going to shoot me in the back? That is what you like to do, isn't it?"

Michael laughed again.

"Do you really think killing two law enforcement officers is going to help your situation? You'll have everyone in the state looking for you." Bet looked around while she spoke, hoping to find another way around him. All she found were more dead ends.

"I'll be long gone before they find you. If they ever do." He started to sing a few bars of "Oh, Canada."

"Getting out of the country?"

"New identity. New country. I'm not afraid to start over. I've been a ghost for a very long time. Besides, with you dead, how will anyone ever know I was here?"

True.

Bet decided she couldn't stay where she was and made her way along the edge of the drop-off, crouched down out of his line of sight. She reached a rock formation at the end and peered around the edge. Something moved near another set of columns. It was difficult to see; the farther she moved from the work lights, the darker the cave. But she thought she might have a chance to make it around if she set up a volley of shots while running across a relatively flat section of the cave floor. If she could get to the stalagmites where Michael stood when he'd first shot at her, there was a chance she could outrun him to the surface.

One, two, three . . . go!

She launched herself out from behind the rocks, sprinting as fast as she could across the expanse, spraying the area with bullets where she thought he stood.

And it might have worked, but just past the point of no return she realized her mistake.

THIRTY-SEVEN

A piece of fabric had snagged on one of the columns and was backlit by the work lights. The air movement in the cave had made it flutter, so she believed she knew where he stood. Now she was lit up, making her an easy target. She did the only thing she could think of to even the playing field. She shot at the generator and the cave went black.

"Clever, Lizzie," the voice called out to her. His voice echoed through the cavern, even more terrifying as it came from all around her in the darkness. With the noise from the generator gone, only the sound of the river broke the oppressive silence.

Bet came to an abrupt halt and looked carefully for the first of the glow-in-the-dark arrows. She hoped desperately he wouldn't realize she knew about them and that he charged them when he arrived. Spotting the first arrow, Bet slowed her breathing and crept toward the entrance to the tunnel.

Inch by painful inch, Bet moved across the pitch-dark expanse of the cavern floor. With her hands out in front of her, fearful of running into a column or tripping on the uneven ground, she moved toward the arrow.

"Don't you want to talk a little more about your dad?" The voice came from Bet's left. She didn't take the bait.

Continuing her glacially slow progress, she spotted the second of the arrows and corrected her course. In front of her, she heard a click and the room around her filled with light as a flashlight turned in her direction. Michael had shifted around between her and the arrows, guessing where she planned to go.

"Following my little arrows?"

Bet fired toward the flashlight, but missed her target. The slide on the Glock locked open.

Now she was in the open and out of ammo. Bet launched herself in the direction of the river. She didn't know what to do if she reached it, but for now it was the only direction to run.

Bullets whizzed past her. Caught in the beam of Michael's flashlight, Bet let her forward momentum carry her up to her knees in the cold, rushing water.

"It doesn't have to be this way, Lizzie. Maybe we can work something out."

Not relishing a gunshot in the back, Bet stopped and turned around. The man stepped out from behind the rocks. Raising her flashlight, she saw a grotesque figure emerge from the darkness. At first Bet thought she faced a monster, one of George's ghosts made real, but the man wore a breathing apparatus used for working in a mine. It covered the lower half of his face. He also wore a hat pulled low, and his eyes were shadowed. His body looked bulky, as if he wore multiple layers, obscuring his body type. Was this really Michael Chandler standing in front of her?

"Water getting cold?" The mask over Michael's face muffled his words. It explained the sound of his voice, which turned coaxing. "You can come out if you want. I'm not going to kill you. I just want to know what you know."

"Worried my corpse will float downstream and end up in the lake like Emma Hunter?"

That was a guess on Bet's part, but it could be how Emma had ended up on the surface. Or there could be another river into the lake and this river remained underground.

"Who's Emma Hunter?"

Bet tried another tack. "Dad wouldn't like his old friend Michael Chandler killing his only child."

"Your father saved my life once, did you know that? He was a hero. The genuine article."

"Doesn't that count for something?"

Bet waited, but the gun remained trained on her, steady in Michael's hand.

"Funny thing about combat," he said. "It does different things to different people. It made Earle despondent. It just made it hard for me to come back home. It made me abandon my son. I couldn't pick up where I left off like Earle did with you."

The water numbed her above the knees. Slowly Bet stepped backward, farther into the water. It beat against her, the current strong enough to make it difficult to stand. The cold contrasted with the fire she felt in her arm from the bullet wound. She gritted her teeth against the pain and stepped backward again.

"I wouldn't go any farther if I were you," Michael said. "I'm a good enough shot to put a bullet between your eyes from here."

Bet's mind returned to the memory of him standing in the Clark Fork River in Idaho, pointing out the beauty of the fish, how some things shouldn't die. Was this really the same man?

Shoving the memory aside, she focused on her current predicament. She knew she wouldn't make it out of the water to the other side without getting shot in the back. If she stayed in the water any longer, hypothermia would kill her where she stood. Getting out of the water on Michael's side just made his job of killing her easier.

"Come on out of the water, Lizzie," he said, lowering his gun. "We can—"

Taking a deep breath, Bet fell backward. The current took her immediately, and when she surfaced again, the last thing she heard before the river sucked her into the side of the mountain was the sound of his voice shouting behind her.

Then everything went black.

She dropped her service weapon. Her father was right; out of ammunition, it was just a chunk of metal heavy in her hand. She hung on to her flashlight, though, and, after surging into the hole in the rock wall held it above her, out of the water. The ceiling of rock sat only a few inches over her head, but it left enough room to breathe. When she turned on the light, the smooth stone flashed by above her.

The cold enveloped her completely, and sodden clothing began to pull her down, boots like leaden weights on her feet. She'd started to think she would die from the cold when she streaked into another cavern. Pulling herself from the water, she removed her boots, belt, and holster, then stripped down to her underwear. At this point, no clothes beat a waterlogged uniform.

The wound on her arm continued to seep through her make-shift bandage, but the cold brought it mostly to a stop. Bet didn't think the wound too serious, especially compared to being stuck in a cavern, wet and cold, with no way to get back to the surface.

Bet shined her flashlight around, thankful it still worked despite the dousing. The space was hardly bigger than her bedroom, but the walls glittered. She looked closer at the granite walls and saw what looked to be veins of gold coursing around her.

"Gold won't help me now," she said through chattering teeth.

A quick inspection showed no exits other than how she'd come in and the tunnel in front of her. She knelt down, wrapping her arms around her legs to try to generate some warmth. She was probably not going to live through this. She couldn't wait and go back up the channel she'd come through. Even if she was strong enough to swim back up against the current and wasn't felled by hypothermia and shock, Michael might still be in the cave waiting to put a bullet in her head.

The only other option was forward. She guessed the river came out in the lake; the question was, how deep? How long was the tunnel into the lake? And if she did make it into the lake, how far would it be to the surface? Twenty feet or three hundred? Bet thought about other options, but nothing better came to mind.

I'd rather die in the water on the move than sitting here waiting for help that will never come.

That's my girl.

Bet wondered if that would be the last thing she'd ever imagine her father to say.

Before she could dwell on it too much, she removed her underwear and slid back into the water. She didn't want the clothing to catch a snag on the rocky surface. Better to swim the River Styx naked, going out of the world the same way she'd come in.

Bet hyperventilated while she still had air to breathe. Free divers used the technique to stay under longer, and any edge it might give her seemed worth the risk. She held on to her flashlight as long as she could, but the time finally came when there would be no air above her. She took one last deep breath and dropped the light. Blackness engulfed her as the current sped her on.

THIRTY-EIGHT

Time slowed, but Bet guessed it was less than a minute later when she felt a shift in the water pressure as she raced through the underground rift and shot into the lake. Pulling as hard as she could for the surface, the light of day shined above her. She breached the surface, gasping air into her lungs. Her frozen limbs refused to cooperate and she started to sink.

As Bet struggled to rise back to the surface, a dark shape moved in above her. With her last burst of energy she broke the surface again.

"Grab this." Peter reached his oar out to her. She grabbed for it blindly and managed to latch on before she sunk. She held tight, choking as lake water spilled into her mouth. Peter pulled her over to the side of the boat.

"You can do it." He helped her struggle into his canoe. She climbed over the edge and ended in a heap next to Peter's video monitor. The air was warm and the sun was hot, and Bet started to laugh and cough simultaneously.

"What just happened?"

"I'll explain." She panted her answer. "Can we just . . . head for shore?" Bet continued to gulp air into her tortured lungs.

"You just came through that underground fissure, didn't you?" Peter's voice carried his disbelief as he reeled in his camera as fast as it would go. "Holy moly, I didn't think that was possible. I can't believe you didn't drown. What was it like? What did you see?"

"I'm lucky you were here. I don't think I could have made the swim to shore." Bet managed to get out the words over her chattering teeth.

"I was over here because of the currents I found about forty feet down. I thought this might be an access from an underground river like you asked about. I couldn't believe it when I saw you, shooting out of the granite wall."

Bet put her hand on the wound on her arm. "That's not all. I've been shot too, and electrocuted."

"Crap. Should I tend to that?"

"Just get us to shore. Do you have your cell phone out here? I need to find Dale. I need to get back down in that cave."

"Here's my cell." Peter brought the camera onboard and tossed her the phone. "I'll get you to dry land as fast as I can." He leaned back to row.

"Hey, Peter, one more thing?"

"Anything, Sheriff. Anything."

"Can I have your shirt?"

Peter turned bright red, as if he hadn't noticed she was naked. He took his shirt off and handed it to her. She knew that if she weren't so thrilled to be alive, this would be a lot more embarrassing.

"At least you're finally calling me Peter."

Once back on dry land, Peter ran to his trailer to get Bet a towel and a dry pair of sweats. He also came back with a roll of duct tape.

He inspected Bet's arm. "I'm not sure if this will work."

"Perfect." The two of them set about wrapping up her wound.

"What else can I do?" Peter's Adam's apple bobbed up and down like a cork. "How can I help?"

"What do you have for shoes?"

Peter raced back into his trailer and came back with a pair of ancient running shoes and two thick pairs of socks. "These aren't much to look at, but—"

"Good enough. I need to borrow your Suburban and take your cell phone with me. I promise you'll get them back."

"Anything, anything." He darted off again to get his keys and the cord for his cell phone. "Just in case you need to charge it." He showed her the code to access the phone. "Should I come with you?"

"No. Stay here. I'll bring these back to you as soon as I can."

Bet climbed up into the big truck, her feet awkward in his shoes. Even with two pairs of socks on, they were way too long. Peter made sure the cell was hooked up to the Bluetooth so she could begin making calls as she started off toward Rob's house.

Struggling with the unfamiliar phone, she managed to call Clayton, glad she knew his number by heart, but it went to voice mail. She left an urgent message that Dale might be injured at the cave.

She called Randall Vogel, asking him to fly back over to the clearing where they'd picked up Seeley Lander.

"Sure thing, Rivers," Vogel said into the phone. "Penny and Paul are with me now. We'll hover until we see you."

Bet managed one more phone call as she turned onto Rob's private road. She told Alma to get an all-points bulletin out on Michael Chandler.

"Michael Chandler!" Alma's voice cracked in surprise. "What makes you think it's him? He hasn't been back here in—"

Bet cut Alma off, saying she'd explain it all later. Alma promised to dig up an old photo of the man and send it out to law enforcement agencies and the border crossings into Canada.

The Collier house perched dark and quiet. Rob's Bronco sat in the garage, but Figure was nowhere to be seen. She left a note on his door and started to jog up the well-worn track to the tunnel, praying she'd find Dale alive.

When Bet saw Dale's still body lying in the woods, she felt rage come over her. Sad as young Emma Hunter's death had been, Dale's would be personal. No matter what their current situation, Dale was one of hers. She wanted the opportunity to set things right between them.

She rushed to where he lay, facedown in the leaves. She knelt beside him, shaking with anger.

Then he moved.

When she put her fingers on his pulse, it was faint, but there. Turning him over, she ripped his shirt open to reveal bullets buried in his vest. One had missed the vest and dug itself through his armpit at an angle. It could have gone into his lung. The ground was soaked with blood. She rolled him injury side down to help gravity keep his lung from collapsing. He groaned. A gash on his forehead showed where he'd hit a rock when he fell.

The shooter had made a mistake. He'd mistaken Dale's unconscious state for death.

Bet looked around. The Vogels should be arriving in the helicopter soon. She hated being a sitting duck if Michael came out of the cave or hadn't left the area.

Rob Collier chose that moment to arrive on the scene.

"I read your message. What the hell happened?" He swung down off Figure. "I must have just missed you at the house . . ." His voice trailed off as he caught sight of Dale.

"He's alive, but I have no idea if the shooter is down in the cave still or on the run. I need your help with Dale—"

The sound of Vogel's rotors cut off her words. Rob pulled Figure into the trees, then moved over to help Dale while Bet waved her arms to get the Vogels' attention. She signaled for Penny to drop the litter.

Bet and Rob situated Dale onto the rescue litter, then looked on as Paul and Penny pulled Dale into the helicopter. Paul gave a thumbs-up signal, and Bet watched as the giant bird flew away.

As the sound of the helicopter faded, Rob eyed her appearance. "What happened to you? Were you here when Dale was shot?"

"No. Well, yes, but I was down in the cave. It's a long story and I don't have time to explain, but our shooter might still be down there."

"You saw him?"

"I fought with him," Bet said, pulling her sleeve up to show the duct tape wrapped around her arm. "He winged me."

"You've been shot!"

"I'll live. First things first, I have to go back down in that cave and find out if Chandler's still down there."

"Chandler? As in Eric?"

"As in Michael. He won't expect me to reappear. He's going to assume I drowned."

Rob stopped himself from asking any more questions. "What's the plan, Elizabeth?"

Bet had removed Dale's duty belt before they loaded him onto the litter. Now she strapped his service weapon around her waist, made sure his gun was loaded, and pulled out his flashlight.

"I'm going back into the cave. It would be great if you could stay here until I get back out safe or my deputy Clayton arrives. You can fill him in."

Rob started to argue, but Bet cut him off. "Will you do it or not?"

He agreed, and Bet went into the cave.

She'd barely reached the top of the stairs when a tremendous boom shattered the quiet. The earth shook. Clouds of dust rolled up the tunnel as the concussive force knocked Bet off her feet.

The shaking finally stopped, but the air remained thick with dust. Rob called her name as he navigated the rocks strewn across the tunnel floor to reach her.

"Are you all right?" Rob asked, kneeling down at her side..

"What just happened?"

He helped her stand. "From outside, it sounded like an explosion in the cave."

"The dynamite," Bet said, remembering the crate she'd seen.

"Dynamite?"

Bet explained about the crate she'd found in the cave. "There were holes marked with glow-in-the-dark paint. I think Michael rigged it to blow the place if he was ever discovered."

"Was there a timer or anything else in the box?"

"Not that I saw, but I didn't look too close."

"How would he get out in time if there wasn't a timer?" A few more chunks fell from the ceiling. The tunnel was filled

with piles of rock. "We'd better get out of here," Rob said. "This whole place could collapse."

Bet felt the adrenaline wearing off and shock setting in. Her arm burned and her head felt light. The two stood and made for the mouth of the cave. Bet stumbled out into the sunlight and almost dropped to her knees.

Rob caught her before she fell. "Whoa there, Elizabeth. You better let me look at that arm. You may have lost more blood than you realize."

"We have to check and see if the dirt bike is parked at the lean-to."

"Let's get you up on Figure first."

Half carrying her over to the horse, Rob helped her onto the steady mount before climbing into the saddle himself. The three of them walked through the trees to the small shed. A moment later, they could see the dirt bike parked inside the structure.

"Do you think he blew himself up by accident?" Bet asked.

"It's possible. Dynamite can be unpredictable, especially if it's old."

"Is there a license plate on the bike?"

Rob hopped down and inspected the bike. "There is. I'll take a photo of the plate and VIN numbers and see if those lead you anywhere."

"Disable it too," Bet said. "That way no one can ride it away."

Finished with that, Rob remounted Figure. Bet felt herself slip toward the ground, but Rob put her in front of him this time and held her tight as they rode.

"You all right there, Elizabeth?"

"Yeah. Good." Somehow she managed to make words come out of her mouth.

"Stay with me," he said. "We're almost home."

"I think you have something more to tell me." Bet's mind went back to his abrupt departure the night before.

"Always angling for a confession, huh, Sheriff?"

"Confessions are good for the soul." Bet started to fade again. She shook her head, clearing the cobwebs.

"I think you have a story yourself," Rob said. "How did you end up with a gunshot wound, why are you all wet, and how do you know that was Michael Chandler in the cave?"

"I'm not sure you're going to believe what I have to tell you."

Rob urged Figure a little faster as they caught sight of the big house in front of them. Clayton showed up on the ATV, so while Rob put Figure up, Bet sent her deputy to search the trail from the cave entrance to Ingalls Creek Road. He might overtake Michael Chandler if he'd left the tunnel on foot before the explosion.

"You know how to put in stitches, Mr. Collier?" Bet asked as they went into the house.

"You can't be serious."

"I don't have time to get to the clinic in Cle Elum," Bet said, referencing the closest thing Collier had to medical care.

"Sure. I can stitch you up," Rob said. "But it won't be pretty."

"I don't need pretty."

"It's gonna hurt."

"How about another shot of that fancy scotch?"

THIRTY-NINE

Bet lay on a bed in one of the Collier guest rooms while Rob finished putting the last adhesive butterfly on her gunshot wound. They'd covered the nice down duvet with a giant plastic trash bag to keep Bet from bleeding all over the bedding. To distract herself from the pain, Bet focused her attention on an oil painting of a hunting scene hanging on the pine wood wall.

The worst part was when Rob cleaned the wound. He'd pulled his first aid kit out, one that included the type of field dressing used by the military, the stick-on stitches that wouldn't require Rob to break out the needle and thread from a sewing kit.

"And here I thought I'd have a great story about biting down on the cartridge from an old Colt forty-five while you used dental floss and a darning needle to put me together again," Bet grunted as he applied pressure to the wound.

"Cartridges are bad for your teeth." Rob wrapped clean gauze around her arm.

While he tended to her injury, Bet outlined the events in the cave, glossing over her time in the water as fast as she could.

"I can't imagine what that was like." Rob shuddered. Bet was glad she faced the wall so he couldn't see her expression.

"It happened so fast I hardly thought about it."

Rob let it drop.

"Want to explain your quick departure last night?" Bet was exhausted and in pain and didn't feel like playing games with Rob Collier anymore. The guest bed was soft and the air was warm and the room was hushed and rich and she really just wanted to sleep, but she had to stay awake until she knew Dale's condition.

"I have something to show you," Rob said. He stood up and left the room, his footsteps fading down the hallway, then returned a few minutes later. Rob carried a sheet of paper, which he handed to her. "My mother wrote this to my father before she left."

Bet took the letter and looked at him for explanation.

"I'll be downstairs in the kitchen when you're ready to talk." Bet looked down at the faded paper to find a typed letter.

Dear Robert,

By the time you read this letter, I'll be gone. Don't come after me, though perhaps I'm giving you too much credit, or myself too much influence, to think you might try. The only good thing to come of our marriage is our son. I thought of taking him with me, but a boy needs his father, and I'm not built to raise a child on my own.

I turned a blind eye to your infidelities for a long time. You had your life and I had mine, and that has been the way of things, but this, you being the father of another woman's child, is too much for me to bear. That is a pain I will not endure, year after year, watching that child grow up in front of me, a constant reminder that I have never been exactly what you need.

I don't blame her, you are a man that is difficult to ignore and harder to say no to, but I hope for her sake, and the child's, you leave her well enough alone. We both know you aren't going to marry her and live happily ever after, you aren't built for those kinds of promises.

I will get in touch in a few weeks. I expect a reasonable amount of financial support in exchange for my silence.

Bet let the contents of the letter sink in. She looked at the date. It was six months before she was born. If her mother was Collier's other woman, then Bet was no longer her father's child.

———

After lying on the bed a while to pull herself together, Bet stood up and found the guest bathroom. She used the facilities and took time to take the pins out of her sodden hair. She picked up a guest towel—remarkably fresh, given it had probably hung there for years—and dried her hair. She used her fingers to straighten her curls the best she could, then repinned them. The time allowed her to regain her equilibrium. She felt like someone had pulled a rug out from under her feet. Finally, she felt ready to face Rob Collier again.

Entering the kitchen, Bet found him sitting on one of the stools at the island.

"This is what you and your father fought about?" She walked around to face him.

Rob nodded. "He let me think she left because of me. I believed that until I found this letter, just before I graduated high school."

"Do I look like your dad?"

Rob searched her face for a long moment.

"What?" Bet's voice croaked, barely audible, unsure what she wanted to hear him say.

"I don't know."

"Would it be so bad? If I was your sister? Half, anyway?"

"Are you asking if I could love you, Elizabeth? Make you part of my family?"

Bet didn't know what she meant by her question or what he meant by his response. Her head whirled with the idea that her dad might not really be her father.

"Why do you think he kept the letter at all? Why not burn it? Or throw it away?"

Rob shrugged. "Why do any of us do any of the things we do? He never thought I'd find it, I guess."

"But you did."

"But I did. And I told him I was no longer his son."

"You never looked for her? After finding this?"

"Nothing in this letter made me think she wanted me to. She never contacted me."

"Why come back to his house?"

"The house doesn't belong to my father. It belongs to me. I inherited it from my grandfather. It was time to find out if I had a half brother or sister. That's the other reason I came back. Now I guess I also have to find out if we're polluting the lake." Rob raked his fingers through his hair in frustration. "And who killed my mother. What a family legacy."

Bet thought about the things she'd believed her whole life that now felt false.

"Your mother's letter says nothing about leaving with Michael Chandler. Do you think she did because of your father's actions? Or was that a lie?" Bet thought about the conversation she'd had with Eric about her mother's affair with Rob's father.

"I don't know any more. But I think we have more pressing problems."

"I have to figure out what happened to the guy who shot at me down in the cave," Bet said in agreement. "I have to know if he died down there or left the area before I returned to the tunnel. He could have set the dynamite on a timer and fled before I had time to get back here."

"Why would he leave the dirt bike?"

"To throw me off? If I think he's dead, he's home free."

Bet drove Peter's Suburban back to him, with Rob following. Then Rob took Bet home to clean up. She learned Dale had made it to Seattle still alive, though it had been touch and go in the air, his heart stopping twice before they arrived at Harbor View. He'd gone into surgery with the same doctor who saved Seeley's life. He'd survived the surgery, but whether or not he would suffer permanent damage from brain hypoxia, the doctor wouldn't know until Dale woke up.

Seeley had regained consciousness, though without any memories of the events around Emma's death. The last thing he remembered was stopping for coffee at the market.

The surgeon said he might regain his memories, but there were no guarantees.

"Trauma like this," the doctor said, "he might never remember what happened. The mind sometimes protects us when our body can't."

"He remembered something," Bet said. "On the flight in, he woke up enough to tell Clayton he knew his friend had been shot."

"The mind is a mysterious thing," the doctor continued. "What he knew at that point might have been lost to him during surgery, the anesthesia, the shock, the trauma; all of those are against him remembering what happened." Bet knew something about forgotten memories. She wondered if Seeley would be haunted in his dreams too.

Now Alma, Bet, and Rob sat in the station as Bet decided what to do next.

Alma kept albums of community photos for every year. She pulled a few out from the final year Michael Chandler had still been around.

"He's hardly in any pictures," Alma said. "At first I thought he didn't participate in community events, but then I remembered. He was usually the one who held the camera. Keeping little pieces of the community on film."

"A collector," Bet said, thinking of all the stolen items in the cave. A collection from the community he struggled to be a part of.

Alma held out one of the photographs. It was a candid shot of Michael Chandler and the Riverses. Bet's mother and father stood next to each other, laughing together at some shared joke. Michael stood off to one side, arms crossed against his chest, the look on his face one of sadness, watching the other two.

"This was a lot of years ago," Alma said. "He'd be about sixty-six now. But I sent his image around, explaining he's older. You didn't say if he looks the same."

Bet explained why she wasn't sure. "I couldn't see his face very well; he had on that weird mask, it was dark, it all happened so fast. But an old picture is better than nothing."

"You'd think so, but the highway patrol has no imagination," she said, spitting indignation. "They want things like a type of vehicle and a destination point for the fugitive a little less vague than 'Canada.' It sure would help if we knew whether or not he was in the mine when the dynamite went off."

"And tangible evidence it was Michael Chandler." Bet thought about what she knew for sure. "There must be a way to compare the unknown set of prints Todd found in the cave to his. That could at least prove he'd been down there at some point. The military should have Michael Chandler's prints on file, but that's a database Todd probably didn't access. I'll call him and make sure he contacts the military."

Life would be a lot easier if all the fingerprints in databases were cross-referenced and there weren't almost a hundred thousand missing persons cases every year. For now, Bet would have to rely on Todd.

"I'd like to ride back out and see how Clayton is doing. He's been watching the dirt bike ever since his ride to Ingalls Creek."

Her deputy had called in from the trailhead. He'd traveled the entire length of the trail from the tunnel without spotting any signs of Michael Chandler. Now he sat hidden in the trees near the dirt bike with the hope the owner would return.

"I don't like the idea of any of you alone out there," Alma said sharply. "Enough of my people have been shot in the last twenty-four hours."

"I'll go with her," Rob offered.

"No mistakes, Mr. Collier," Alma said, not meeting anyone's eyes.

Rob raised an eyebrow at Bet, no doubt wondering at Alma's sharp tone. Bet signaled him to leave her alone with Alma. "I'll get us coffee and meet you at the car," Rob said, taking the hint.

Bet sat for a long moment after Rob left, eyes trained on Alma, who refused to look at her.

"I'm all right, Alma," Bet said.

"I don't know what you mean."

"And Dale will be."

"I know that."

Bet had started to walk out the door when Alma stepped up behind her. The old woman wrapped her arms around Bet's waist and put her head on Bet's shoulder. "I'm just so glad you're safe. Collier can't get by without you."

FORTY

Bet and Rob rode Figure to the cave entrance so they wouldn't announce their presence as they arrived, and Bet would drive her ATV back. Clayton reported that everything remained quiet. The dirt bike in the lean-to was exactly as they'd left it. Bet decided not to keep watch any longer and sent Clayton home.

Meanwhile, she needed to have a heart-to-heart with her old friend Eric Chandler. She arrived at his house to find him working on his computer in the back room. Now Eric sat in the chair by the window in the living room, looking out at the meadow visible from the Chandlers' house.

"Hard to believe my old man was still around, let alone that he killed that girl, and tried to kill you." Eric hung his head as he took in what his father had done.

"I know."

"And now? You think he died? Down in that cave?"

"Maybe. The registration on the dirt bike we found is expired, but it belonged to your brother; we think your dad must have been using it. It probably wouldn't still be there unless . . ."

"Unless he was still underground."

Bet let Eric take in the news that his father might be dead.

"I wonder what my mother knew," Eric finally said.

"Do you think that's why she never divorced him? Was the affair with Lillian real? Or did she just let people think that's why Michael left?"

"I have no idea. None of this makes any sense to me."

"Do you think she loved him?" Bet wondered if Tracy Chandler hadn't bothered with a divorce because she couldn't find her husband or from a misguided belief he'd come back to her one day.

"I don't know. I wish I could ask her."

Eric turned from the window and looked at Bet. In his smile, she could see the boy he had been. His hair had receded and laugh lines bracketed his eyes, but the boy remained, hidden in the skin of a much older man.

"I've missed you, Bet."

"I've missed you, too."

Schweitzer nudged Bet's hand and rested his head on her knee. She scratched him behind the ears, and he groaned in pleasure. Eric chuckled.

"Looks like you found the perfect man."

"I did," Bet said. "It took a long time, but I did." She fondled Schweitzer's ears as he leaned his weight against her. A sign she was his person. For better or worse.

She watched Eric and felt something let go inside her for the first time in years. The frozen part she'd carried around in her heart since the moment he'd walked out the door broke loose from where it had been moored. It wasn't anger she'd kept alive all these years. It was disappointment. Disappointment in herself for not being "enough."

"What are you going to do with the house?" Bet asked. "I know Dylan likes to come up here sometimes. Brings his kids."

"We'll keep it. It's paid for, and in this economy it would be tough to sell. No one is moving to Collier these days. I'm going to live here for a little while. Write my next book. Find out about the water in our well, in our lake. Then, who knows? I'm not sure what the future is going to bring. Or who will be in it with me."

Bet didn't want to know if he meant her; that wasn't a road she planned to take again. She stood, ready to go. Eric looked out the window, his eyes reminding Bet eerily of Michael's as she remembered them.

"So you solved the crime." Eric's gaze never left the window.

"I solved the crime."

"Does it make you angry no one will pay?"

"We may still find him," Bet said. "It's possible he's still alive. You will let me know if he contacts you, right?"

Eric shook his head. "I can't imagine he would—he never has in all these years—but of course I will."

Bet thought about the idea of justice. She'd gone into law enforcement because of her father, to be like him. She'd gone to LA to make a name for herself, but understood now she could do that here. Bet Rivers, Sheriff of Collier.

It suited her.

Maybe part of her father's reserve had been because she wasn't really his child. He'd only ever dispensed advice to her about practical matters; he'd never spoke from his heart. Or had he even known? Maybe it had just been her father's way. Maybe her mother's affair had died with her. Or maybe that secret had driven her mother to take her own life, a secret she could no longer live with, Bet a constant reminder of a mistake.

"Have to take care of the living," Bet said.

"I don't understand."

"No. I wouldn't think so. But I do."

Bet and Schweitzer stepped out into the perfect late-summer day. The endless blue sky, the leaves of the deciduous trees red and orange and gold, but the air still warm.

"I just wanted you to know," Bet said, as Eric followed her out onto the porch. "This will be all over town eventually. I'll be going public with Emma's death and your father's part in that."

Bet didn't mention Lillian. She and Rob still had much to learn, though that story might have died with Chandler down in the mine. Bet hoped they could discover what happened, even after all these years. There was still another living witness, after all, even if Robert Collier Senior might not want to tell them the truth. Since Jamie Garcia was holding up her end of the bargain, she might get that exclusive too.

"I'm glad you decided I wasn't involved," Eric said. "I feel better knowing you chose to trust me."

"I didn't," Bet replied, putting her hat back on and tucking an errant curl back under the brim. "I trusted the evidence."

She walked away and didn't look back.

Alma went home while Bet finished up some paperwork. In the silence of the quiet station, she could hear the sound of a cell phone ring. Tracking the noise to the locked cabinet behind Alma's desk, she opened it to find the sound coming from Dale's backpack. They'd recovered it from where he'd hidden it in the woods and locked it up for safekeeping.

Digging into the pack, she found a cell phone with a number of missed calls. She didn't plan to invade his privacy, but the number on the screen popped out at her.

Jamie Garcia.

The phone rang again, same number.

"Hello, Jamie."

Nothing but silence on the other end.

"This explains who your source was," Bet said, though she couldn't blame the woman for wanting to further her career.

"Why are you answering Dale's phone?" Bet could hear fear in the young woman's voice and wondered how intimate she was with the deputy. He had been seeing someone new. "Is Dale all right?"

The shooting of a sheriff's deputy in Collier was newsworthy. "Shot in the line of duty," was all Bet would say, but she told Jamie what hospital she could find him in. If Dale didn't like it, he shouldn't have sicced the reporter on her in the first place.

Bet stuffed the phone into the backpack and locked it up again. The text to her had come from the same phone. At least that tied up one more loose end.

Back in her own office, she looked at the file on her desk. Her findings that Michael Chandler had killed Emma Hunter and shot

Seeley Lander and Dale, along with attempting to kill her. His whereabouts unknown. He was either on the run or dead in the mine. She and other law enforcement agencies would continue to look for him, but there was little she could do.

Turning off her computer, she leaned back in her chair, resting it against the wall. She could just make out the glimmer of Lake Collier. The surface was ruffled, silver and orange in the dying light. Twilight was one of Bet's favorite times of the day. Not yet night, not quite day. An in-between time when anything could happen, the possibilities that lay in darkness hiding trouble from the light.

Bet caught sight of a piece of paper on the edge of her desk. Picking it up, she realized she hadn't filed the information about Eric's fingerprint on the flashlight into the case file. Though it had turned out to be a dead end, she had to include it in her final report. Unfolding the sheet of paper, she read back over the information. Something gnawed at the edge of her consciousness. It wasn't the fingerprint; Eric had readily admitted being there. He'd explained his interest in the mine, and his letter to Robert Collier Senior several months ago—prompting Senior to contact Peter Malone—supported his story. She had no reason to doubt he'd told her the truth.

Except history.

Eric was a perpetual liar. Nothing on Todd's note changed anything. A fingerprint belonging to Eric Chandler. Check. Blood type B positive.

Sixth grade. Science class. Learning about blood types. Bet and Dylan had discovered they shared the same blood type. Eric's was the same as theirs. It had meant something to Bet, all those years ago. It made her feel like Dylan and Eric really were her brothers. Their blood was the same.

And Bet's blood type was not B positive.

FORTY-ONE

Bet called the medical examiner at home for the first time. She waited twenty agonizing minutes while Carolyn drove over to her office.

She confirmed what Bet had guessed. Emma's blood type was B positive.

It could take weeks for DNA testing to be done on Emma Hunter and the blood on Eric's flashlight, but Bet already knew what the results would say.

―――――――

Bet waited out front for Clayton to appear. He pulled up in his Trooper dressed in black and wearing his bulletproof vest under a windbreaker with *SHERIFF'S DEPARTMENT* stenciled across the back.

"What's going on, Sheriff?"

"I think Eric played me." Bet went on to explain the flashlight, with Eric's fingerprint and someone else's blood. "I'm not sure that was Michael down in the cave at all. I think that was Eric. Something he said wasn't right; it came to me later on."

"What was that?"

"He spoke about how the war changed him, how it made him abandon his son. Singular, not *my sons*."

"Eric pretended to be his father so it would take the suspicion off him, then pretended to die in the cave so you'd close the investigation. Except he blew it with that slip."

"Exactly," Bet said. "In Eric's mind, he was the one Michael abandoned; Dylan didn't matter."

"So what's the plan?"

"I want to talk to Eric, but I'd like you nearby. Just in case."

———————

Bet and Clayton arrived on Eric's street to find the house dark except for a single light on in the back. Eric's writing room. She pulled up behind Eric's car in the driveway and doused the lights of her SUV.

She waited while Clayton moved over into the shadows on the side of the house before she crossed up to the front porch and knocked on the door.

Lights came on throughout the house, and Bet felt the sensation of someone looking through the peephole.

"It's me, Eric," Bet said. "Can you open the door?"

"Just a minute."

She heard him fumble with the lock. He opened the door, dressed in sweats and a T-shirt. Barefoot, he looked like the teenage boy Bet remembered.

"Come on in, Bet."

"No. Let's chat out here."

Eric gave her a quizzical look, but he stepped out onto the porch and gestured at the two rocking chairs.

Bet chose to stand, leaning against the porch rail instead of sitting in a chair she might not get out of fast enough.

"When were you really down in that cave?" Bet asked after Eric settled in.

"I told you, Monday."

"You've told me a lot of things in my life, Eric. How many of them were lies?"

Eric's body stilled, and Bet tensed. She could see his eyes glowing silver in the scant light thrown by the moon. Bet could also see the wheels turning in his head.

He's looking for a place to run.

"I'm not lying to you, Bet. Why would you think that?"

"History."

"I can see you're riled up about something. Why don't you wait here while I go get us a couple beers and we can talk this through?"

"I'd rather you didn't go anywhere, Eric."

He stood up. "I'm just going to get a beer," he said, untangling himself from the rocking chair. He moved to the front door.

"I think you should stay right where you are, Eric."

Reaching the front door, Eric bolted, Bet hot on his trail. The two ran through the house, Eric pulling books and a chair into Bet's path. She managed to jump over the books, but the chair slowed her down enough that Eric hit the back door ahead of her.

"Eric, stop!"

He yanked open the door and launched himself across the back porch. She heard a cry and rushed out to find Clayton holding Eric against the side of the house, arm pinned behind his back.

"Did you really think I wouldn't have backup, Eric? And where the hell did you think you were going to run?"

Bet pulled her handcuffs out and placed Eric under arrest for the murder of Emma Hunter and the attempted murder of Seeley Lander, Dale, and her. After reading him his rights, Bet and Clayton maneuvered him to the SUV and locked him into the back seat for their ride back to the station.

Eric kept his mouth shut on the quick trip back, and he didn't try to struggle as Bet and Clayton escorted him into the vintage cell. Pulling the giant skeleton key off the wall, Bet unlocked the barred door, and Eric meekly went inside and sat down on the cot.

With Eric secured, Bet walked out the front door with Clayton.

"Now you can finally get some time at home with Kathy. You have tomorrow off."

"Thanks, Sheriff. But I'll see you the day after." Clayton would be full-time for now. Bet hoped he would stay on even after he became a father.

Bet went back into the station to find Eric looking miserable. He didn't even glance up.

"Need anything?" Bet asked him.

"What happens now?"

"Tomorrow I drive you down to Ellensburg and you'll be transferred to the jail there."

Eric nodded, his eyes bleak.

"What happened down in that cave, Eric?"

"Anything I say will be used against me, right?"

"Probably," Bet said. "But I think you want to tell me. Start with your dad. You knew he'd been here over the years, didn't you? That wasn't true, was it, about not seeing him?" Bet hoped she could trip Eric up in a web of lies.

She could see his desperation as he looked for a story that would help him out.

"You're right, Bet. I did know my father was around. He's been sneaking in and out of town for years. He knew the house was empty, knew Dylan would only be up on a weekend or a holiday. Any other time he could come and go as he pleased. He used Dylan's old dirt bike. It's easy to get through the woods to the back of our place without being seen, and Mrs. Villiard wouldn't hear it if a cannon went off in the middle of the night. None of the other neighbors are close."

Bet stood silent, waiting to hear the rest.

"I was so surprised to see him," Eric continued. "I asked where he'd been all these years and he told me he came around, he just didn't know how to be with people anymore. I promised I wouldn't say anything. I wanted to know him again. I didn't know he'd done anything wrong."

Eric began to pace the floor of his cell. He started up again, back turned to Bet.

"That night, I heard him slip out. I grabbed a flashlight and followed him. He went into the cave. I could hear him cursing. After it fell quiet, I went up to the entrance and saw the gate sawn through. It must have been those kids. They must have done that to get inside. I followed after him, into the tunnel."

He turned back around to face her.

"What did you see, Eric?"

"We went all the way down into that giant cavern. There were two young people there. Dad yelling at them, asking what they were doing in his cave. Then everything happened so fast. It was dark. I thought I could help, so I came into the light."

"What did your father do?" Bet asked, when Eric stopped telling his story.

"I saw Dad point a gun at the boy. I reached out and grabbed at his arm; the bullet just grazed the kid, I thought. Then Dad raised his gun again. The girl looked so scared." Eric's voice trailed off again.

Bet decided to take a chance at rattling Eric's cage.

"That's not what Seeley told us."

Eric's face went white. "I thought he didn't remember anything that happened."

"Memory is a funny thing," Bet said, thinking over what the doctor had said about Seeley. "Seeley's memory is coming back. One thing he remembers is there was only one man in the cave with them. One man who shot at him, and his description matches you, not your father. If you tell me the truth, I can help you."

"I am telling you the truth. It was my father."

"We recovered evidence from the cave to prove it was you," Bet said.

"The cave was blown up by dynamite. There's no way you have anything on me."

"I never told you it was dynamite. I just said there was a cave-in."

Eric stopped. "I just assumed it was dynamite . . . isn't that what people use? To blow up a cave?"

"You're backtracking, Eric, but we both know you aren't telling the truth. You set off that dynamite, after trying to make me believe it was your father shooting at me. You're covering your tracks. You tried to kill me."

"No! Never." He sounded adamant. "I thought I'd scare you enough to get you out of the cave before I blew it up. I thought you might let Michael go to save your own life. I never thought you'd go into the water."

Bet watched Eric's face as he realized what he'd admitted to. He couldn't very well deny his involvement in the shootings now.

"Why kill Emma, Eric?"

At first she thought he would spin a new story, trying to maintain his father was to blame. But he shifted to a new tack.

"I never meant to. It was an accident. I was down there. It was dark. It happened so fast. I was in danger. Seeley was armed. With an old gun. It was self-defense."

"That's how you hurt your arm?"

Eric said nothing, proof enough for Bet she'd guessed right.

"How did you know about the cave to begin with?" Bet asked to keep him talking.

"My father knew about that cave. That part's true. He showed it to me, years ago, when I was a kid. Dylan was still too young. I promised never to tell anyone it was there. He stole little things for years, from the community, and hid them in the cave."

"Why?"

"I think it started as a joke. He always loved the rumor the items were stolen by the ghosts, but then it became a habit. Dad . . . combat did things to my father they never did to yours. He couldn't be a part of anything. I think this was his way to try to keep his community close. He always knew he could visit his things."

Like the rainbow trout in the pool.

"Why keep doing it, Eric? Did you think someday he'd come back and see you were waiting for him?"

Eric looked away from her then, as if she'd hit him with her words.

"You thought one day he'd come back and see you'd been the good son."

Eric looked like he might cry. "I really did want to investigate the lake. That's how it all started. Then it seemed like a way out, to blame my father. I knew I could throw suspicion on him."

"Do you know where your father is?"

Eric shook his head. "I have no idea."

"I thought he was with Lillian Collier," Bet said. "Isn't that why he finally left town for good?"

"Right," Eric said. "I . . ." Eric's eyes darted around the cell as if the plain walls and metal bars could give him answers. Bet replayed the night Lillian was dumped into the lake. It had been a terrible time in her life. Bet and her father had gotten through their first Christmas without her mother. They had spent it with the Chandlers. Michael was still coming and going to visit his sons, though his visits were more and more sporadic. Further and further apart.

"Why did your father stop coming home?"

"He would never break off his relationship with Lillian," Eric said, but he still wasn't meeting her eyes. "Mother finally had enough, I guess. Told him not to come back."

"That's not true, Eric. Lillian died seventeen years ago."

"How could you possibly know about that?" Eric's face showed first shock, then dismay as he realized what he'd said.

"What did you do?" Bet asked.

Eric dropped onto his cot and buried his head in his hands. "Oh, God, Bet. I've carried this thing around with me for so long."

Bet held her breath, waiting to see what Eric would say. "It really was an accident."

"What was an accident, Eric?"

"I saw Lillian and my dad drive into town together. I saw them turn in, up at the Collier place. I followed them. I thought he left us for her."

For the first time, Bet thought Eric might be telling the truth. "And then what happened?"

"School hadn't started yet. You and Dylan went with my mom down to Ellensburg for something. I don't remember what.

I had my twenty-two. The one Dad bought me for Christmas. I was just out, I don't know, shooting at things. Tree trunks, rocks, stop signs. No one else was out. It was cold."

He paused again, his eyes a thousand miles away. "I saw them. And I was so angry. That woman, I thought she took my father away. I wondered what they were doing in Collier, so I went through the woods, to the house. I snuck in through the back door."

"Was anyone home?"

"Robert Collier was there."

"Senior."

"Yeah, Senior."

"You heard them talking?"

"Lillian wanted to see her son. She said he was eighteen now and she wanted a chance to talk to him. She wanted to say she was sorry."

"And Senior was angry?"

"He said he'd pour them all a drink so they could talk about it, and he left the room. I heard the two of them, Lillian and my dad. She asked him if he wanted to go out and visit us, Dylan and me, and he said, 'No.' Just like that. He said he was there to make sure she was safe and he'd stay until she was ready to leave."

Eric's voice became younger and younger as they talked. His body shrunk in front of Bet as he curled in on himself. He looked more and more like the teenager Bet remembered.

"Did you confront him?"

"I went into the room. I still had the gun in my hand. And I pointed it at them. At my father. I started yelling at them, 'Why?' Not really making sense, just 'Why not come see me?' 'Why are you with her?' Stuff like that. Dad tried to calm me down. Saying I had it wrong. Then Senior came back in and started yelling at me, and my dad was yelling at him, and Lillian was yelling at everyone. I fired the twenty-two and I guess I shot my dad. In his leg."

Bet could picture the figure in the dark woods. She remembered the hitch in his gait.

"Not bad, but he's bleeding and Lillian's screaming, and Senior left the room again. I thought he was going to get a gun of his own. So I hustled Lillian up the stairs. I don't know why. To get away from my father, I guess. Or to ask her to leave my dad alone. Maybe I was afraid of Robert Collier." Eric shook his head as if to dispel his memories. "So I'm pushing her up the stairs in front of me, poking her with the gun. We get up to the top and she lurched against the railing, at the top, and before I knew it, she just fell. Onto the stone floor. And the screaming stopped."

Eric sat quiet, his breath heavy and ragged, as if he'd just run a marathon.

"She broke her neck and your father disposed of her body. To protect you."

Eric nodded.

"Why didn't Robert Collier report what you did?"

"I don't know. Maybe he felt guilty about what his wife had done, sleeping with my dad. Breaking up my family."

More likely he felt guilty about what *he'd* done, Bet thought to herself. If Senior hadn't had an affair with another woman, Lillian wouldn't have left with Michael. Or maybe he just didn't want to explain to Rob that his mother had come back to see him and ended up dead. So he decided to hide everything.

"And my father wasn't involved in any of it, right?"

Eric looked at her in confusion. "What? Your father? Earle had nothing to do with it."

Bet breathed a sigh of relief. She hoped at least that was true.

"My father said he couldn't look at me."

Bet watched Eric in the cell for a moment. Had Michael left for good because of what Eric had done? Or let people think Lillian was with him to protect his son?

"Are you going to turn me in? For that too?" Eric's voice still sounded like a child.

"You have to take responsibility for everything you've done, Eric," Bet said. "But so does your dad, and Robert Collier. It may take a while to sort out such an old crime. But you have to admit your part. Rob deserves to know what happened to his mother."

Anger flashed in Eric's eyes. "Oh, Rob does, does he?"

"For what it's worth, I'm not sure Lillian actually *had* an affair with your father. He may have just helped her out as a friend."

Eric's anger drained from his face. Bet could see that sink in. That perhaps Lillian's death had been over nothing at all.

Bet left Eric alone in his cell, then, and walked back to her office, contemplating the intricacies of fathers and sons.

And daughters.

Standing in her office, Bet looked at the portrait of her father, hanging on the wall, the one where he looked like a stranger. She tried to find herself in the man.

"Time to take care of the living," Bet said to Schweitzer, who lay on the floor, watching her.

She took the photo down. Picking up her own portrait from where she'd relegated it to the closet, she hung it in place on the wall. She was sheriff now. For better or worse.

Bet turned off the lights and called for Schweitzer. It was time to go home.

EPILOGUE

Bet walked into the tavern as she had a thousand times before, Schweitzer on her heels. The room felt welcoming, with only a few Lakers at the bar. The jukebox in the corner played an old bluegrass tune.

Walking out to the back deck, Bet saw a familiar figure at her favorite table, his beaver-fur hat balanced on its rim. Two glasses of single-malt scotch sat in front of him alongside a white envelope.

Bet sat down and Schweitzer slid under the table, hopeful a few french fries might fall his way. Bet picked up her glass and sipped the exquisite liquor, tracing its heat as it slid past her heart lodged in her throat.

"Are you nervous?" she asked.

"Are you?"

Bet didn't answer. Instead she looked at the light shining through the slats of the deck onto the cold, black water below. Fall in Collier, her favorite season. With October here, snow was just around the corner and the weather was crisp and sharp, sending summer into hiding for another year. The election had been canceled when it became clear Dale's injuries would prevent him from running. Hypoxia had impacted his speech and movements. It wasn't clear how much he would recover. She decided it was pointless to make Dale's tricks on her public now; she was, after all, fully ensconced as the sheriff of Collier.

At least for the next four years.

"You okay?" Rob asked.

"I will be. I need to know the truth."

"What's the latest with Eric?" Rob asked after a moment of silence, neither moving to open the letter.

"His attorney is trying for diminished capacity; he wants to have the charge reduced to manslaughter. Along with the divorce and the death of his mother, the attorney is using Eric's bizarre hoarding down in the cave as a way to show he suffered from psychological issues and that the shooting was in self-defense. Seeley had that old revolver, which we think he discharged; tests on the gun showed it was fired recently. Eric states Emma was caught in the crossfire. With Seeley still unable to remember, there isn't a lot of evidence to the contrary."

"Why not go for an out-and-out insanity defense?"

"Eric evaded prosecution, lied to me for days; he appeared perfectly sane to a lot of people long after the crime happened. I think the attorney knows he can't win that one, so he's trying to figure out what he can win. They may plead him out."

Thomás came out, but Bet waved him away, asking for a few more minutes.

"Want to know the worst part of all this?" Bet said.

"What's that?"

"Those kids, with their diary and hope to find gold. If they'd only waited and told me about it, I would never have let them go down there. They wouldn't have surprised Eric in his cave and none of this would have happened."

"Most violent deaths are that way, Elizabeth." Rob touched her arm, his fingers warm. "One little thing would have prevented a tragedy. You can't let that get to you."

"I know. It's just sad." The two sat for a moment with thoughts for the dead.

Bet couldn't imagine the terror Seeley had gone through, down in that cave all those days alone, endlessly searching for a way back to the surface. Victim of a gunshot because Eric had protected his father's legacy at all costs. Emma dying because Eric had hoped his father might one day return.

Bet reflected on Lillian's death. She thought Eric's story was probably true and Lillian had died in a terrible accident. The medical examiner had confirmed that Lillian had died from a cervical fracture of the fourth vertebra. She would have died almost immediately from asphyxiation brought on by paralysis, consistent with a fall.

Bet returned to the reason she'd met with Rob this evening.

"If it's not me, it has to be Dylan, right? We were born at the same time. We're the only two children in Collier that make sense. The affair with your father had to be my mother or Tracy Chandler."

Rob nodded, but Bet couldn't tell what he was thinking. They'd spent a lot of time together over the last month. He'd helped her move the last of her father's personal stuff out of the house, they'd shared meals and long walks, but he remained very much a mystery.

Bet looked at the envelope. "Let's find out."

"This won't tell us everything."

"I know. There will still be unanswered questions. But it's a start."

Bet imagined the miners, their bones entombed in the earth. And the gold. The veins she'd seen in the little room before her last ride into the lake. She'd never told anyone, not even Rob.

Rob picked up the results of their DNA tests and tore the envelope open, staring for a long moment at the piece of paper in his hand, his face expressionless.

"Well?" Bet prompted him. "What does it say?"

"What are you hoping the answer will be?"

Bet had thought about that question ever since they'd decided to send their DNA in to be analyzed. She'd never had a brother. She'd always been an only child. But then, she'd had Dylan and Eric. They had been like brothers once.

But that wasn't the relationship she pictured with Rob.

She looked at his face, lit in the warmth of the Christmas lights tacked to the walls above his head, and knew her answer.

"I don't want to be your sister, Mr. Collier."

Rob leaned over and kissed Bet, gently, on the lips.

"Be careful what you ask for, Elizabeth."

Acknowledgments

A writer never works alone. I rely on experts for their insights, the professional writing community for the publishing process, fellow writers and readers for feedback, and friends and family for emotional support.

I love research, and one of my favorite parts is talking to experts in various fields. First and foremost, I thank Diego Zanella, my go-to expert on police procedures and homicide investigations. I treasure your friendship. To Paul Goldenberger, who really can save people from helicopters; Officer Jennifer Rogers; Nick Henderson, Kittitas County Coroner; Alison Duvall, assistant professor, Department of Earth and Space Sciences at the University of Washington; and everyone at Adventure Protection, especially Curtis Bingham, for teaching me about firearms and answering my sometimes random questions about guns.

Any errors of fact in this novel are solely mine.

I'm very grateful to my agent, Madelyn Burt at Stonesong Literary Agency. I'm looking forward to many years and many books together. To everyone at Crooked Lane Books, especially my amazing editor Jenny Chen, Rachel Keith, Ashley Di Dio, Sophie Green, and Nicole Lecht.

Thanks to developmental editor Erin Brown for her belief in the viability of a very early draft of this novel. You can check her out at erinedits.com. To my longtime writing partner, Andrea Karin Nelson—I hope I never, ever have to write a book without you. You can learn more about her at Allegoryediting.com. To author Sheila Sobel, the best beta reader I could ask for. And to Sherry Hartwell, who fits into two categories: first, my favorite proofreader, and second, my mom.

Which leads me to the last group: the friends and family who have helped me build a writer's life. Special thanks to the two stalwarts in my corner: my mom, Sherry, and my husband, JD Hammerly. There are too many other people to list, so let me just say I hope you know who you are, and I hope you know how you have enriched my life and made all the hard work pay off.

Last, to my father, Steven Hartwell, who died October 19, 2019. I wish you had lived to see this novel on the shelf at the bookstore. I'm glad you were able to see the artwork, and I will never forget your words: "That's the most beautiful cover I have ever seen."

My father taught me how important stories are to understanding the human condition. Though he was never much of a fiction reader himself—nonfiction was more his style—he read out loud every night of my childhood. From fairy tales to C.S. Lewis to J.R.R. Tolkien, even now, when I think of the greatest literature I've ever known, I hear my father's voice.

I'm grateful to have been with him in his final days, when I read to him, as he did to me so many years ago.

I love you, Pop. A part of you is in every word I write.

EMHT
Hapuna Beach, Hawai'i
December 5, 2019